RICE
BOWL

**A FIRST NOVEL FROM THE FIRST
SINGAPORE LITERATURE PRIZE WINNER**

SUCHEN CHRISTINE LIM

TIMES BOOKS INTERNATIONAL
Singapore • Kuala Lumpur

This is a work of fiction and any resemblance
between the characters in this book and real
persons is coincidental.

National Library Board (Singapore) Cataloguing in Publication Data

Lim, Christine Suchen.
    Rice bowl / Christine Lim Suchen. — Times Books International, 1984.
    p. cm.
    ISBN: 981-204-099-4 (pbk.)

1.   Title

PR9555.9
823 — dc21   SLS88069395

Published by Times Books International
An imprint of Times Media Private Limited
A member of the Times Publishing Group
Times Centre
1 New Industrial Road, Singapore 536196
Tel: (65) 2848844 Fax: (65) 2854871
E-mail: te@tpl.com.sg
Online bookstore: http://www.timesone.com.sg/te

Times Subang
Lot 46, Subang Hi-Tech Industrial Park
Batu Tiga, 40000 Shah Alam
Selangor Darul Ehsan, Malaysia
Tel & Fax: (603) 7363517
E-mail: cchong@tpg.com.my

Printed in Malaysia

ISBN 981 204 099 4

For
Chi-Minh,
Chi-Sharn
and
Shannan

About the Author

Rice Bowl is Suchen Christine Lim's first novel. Her other novels are *Gift from the Gods* (1990), *Fistful of Colours* (1993), which is the first Singapore novel awarded the Singapore Literature Prize, and *A Bit of Earth* (2001). She also co-authored a prize-winning play with Ophelia Ooi—*The Amah: A Portrait In Black And White*. She is a curriculum specialist with the Ministry of Education, Singapore, and has written several children's books and English textbooks. In 1997 she was awarded a Fulbright grant to attend the International Writers' Program in the University of Iowa, and in the spring semester of 2000, she was the university's Writer-in-Residence.

A Bit of Earth

Malaya. A land of unparalleled richness. For centuries, the peninsula has attracted fortune hunters, money-grabbing pirates and migrants seeking a better life. Among those whose lives are rooted in the Malayan soil are three families—the Wongs, sons of the Chinese earth; the Wees, subjects of the English gods; the Mahmuds, scions of the Malayan soil—each with different dreams for the bit of earth they live on. Their destinies meet and this clash of hopes inevitably leads to tragedy.

In *A Bit of Earth*, Suchen Christine Lim deftly weaves historical fact and a fiery imagination in a visually powerful multicultural story that spans three generations and four decades—proving once again that she's one of Asia's leading fiction writers.

ISBN 981 232 123 3

CONTENTS

Convent	9
Ser Mei	49
University	112
Jurong	156

CONVENT

Spirals of hope rising white . . .
and pure in the morning light;
Circles of red – courageous and strong
Hand in hand marshalling
the nation's throng.

Pleased with her own little rhyme, Marie watched the dance, fascinated, letting the words form in her head.

'Clichés for the occasion,' she muttered as she viewed the five hundred waxed-paper umbrellas, flashing red and white spirals, twirling and whirling in the school field down below in the heat of the noonday sun. She turned away from the window. The needles of light bouncing off the glossy red and white umbrellas were hurting her eyes.

'Higher, higher! Hold them up higher and point your toes!' a voice screeched into the megaphone. 'No, no, no! What's the matter with you all today? Can't you count? One, two, one, two, and turn with precision! You're supposed to do a ninety-degree turn – not a half turn nor a quarter turn. Stop the music!'

From somewhere in the belly of the school, a switch went up and the music stopped. The circles of red and white disappeared. The students had folded their umbrellas and stood raising their heads and flexing their arms and legs. The field was now a mass of moving white and blue which froze when Mrs Khoo shouted, 'S J I boys, if you don't stop talking at the back there I'll keep you here till two o'clock. And stand up straight! Straight, don't drape over your umbrellas like wilting daisies! You're supposed to be young and rugged – look at you!'

The convent girls tittered and giggled, a moving mass of blue. Marie, who had gone back to the window, was amused too. Poor guys, she thought, as the boys standing ramrod straight, stared ahead into space; their faces grim with anger and embarrassment. There was just the trace of a smile on their faces when Mrs Khoo, always fair in anger, shouted at the girls.

'Stop giggling over there! Don't think you were any better – all of you were like water buffaloes. You're supposed to lengga-lengga and sway gracefully. And what were you doing? Stomping around like elephants! Now dance properly this time.'

The music blared out from the loudspeakers again. The umbrellas opened and the circles of red and white were soon spiralling. Ah, brave symbols of a young nation. Red and white. Courage and hope. But not joy, Marie sighed. All those responsible for this first National Day celebration were carrying out their duties with such grim determination that come rain or shine, this would be a success, fearing that otherwise heads would roll. She only wished that the students did not have to suffer so much humiliation 'all in the good name of the school'. She got up to go to her first Ethics class with Pre-University One.

'Don't take the subject too seriously, it may be scrapped next year. The Ministry wants to introduce Civics next year – Citizen Formation,' Mrs Chow was saying.

'Ya, ya, listen to this, June,' someone else shouted,

'your hero said last night that "a disciplined and rugged population must be forged, steeled to meet the problems of nation building and the schools must take on this task of citizen formation." '

Marie smiled and turned away from the general chatter for it was a well-known fact in the staff-room that Mrs Chow was an ardent admirer of the Prime Minister. 'Not that he's handsome but he's got brains,' she used to tell her students. She could be so childish at times, Mrs Chow, with her pure acceptance, no questioning; and she had always thought that teachers, at least those teaching the upper levels, were supposed to instil in their students a spirit of inquiry and objectivity, not this blind acceptance of 'he's got brains'.

The martial music had stopped and Marie could hear the tramping of the students' feet along the stairs and corridors. She stood up and straightened her blouse. It would be fun teaching this Pre-University class since the boys from St Joseph's were joining the girls for Ethics each week.

'My, my, aren't we getting permissive,' the teachers laughed.

'Be careful, Marie, don't let them take advantage of you,' Mrs Chow was again giving a maternal pat on the shoulders of one of her former students. Marie nodded. She knew that her teachers meant well but she did not need their protection. No student would ever take advantage of her; all she had to do was to treat them as persons, not just names on the school register.

Enveloped in this certainty she strolled down the dark grey corridor of her beloved convent, pleased at the younger girls looking out of their classes trying to catch her eye.

'Class stand!' a girl's voice rang out, and forty-four boys and girls obeyed as Miss Marie Wang entered. They liked what they saw. She was small and very young; tastefully dressed in a dark skirt and pale pink blouse. Her eyes twinkled as they chanted:

'G-o-o-d-m-o-r-n-i-n-g Miss Wang.'

'Good morning,' she answered and waved them to sit down.

'I'm new.'

Everyone laughed. 'We know.'

'I mean, I must confess I don't quite know what I'm supposed to do with you.'

'Teach ethics.'

'I know, but it's so vague . . . what's ethics all about?'

There was something attractive in her tentative manner. Such a contrast to those who came dressed in their suits of knowledge ready to enunciate and elucidate.

'Do you know what ethics is all about?'

The class looked at her. Why on earth was she asking them? Was this a new teacher's trick to expose their ignorance? Not used to being treated like this they remained silent, heads bent. Wasn't she going to continue and give the answer? Why didn't she just teach instead of asking them questions knowing full well that they wouldn't be able to answer?

'Hey,' she said softly, 'you're not used to answering questions. Why?'

'Scared!' someone offered, but she was not quick enough to see who it was.

'Scared of what?'

'Of being wrong!' and this time Marie caught the girl's challenging eye.

'Scared of being wrong? Young Singaporeans like you?'

Unsettled by her tone the students looked at her blankly. She returned their look, sizing them up in turn.

'How long have you had this fear?' she asked, clinical now, like a doctor.

'Oh, ever since we can remember.'

'Then you haven't been educated.'

Enjoying the surprise that flashed across their faces she continued, 'Education is freedom from fear, especially the fear of being wrong. It is a liberating process. Only when we are free from these fears do we dare to do new and unfamiliar things.'

'But we will be shamed if we admit that we don't know.' Tan Siew Yean, the girl who had just responded, felt that the new teacher needed to be told how things stood.

'Who will shame us?'

'Our teacher or our classmates. We know they don't mean it but we might feel it all the same.'

'If that's the case, what you've experienced is not education but competition. We're all caught in a power struggle, the teacher to maintain his superior position and you, not to be put down, must show your mastery over whatever knowledge doled out to you by the expert.'

Pre-University One looked at Marie. Here is someone different.

'In a power struggle who wins?' Marie was gaining confidence.

'The teacher.'

'Why?'

'Because he has more power.'

'Where did that power come from?'

'The Ministry of Education.'

'I see, the Ministry appoints them and automatically

they have power and authority over you.'

'No, not if they do not know their stuff.'

'So it is their superior knowledge that gives them authority too, right?' The class nodded their approval; this was much more fun than the usual monologue of the Ethics class.

'What happens to those who are not appointed by any power and have no special knowledge?'

Silent this time; they had not thought of that before.

'Surely the rest of us have some authority. As the children of God, aren't we worthy of respect too? What about the authority that comes with age, experience or wisdom? Do we always need an outside source to give us authority?'

Perhaps a habit of acceptance was being broken here; at any rate some of the students had been openly surprised by Marie's assertion that teachers were only paper tigers.

'Yes, we are paper tigers, didn't you know? We have power only so long as you feel you ought to obey us. But if you decide to disregard me by yawning or folding your arms like this to challenge me, what can I possibly do? I can't send all of you to the principal simply because you looked bored. What would she think? Ever thought of that?' And she was teasing them now, 'The teacher tyrant is helpless in the face of group power!'

* * *

Marie took off her shoes and entered the school's chapel. She sat on the bench, hugging one of the scatter cushions, luxuriating in its comforting warmth as she gazed into the dim red glow of the tabernacle lamp.

Daily duties and activities settled to the bottom of her mind. She straightened her back, leaned against the wall, pulled up her legs on to the bench, crossed them and rested her hands lightly on her lap, yoga-style. In this posture, she closed her eyes and following her instructions, emptied her mind and turned her thoughts to God.

'Dear Lord,' she intoned, 'thank you for the pains and joys of all these months. Although I resented them at that time they have been good for me. Now I'm beginning to see the unfolding of your design. Failure has forced me to re-arrange my priorities. I had been selfish, thinking only of my own accomplishments, now I want to be able to do some good quietly – to help these students grow. Give me the grace to help them grow.'

Marie sat there for another few minutes and then sensing she might miss out on something going on outside she made her apologies to the Lord and slipped out. Her restless feelings were accurate; girls were waiting to talk with her. She would have to hurry them today since Paul was coming to fetch her. Nevertheless she was mightily pleased with herself. Barely six months in the school and already she had acquired the reputation of being the most understanding teacher on the staff.

> I walked one morning by the sea
> and all the waves reached out to me
> I took their tears and let them be.

The hymn came naturally to one who knew that she was doing the Lord's will, and Marie was proud to have taken their tears and let them be. As she had always told her students:

> Love is free with no strings attached.

The driver in the red Mini-minor had been waiting

for more than an hour. Paul Tan Wei Jin, his face an impassive blank, stared ahead at the chapel door as if his determined gaze could will Marie to come out sooner. A young man in his early twenties, Paul was short-haired, clean shaven and immaculately dressed in a light blue shirt, dark blue tie and dark blue pants. He had what the local ad-men called 'the young executive look'. Today his usually handsome face was dark and angry because of the long wait. Leaning back into his seat while his hand rested on the steering wheel, tapping out the seconds and minutes, he was trying not to fume at a pattern which had become all too familiar – Marie, torn at the seams unable to say 'no' to a request for help, and Paul left to fend for himself while the angel of mercy went about her work: somebody having trouble with parents or teachers, with boyfriends or girlfriends, with dogs, cats or mice!

He liked her generosity but just couldn't understand her involvement with her students, with her constant need to be needed. He resented having to wait like a beggar for what was rightfully his, their evenings together. Too often he had wanted to yell, 'You take me for a priest!' but she had remained blithely unaware and they continued to discuss the affairs of the world, the complexity of living and the spirit of loving, the dry rot in Singapore, in education, politics and religion, on and on and on. In this cage of silence Paul was compelled to witness Marie's placid patience with him one minute and exuberant enthusiasm over school kids the next. He had always counselled moderation but with Marie it seemed to be all or nothing. Compromise was a bad word. Paul sighed. She was totally unaware of her power to move feelings in him which he longed to release. He longed for those wonderful schooldays when he was her 'special' and she had looked up to him depending on what she called his silent strength. He had been the rock of her life then, and when she failed to win her prestigious government scholarship he had comforted her throughout all that clucking sympathy. Now this silence was merely that of the inarticulate Singaporean male, limiting and rigid. Marie had forgotten this in her talk, talk, talk when all he wanted was to hold her after a long tiring day.

*　　*　　*

In his office, Paul pushed the files away. Tomorrow was the interview by the Public Service Board for his scholarship to Harvard. Top student of his year in the University, he was confident of getting it. It would compensate for all the sacrifices his parents had made, and the pride and prestige of having a Harvard scholar in the family would be their reward. He knew already what the gist of his statement to the press would be: 'hard work and endurance are the keys,' and he smiled at the thought of his friends and relatives reading of his achievements in *The Straits Times.* How proud of him they would be! Not Marie though. No, she would see herself on the other end of the see-saw balancing all that praise by plucking out what she would undoubtedly call his peacock feathers. He banged the drawer shut, turned the key and stood up, determined that Marie should not be allowed to destroy his moment of triumph when it came.

Driving out of the car park he backed into a pillar and jerked forward. 'Damn it,' he cursed beneath his breath, angry that he had allowed thoughts of Marie's reactions to affect him like this. He had worked hard. He had given up a lot of things for this moment of success. He deserved it and if the government chose to recognise his merits (and this is a meritocracy isn't it?) why should he be made to feel guilty because others couldn't go to Harvard? No, he was not going to allow Marie to do this to him. It was too bad she hadn't made it to the top. He was sorry about it but since he had not stopped loving her, she should not grudge him this. Yes, she had changed. She had grown more critical of the system now that she was no longer one of the 'cream' as she would have put it. A case of sour grapes, Paul's mind whispered; a thought he quickly pushed aside, guilty that it should have even crept into his consciousness at all. No, Marie was too generous a girl to be like that. They had been together all the Pre-U days when she was his most ardent admirer and supporter; their minds and hearts in total agreement. So, could she be right after all about the ill effects of meritocracy? But countries like Singapore, short on natural resources, needed men like himself. And not everybody could be a leader. Leaders had to be nurtured and what was wrong in giving the best to those who best deserved it, and would give the best return. 'But surely you're a human being not an investment?' He had ignored the mockery in her question. Singapore had to make the best possible use of her limited resources, she had no other choice. Paul turned on the engine of his car and smoothly guided it into busy Robinson Road. He felt vindicated. He would be one of those who would contribute to the development of his nation and he was not going to shirk his responsibility.

A red traffic light reminded him of his angry outburst at Marie's decision to enter the convent. Such a sentiment she had voiced to him time and time again but he had never taken it seriously, confident that she belonged to him. All along he had thought that this was but a way of coping with her failure to live up to her father's expectations and also a religious fervour carried over from the days when they were both in Christian Youth. He had never expected it to materialize into a definite commitment. He pressed the accelerator hard and the car zoomed forward. She simply didn't realize how sexy she was! A nun! She would never make it, and Paul was determined to let her know it tonight.

*   *   *

Marie closed the front door with a soft click. The family was still asleep. Sunday was for sleeping late. They had all done their duty by God at last night's mass. Saturday evening was for God; Sunday morning was for man. To rest his work-weary limbs? Yet those who were truly weary would still have to work on Sundays to make ends meet.

Onan Road in the grey light of dawn looked beautiful. A light breeze played among the leaves of the angsana trees and sent cascades of small yellow blooms covering the sides of the road with a bright carpet. The family sedans were parked in a haphazard zigzag fashion, shoved into whatever space was available. The human spirit, she mused, would defy and subvert all attempts to control it and make its movements more orderly. These drivers would resist all the government's attempts to box in their cars as it had tried to box in their Singaporean soul. Neat little rows of cars and neat little souls housed in neat little H D B blocks. Three cheers for the spirit of man; alive and tingling right down to his fingertips; conscious of the life flowing in him and in all living things . . . with this, Marie stopped, smiled to herself and thought of Paul. He would have stopped her too, if he were with her now. Paul, dear Paul, he could never understand her nor see what she saw. He would look only if she told him to, pushing his spectacles further up the bridge of his nose to give himself a clearer view. Then he would look and nod in agreement but soon enough begin his lectures again. He was not interested in Man's defiant spirit. His special interest was in Man's ability to adapt to changing conditions and survive. The laws of survival, the ethics of hard work, thrift, stability and orderliness and the defects of her own thought processes were his eternal interests. He would methodically and quite clinically tear her arguments to shreds and in a tone of infinite patience point out that the errors of her concepts and criticisms of society were the results of her irrational feelings. How he had scolded her when she had brushed off his pleas for reason.

'Singapore is a small nation. We cannot afford defiance, rebellion and constant questioning of government policies. To survive in this tough world we must be a tightly-knit unit; nobody owes us a living, we must look out for ourselves . . . '; on and on and on. How they had argued! She was fighting windmills with a broomstick, he had said. And she had laughingly supplied a local equivalent – using a candle to chase away the shadows of the coconut palms. Then, angry, he had accused her of being the eternal rebel refusing to grow up! Spoilt! Pampered! Cloistered! Armchair critic! How she had cried whenever he used that term. It stung her hard and made her want all the more to do something, anything, just to show him how wrong he was. But he had quickly acquired a new set of invectives when he learnt that she was entering the convent. Only the word, Cloistered, remained. And with that he had added Martyr! Nun! Escapist! The perfect Bride of Christ! Yes, he could imagine her in the dim light of the convent's chapel offering herself as a sacrifice – the perfect virgin; cold, calm and collected. But untouchable. And she had retaliated then with Conformist! Strait Jacket! The numbered Singaporean slaving for 4 wheels, 3 rooms, 2 kids and 1 wife as the supreme goal in life. How mad Paul became at this. And finally it had become intolerable. The break was inevitable, also they might have destroyed each other, stabbing and cutting, returning thrust for thrust. The grief and anguish of their last meeting before he left for the States on a government scholarship stung her still. He had sold his soul. She could see him in the next few years coming back as the brilliant administrator of a government department; one of the 'bright boys' trained abroad and respected as 'a returned scholar'. A systems analyst – patient, stable and methodical; driving a German-made car because its engine was reliable and buying a house in the Holland Road area because it was a good investment. With a sigh, she dismissed him.

She stood for a moment at the junction of Onan Road and Katong Road and looked across at the Holy Family Church. Filing in for the 6.30 mass were sober-faced women, their hands strangled by dark strings of rosary beads. How childishly trusting and simple in their faith! O God, forgive me. She had no right to deride these innocent women. Who was she to judge their faith? Only the Creator could know and decide.

Boarding the bus she took a corner seat at the back. Pleased at finding the bus quite empty, for not many people travel to town so early on Sundays, she settled into her seat. She could now think without having to be ready to give up her seat to an older person. Following Reverend Mother's advice, she had waited three years to come to this decision. Now she was ready. The coming meeting would merely confirm what was in her heart from the first. In the nooks and crannies of her mind she searched for the time when she first said Yes to Christ but only broken phrases returned like parts of a musical theme. My God comes to me on the wings of the breeze, she had told Paul. I cannot give you facts, figures and reasons one by one. I don't think this way. I just know it. He calls me and I must go. Paul had dismissed her with one word, Dramatic! She had kept quiet. She didn't want to argue with him any more. Other bits and pieces returned to her as she searched like one looking for some coins flung into the lallang and as she parted the tall grasses, here and there, she came across forgotten things carelessly tossed away, long ago when she was much enamoured of Paul.

> I cannot escape You.
> You are in the sky
> Among the clouds.
> You are in the valleys
> And up the mountain tops.
> If I sink into the ocean
> You are there too.

Maybe this was part of a psalm she had heard somewhere. Her soul quivered delicately at being so pursued, and in the near-empty bus Marie closed her eyes and bowed her head, grateful to have been so chosen and called. I'm yours, my Lord, take me with all my warts and faults. I leave me in the palm of Your Hand; only give me the grace to do Your work and accept Your will. *Yours,* not *my* will be done. A cloud of calm descended upon her and in this state she got down from the bus and passed through the gates of the convent like the pilgrim welcoming the desert that he knew awaited him because he was sure that after forty days he would be stronger and freed to do the work of his Father.

' "In each individual the spirit has become flesh. In each man the creation suffers, within each one a redeemer is nailed to the cross." Herman Hesse – that's all for tonight'. Marie closed the book and got up.

Stifling a yawn, Tan Siew Yean got up too. She was too tired to let Miss Wang know that once again what she had just read was way above their heads. She was pleased, though, that this school camp was not at all like the usual stuffy, serious, silent retreat that all Catholic students were compelled to attend each year because in this camp, the twelve of them, selected by Miss Wang, were getting to know one another and were learning to relate to each other 'as persons not as roles' as Miss Wang had put it. With the exception of Siew Yean herself, all the students were claiming that the success of the camp was largely the work of this engaging new teacher. So stupidly admiring, thought Siew Yean, trying to resist Miss Wang's charm, although she wished she could be more openly enthusiastic like the others. She was awkward in Miss Wang's presence. A dumbness would descend upon her whenever Miss Wang drew near. No feeling. Her mind just a blank. Miss Wang was a blithe spirit and Siew Yean simply clay. She liked and resented her at the same time. She wanted to be in Miss Wang's presence but she was all too conscious of those millions of eyes on her when she walked through the canteen at the heels of this popular new teacher. What would the others think? That thought gnawed at her guts although she knew it shouldn't. But it did. It so tightened her intestines that in Miss Wang's presence, words could never come out of her mouth no matter how desperate her desire to please, knowing as she did how Miss Wang prized a student's ability to articulate thoughts and feelings. And Heaven knows she wanted to please though at eighteen one was hardly supposed to find one's teacher attractive, still less need her approval so desperately. One was supposed to have outgrown such stuff and adopt a more blasé attitude. And yet, there she was – hopelessly heroworshipping Miss Marie-Therese Wang!

Yean returned to the dormitory of the Friary, irritated both with herself and with the others. First night at camp and already they were breaking all the rules. It was way past bedtime and the boys were still playing cards in one of the girls' rooms. That was just typical of Miss Wang – breaking rules – and she was supposed to be their chaperone. No wonder the others liked her so much. Resolutely, Yean changed into her pyjamas and plumped herself into bed. The sounds of laughter down the corridor made her feel lonelier than usual.

The door opened. Miss Wang's head popped in. 'Hey, come and listen to this,' she invited and walked off, confident that Yean would follow.

And Yean did, though with a mixture of trepidation, elation and resentment. What was she up to? Miss Wang had been hinting about breaking down walls. Was this an attempt to break down her wall? As a thin bar of yellow light cut across the dark corridor of the Friary, Yean opened the door wider and went in to find Miss Wang sitting on the bed, looking cheerful and relaxed. Yean sat down too, stiff, square-boned and uncomfortable. Miss Wang smiled.

'Listen to this:

> We are separated
> by a title
> (and a few years)
> by a few errors
> (not yet made by you)
> We are unified by the life we see
> (through equally concerned eyes)
> by the way we feel
> (in our moments of
> solitude
> despair
> anger
> grief
> and joy)
> And so we must talk
> (and not avert our eyes and say
> small things about the heat and the rain)
> of life and death
> of hope and despair
> of love and hate
> seeing the world in our lives
> and our life in the world
> touching,
> at least for the moment,
> our common chord.

Do you like it?' she asked and so winsome was her tone that Yean's defences cracked a little and tears welled up in her eyes. Here was Miss Wang being so kind to her while she herself had been so critical.

Marie was a little surprised by the tears, but kept quiet and simply held Yean's awkward hand, waiting, feeling that this must have been the welling up of months or years of suppressed childhood sorrows or yearnings for affection and understanding. She didn't know and she didn't ask, and Yean was grateful for that respectful silence. She didn't know why she cried but she had. She only knew that questions would have embarrassed her. She only knew that Miss Wang had come to her in her lonely need for that special union with another soul. Miss Wang so well-liked and self-assured had found her, after all, acceptable.

Eyes bright with excitement, Yean listened as Miss Wang recited odds and ends of poetry – cummings, Dylan Thomas, Tagore and Gibran – strange names whose sayings made her feel that life was rich, beautiful and mysterious. Miss Wang read on into the early hours of the morning invigorated by her attentive audience of one. Somewhere along that spectrum of timelessness Yean stopped listening and was aware only of that lovely face propped up against the pillow. The bedside lamp threw fine streaks of yellow light upon Miss Wang's thick black hair, and her eyes shone with intense pleasure as she read. On that night, Yean thought that was the most beautiful face she had ever seen.

And Marie was pleased to feel that the hand nestling in her palm had grown less stiff, was now soft and warm. Dark masses of hair brushed against her face: tough, tousled, almost boyish; and Yean's sleepy face, blank an hour ago, was now open with the painful vulnerability of a child. And she knew that she must tread gently, very gently, for this stranger-child-adult had come in full trust and invited her into her private garden.

The plants were tender, fragile and unused to strangers and sunlight. She sat down among them carefully trying not to dislodge them as she listened to Yean's talk into the wee hours of the morning.

*   *   *

That, she reflected, was her forté – an almost instinctive response to the needs of others. She had always felt that her gift was knowing people and for one eternal moment to hold that contact with them so that the other person came away feeling that he had participated in something beautiful and mysterious. And because he couldn't understand he would, she felt, always remain true to her. Is this charisma? Marie did not know but she was not bothered by it anyway. It wasn't as if she could hold sway over everyone all the time. To speak the truth, most of the time she felt she was out on a limb, not quite securely attached to the main trunk . . . like this morning.

Marie was staring down at the school field where students were bunched into one undifferentiated mass of blue in front of the flag, reciting the new national pledge. It still sounded strange and unfamiliar. Its rawness struck her as if civil servants had been told to spell out the aspirations of a nation whose course had yet to be charted by the political leadership. Then the sound of the bell stirred her as row upon row of blue fanned out toward the classrooms. Where was she, where was Siew Yean? And then, don't you have any pride at all? She has forgotten you. You're just another teacher.

But Marie-Therese Wang, used to being well-liked, could not accept this. Nevertheless, the procession of uniformed blue passed her by, chanting,

'Good morning, Miss Wang.'

'Good morning.'

'Good morning, Miss Wang."

'Good morning.'

'Good morning.'

'Good morning.'

'Morning.'

'Morning.'

'Morning.'

With that the convent's daily ritual of corridor manners came to an end.

Yean, too, had passed her. Her face, impassive, mouthing 'Good morning Miss Wang' like the rest.

Why should she resent that? The girl had acknowledged her, but she still felt cheated of her moment. Something more was due to her than just another 'Good morning'. She had thought Yean was part of her select flock, part of the eleven. Didn't Yean realize that something special had occurred that night?

O heavenly Father, I thought I had touched her that night but she has clammed up again. Teach me how to help her grow. The ejaculation strengthened her. She had done her best. The rest was in the hands of the Lord.

She walked into her class, untouchable, pure and crystal clear.

*   *   *

The green field of the Saddles Club stretched smooth and wide toward the thick hedge which separated it from Thomson Road. The noise of the traffic was muted and the evening sun cast long shadows along the edge of the field. The angsana trees were in full bloom again and their tiny flowers adorned the tree tops like so many patches of marigold.

The group of twelve boys and girls known in the school as Marie's Gang were reclining against one another on the grass in the shade of the trees. Siew Yean sat on the fringe. Even after a term she did not feel she quite belonged yet to this select group and envied those who could talk with such ease with Miss Wang while she still suffered the agony of being tongue-tied. They had come out here to relax in each other's company; to share, as Miss Wang had so beautifully put it, the periods of noise and silence in their lives. How she wished she could speak like that!

'Hey, I have a poem here. Shall I read it?' Miss Wang asked.

'Hmmmm, so long as we don't have to do P C and write another cree–ti–kal analysis,' answered Kim with an indolent wave of her hand for she never did like anything to do with 'brainy work' as she had so often confessed to Miss Wang. The group laughed and nodded in agreement.

'Okay,' Marie laughed, 'here goes. "Friends", by Elizabeth Jennings.'

> I fear it's very wrong of me
> And yet I must admit
> When someone offers friendship
> I want the whole of it.
> I don't want everybody else
> To share my friends with me.
> At least I want one special one
> Who indisputably,
> Likes me much more than all the rest

Who's always on my side,
Who never cares what others say
Who lets me come and hide
Within his shadow, in his house –
It doesn't matter where –
Who lets me simply be myself,
Who's always, always, there.

Yean listened with the rapt attention of that night in camp when Miss Wang's voice was sweet as the murmur of a mountain stream and she was the lone select, invited to appreciate it. Was this poem for her too? How did Miss Wang know that this poem expressed her wishes exactly? Yean glanced at Yau Ser Mei sitting beside her. She too seemed to hang upon Miss Wang's every word, nodding as she read, 'I want one special one.'

'Like it?' Marie asked; her eyes shining with the pleasure of knowing that they did.

'Ooooh, it's so beautiful,' gushed some of the girls.

'What does this poem say to you?'

There was a pause as the girls checked their enthusiasm and thought.

'Isn't it selfish to want the whole of someone? To want someone to be always there?' asked Ken who regularly scored As for his Mathematics so his approach to all things was naturally two plus two equals four. He could never see things from anything other than the logical point of view.

'What do you all say?' was Marie's non-committal response. She looked round the group. Yean had her head down, presumably examining the ants crawling in the grass. Marie knew that Yean had been keeping her distance the whole of the school term and yet, she was pleased to note, Yean had after all been to every outing with her group.

And then there was Ser Mei, sitting next to Ken; an intense-looking girl with grim eyes set below a dark straight fringe of hair; eyes which looked out poised somewhere between great kindness and great bitterness as if to challenge her – which quality can you bring out in me? Sitting on the edge of the group, Ser Mei caught Marie with an impassive stare which disconcerted her as much as it did Ser Mei but Mei had never been one to balk at the uncomfortable. Ever since she could remember she had always had to live at a tangent with the rest of her companions who came from comfortable ordinary homes with loving parents.

'Well, Mei, what do you say?'

'Huh? Oh I don't know,' she shrugged, 'everybody is so selfish.' Her matter-of-fact tone flattened the gushing enthusiasm of the others.

'But surely, Mei, it's not wrong to want to be special to someone?' asked Yin Peng, hesitation in her voice as she looked shyly at Marie. Retiring and sensitive Yin Peng was a cripple on crutches who, of necessity, had always been on the sidelines of school life. It was Miss Wang who set her free one day when she told the class, 'Yin Peng wears her crutches on the outside but all of us wear crutches on the inside. Everybody needs a crutch. The difference is – do we have the courage to acknowledge this need and then carry on with living?' After that Yin Peng had joined the fold, full of gratitude and admiration for this unusual teacher whose acknowledgement of her handicap had helped her to be more honest with herself.

'Is it wrong, Miss Wang, to want someone special?'

'No, I don't think so,' answered Marie and she smiled so charmingly and approvingly at Yin Peng for having the courage to push her point that the girl glowed with bashful pride.

'I still say it's wrong to want the whole of someone. It's an impossible demand.' Ken responded with the conviction of a logical male.

'We're not talking about right or wrong in this case. We're talking about the needs of a particular moment in life,' shot back Marie, a little irritated at being contradicted and wanting Ken to realize that it was not only logic that determined human behaviour. 'Feelings, our feelings, are important. At such moments, a person may need to feel that he is special to someone and needs all her attention. Before we can do anything else, even before we can discuss whether that need is selfish or not, it has first to be met. If we want to help someone we have to start at the level of his needs first isn't it?' Marie looked at her group with the confidence of a teacher who knew that eventually she could bring her students round to see her point. And all did except for Ser Mei who remained unconvinced.

'It's all very well to say that, fine, but how many people can do that sort of thing?' she shrugged her dismissal.

Marie smiled. Mei was hard, hard, even harder than Yean. She had never been able to 'touch' her spirit, not even with poetry. And yet beneath that hardness and cynicism there must be a soft spot.

Yau Ser Mei was definitely a challenge. It would be difficult to handle her but Marie would never allow difficulty to stand in her way. She was all the more determined to rise to the task.

Later when the group was going home, Marie, seizing the opportunity, asked Ser Mei, 'Want to come for a walk?'

'Don't mind,' she replied.

As if that invitation was her birthright! Yean was peeved as she watched them walking off, unwilling to admit even to herself that she would have liked to be the one so invited. Such longings were best kept secret, for she regarded them as weaknesses in her own character or, worse still, perhaps, Ser Mei had something which she, Yean, did not. Anger was the best defence in any case.

*   *   *

When term re-opened Marie received this note.

Dear Miss Wang,

> I've been trying to kill your ghost for the past few weeks but I've failed. I'm not exactly sure what I want to say. Probably not very much but I'll try to be honest. Yes, you've become a very special person to me. Why? I guess it can't be understood. Perhaps because you're different; perhaps I need somebody to relate to in certain areas. No, I'm not the cold scientist trying to find a reason for every darn thing but I don't want to sound like the confused school kid who doesn't know what's happening to her either. I want to be able to come up to you and joke, or be very serious or just to be in your company without feeling awkward. I haven't the faintest idea what you can get out of me but if it's any use I promise to be a 100% insult hurler.

> Yean

She had finally accepted that with all the other students she, too, liked Miss Wang. She admired her, so rich in beauty like a piece of rare porcelain specially fired in Life's kiln for the world's benefit while she herself was only a lump of clay.

Miss Wang was so different from the others.

She was not a rice bowl teacher.

She was committed.

She treated her students as persons

and not as empty vessels

to be stuffed with mince-meat knowledge.

She was trusted by everyone.

She touched them at critical points

and they grew.

Ken found solace in telling her of his

loneliness since his mother's death.

Peter became more sensitive to others

after meeting her.

Yin Peng grew more confident on her crutches

and Ser Mei less cynical.

They were all adolescents.

They were all lonely; and inarticulate.

Touched by that sense of loneliness as they moved from the innocence of childhood into the complex world of men and women, of work, study and commitment, grating against the hardheadedness of the commercial world. Into this flood of dark doubts, longing and anxiety, Miss Wang's optimism, hope and sympathetic listening was like an island which offered temporary shelter which they hoped would be permanent.

The tiled murals of the padi planters, construction workers and ship builders along the walls of the railway station stared down at the mass of people milling below. The yellow light of the old-fashioned electric lamps hanging from the high vaulted ceiling cast an unearthly glow on their faces. In the midst of this multi-coloured ensemble a knot of white stood out. These were the sisters of the local convent who had come to send off their novitiates to Bukit Nanas in preparation for their vows.

Marie, glowing with tear-filled eyes, kissed her father and mother; hugged her two sisters and brother.

'Keep well and write often,' she told them. They nodded, a little awed by the solemnity of the occasion. Their elder sister was giving her life to Christ. Her father remained silent. He had hoped she would become a lawyer but she had failed to obtain that scholarship and now, to crown it all, she had joined the convent. He did not wish to say anything more, preferring, as he claimed, not to influence his favourite daughter and letting her make up her own mind. When it was Paul's turn to say good-bye, he smiled and hugged her briefly. 'Good-bye,' he said without looking at her and then abruptly walked away, rejecting the proffered goodwill and sympathy of the onlookers.

Marie, then, turned to her group. The boys lined up and hugged her gallantly while all the girls kissed her.

Yean and Ser Mei each gave her a rose. They looked as if they would like to cling to her a little longer but no, there were others awaiting their turns. The boys helped Yin Peng forward where she leaned on her crutches as Marie hugged her.

'Be brave,' she whispered and Yin Peng smiled through her tears.

'C'mon, you guys, she'll only be away for 3 years, not a lifetime!'

'Three cheers for Sis!
HIP HIP HOORAY!
HIP HIP HOORAY!'

the assembled students responded with gusto. And for a fitting finale, they broke into song.

'It's a long long road to freedom . . .'

Paul's lean face darkened with irritation as he watched from a distance. This was a farewell fit for a princess. She looked so radiant, so pure, so white! Damn it! How could she have talked about their break-up and yet look so radiant? Didn't he matter any more? Was he pushed aside so effectively that she could forget his anguished face? She had just walked out of his life and yet she had been so calm and open about the whole thing. It was something which had to be done for the sake of a higher good. And in the serene voice of one who had removed herself from pain, promised to pray for him to have the strength to overcome this separation. Marie, you cut like a knife. Slice by slice you separate and arrange in order of priority. Could life be lived in this way all the time? And she had sat there, silent; her eyes pleading for understanding and acceptance. And he had most probably been the one who taught her how to 'prioritise' her life as the Americans would say.

Heaving a sigh, he got into his brand new car, a BMW, and drove home. Time would tell which of them had the truer vision.

The train sped into the night, chugging between banks of lallang under a starlit sky. Marie settled into her seat but was too excited to sleep. She needed some quiet time to sort out her feelings. The other novices probably felt the same for none of them was talking. They seemed quite ghastly in this yellow light, and she hoped she didn't look like them, concentrating instead on the radiant figure that was herself a moment ago waving to the throng as the train pulled out.

Again she saw their tears of joy and sadness at her departure and felt again the sensation of pleasant surprise at the large crowd which had turned up to bid her farewell.

How could it be? Was she so well liked? What had she done to deserve this? She was conscious of having some kind of charisma, often been aware of the impact she had on others. People liked her and would often do what she asked. But she hadn't the faintest idea why. To fully acknowledge this power would have seemed like arrogance in one joining a religious community. She believed in showing the way as the apostles had done and if she were a superior being, then, somehow it must be due to the superiority of her faith. She leaned further back into her seat and gazed into the night outside the chugging train. Man's world was chaotic and as brutal as the jungle outside.

She had always felt the need to do something
which would change her society,
uproot its mix of bourgeois complacency

and urban jungle mentality;
of having a vague sense of being burnt
by lofty ideals
for which she would
willingly lay down her life.
To her, life without dreams
and visions
and hopes
was like a bird with a broken wing.
She must needs fly.
It was in her to soar above the crowd,
to look down from the blue above
and point to the way ahead
for those earth-bound below.
Life must be one wide expanse,
with room for change,
variety,
freedom
and action.
Others were drawn toward her
as moths to a light.
As their light she was responsible
to them and for them though
she must live
according to her own conceptions,
with no illusions.
Visions not illusions
were her business.
She would go about
her Father's business
conveying the truth
as she saw it.
At twenty-three she understood a lot

about the Truth,
about what was evil in the world.
It was wrong to treat people
as digits
commodities
and units.
The alienation of man from man was evil.
Faith was the bridge.
Truth another bridge.
Visions were bridges linking the community of man.
How she would love changing these abstractions
into visions of the possible!
As a bridge builder,
a bringer of Good News,
a bearer of the Sword of Truth
in a community of disbelievers,
she would be unafraid of pain;
her life would always be one
dedicated to Love and Truth.

She smiled, pleased with the way she had such facility
in arranging things in her mind. Such pleasures were
often hers these days ever since she walked through the
gates of the convent to say Yes to Him who called. In
her surrender and in her Yea, My Lord, was her
humility and commitment. His Words had thrived in the
rich garden of her mind whose bower-like quality had
already proved very attractive to others as yet unsure of
themselves. For them, she was a suggestion, a possibility,
an alternative, and this was the success of her Father's
work as well as her own. She must exploit this for the
good of others and for the development of their awareness of the misery of the world. But why did she have
to be away for so long? Already, she knew what she

must do. A long novitiate was only for the indecisive. But with this she curbed her impatience; after all, Christ took 30 years to prepare for 3 years' work. She bowed her head, and without quite knowing why, murmured, 'Please, God, forgive me.'

She opened her eyes and looked round the carriage. The other novices had fallen asleep, rocking to the rhythm of the night train moving up Malaysia. Bending down, she opened her bag and took out Ser Mei's letter, the last one given to her just as she left. She smiled. Mei, dear Mei who loved her so and who had resisted the hardest. That just proved that she, Marie, was capable of overcoming such barriers between people. She read Ser Mei's letter again and one statement stood out – 'This is bad; I need you. I hate to admit it but I'm afraid of losing you.' She was touched, and folding the letter carefully she slipped it back into her bag, a little awed by her own ability to touch people so deeply and yet remain so detached herself. She could move in and out like a freelance gardener invited into many private gardens to listen to the murmurings of the leaves, to admire the rare blooms or to cure sick plants. Though honoured and grateful she never did want to stay long in any garden. She must move on for the other gardens needed her care too. She knew she must have disappointed many people but they must accept this transience, this impermanence. It was part of life. It was also part of the condition of loving Marie.

The two-storey bungalow stood in a large garden in fashionable Kensington Park. Ken, Peter, Aileen and Kim waited outside its elaborately wrought iron gate, tired but cheerful after walking a long way in from the bus stop.

'I'm deadbeat,' said Peter. 'Obviously these people here don't go around by bus.'

'Mutt, look at Yean. They all drive or are driven.'

'I hope she invites us to swim in her pool.'

Ken rang the bell again. A huge black and brown Alsatian came bounding down the path, barking.

'Rex, Rex! Come back. Quiet!' commanded Yean as she came running after her dog. Rex obeyed and stood aside, wagging its tail.

'Hi, come in everyone. You are late.'

'We had to wait for a bus and then stroll in, you know,' explained Aileen, as if to inform Yean who probably never had to know about such things.

'Where are the others?'

'They are inside.'

'Anything to munch? I'm hungry.'

'I never knew when you weren't, Kim,' said Yean. 'My servant has cooked something special for tea. *Buboh Cha Cha* with *pisang raja*. Come in.'

Everybody trooped into the house with its spacious sitting room dominated by a grand piano and a curved settee for ten people.

'Hello, Ser Mei,' greeted Peter.

'Wow! Look at her,' shouted Kim. 'Look at these kinky bracelets. Where did you get them?'

'I don't know,' Ser Mei replied with characteristic nonchalance. 'My mum bought them and I wear them.'

She was very attractively dressed in artist's smock, silk scarf, pedal-pushers, white knee-length socks and sneakers. Of all the girls in the group Ser Mei had always been the most fashionably dressed.

'Where's Yin Peng?'

'Oh, she can't come; no one to drive her here,' replied Yean.

'She should have told me, I would have found a car to fetch her,' said Kim, looking at Yean and Ser Mei pointedly.

'Dumb! Don't fantasize, you have no car,' laughed Peter; his maleness was too blunt and blind to perceive the subtleties of women. Ser Mei and Yean exchanged uncomfortable looks.

'Both our cars are being used this morning,' Yean apologised, 'and my mother has taken my car to go shopping.'

'Hey, even if you had offered, Yin Peng's father would have refused. How can he trust a baby – barely six months on the road. Here,' said Ken, 'I've bought a St Christopher's medal for your new car.'

Yean, conscience-stricken by her oversight, was grateful for Ken's protective gesture now that Miss Wang, who was Sis to all of them now since joining the convent, was no longer by her side.

Ser Mei as usual looked impassive; nothing seemed to touch her, and everyone knew that she had come more to listen to the letter from Sis than to socialize with the rest of them.

Hi, everybody,

I'm writing again because I'm a little worried about you. Your letters reveal a fractious group, almost breaking into individual little cells. You're a group with the talent and the willingness to use this talent to serve others. I'm very happy and proud of all of you.

But if we want to be useful we have to share at a deeper level, developing our commitment to Christ and finding alternative ways of expressing our faith in a nation committed to material progress.

If our group is cohesive and strong just imagine what things we can accomplish together as the leaven of the loaf!

'Wow!' Ken exclaimed, partly to express his own inadequacy in the face of Sis's lofty ideals and partly to dispel the group's unease at having failed to live up to her expectations.

'May I keep this letter together with the other two?' Ser Mei asked.

'I'll keep this one since it was sent here,' was Yean's immediate response.

'Oh alright then; I only wanted to read it again.' Ser Mei's voice sounded matter-of-fact but they could see that she was disappointed.

But although she felt a little uneasy, Yean was not to be dissuaded by Mei's feelings. It was as if in refusing Ser Mei's request she had, there and then, fragmented the group – an act which would disappoint Sis and therefore be disapproved of by the rest.

After the group had left, Yean locked the letter in her drawer, determined not to feel guilty over her action. Surely she had as much right as Ser Mei to keep Sis's letters.

★　　★　　★

The usual dignified silence of the gallery leading to the convent's chapel was broken by the excited whispers and laughter of their group. Yean felt her happiness straining for release like the thousands of airborne balloons and pigeons on National Day. Like the apostles her group had waited and prayed and their Easter had finally dawned. They had all been accepted into the U. All their anxieties were over, their prayers had been answered, their hard work amply rewarded! But the best reward of all was – their Sis was also going to the U.

'Let's celebrate, this is God's will,' Peter shouted.

'Shhh!' the rest calmed him, and settled down to wait under the arches of the gallery for Sis's arrival. The pink and white crinium lilies nodded in the breeze and the carved cherubims and seraphims smiled in silent joy.

'Hey,' a soft voice called from behind, and before they knew it Sister Marie-Therese, without a thought for her new status, had sat down on the floor beside them, looking a little self-conscious in her snow-white habit. This gesture, so characteristic of her, warmed Yean's heart. Formality was for the other nuns and priests!

'Wow! Sis,' the boys hooted and the girls hugged her.

Ser Mei gave one of her rare warm smiles, looking deep into Sis's eyes with pleasure before hugging her and Yean noticed, pressing a note into her hands.

'Hey, what subjects are you doing, Sis?' Peter asked, pleased that Sis was still the same.

'Why are all of you going to the university?' Sis asked, stopping the excited chatter and, as usual, prodding them into thought.

'Why not? Our results qualify us.'

'But why not do something else instead?'

'What else can we do?'

'So you are going because you have no choice?'

'Sis, ah, Singapore's a meritocracy, you know. Qualifications count! You wouldn't want us to be salesmen,' Peter laughed a little uneasily because he was not sure whether he wanted to be taken seriously.

'What's wrong with being a salesman? It's a decent job.'

'Nothing wrong; just near the bottom of the ladder that's all.' Peter was already a little defensive.

'Is this what you mean by meritocracy? Just fighting to get to the top?'

Yean knew what Sis wanted their answer to be, but to test her response they answered in the affirmative.

'Is that really what you want? What happens to the underdogs? Do I detect an attempt to suppress the heart?' and Sis laughed: she had won again.

*   *   *

Later, in the convent's recreation room, Marie looked at the two letters on her lap. One was Ser Mei's, the other from her father. She took up Mei's letter first and as she read it a slight frown creased her brows: 'Now that you're back it's going to be worse. You are so near and yet so unapproachable. Why do you do this to me? Why didn't you leave me alone?'

She would have to see Mei soon. That girl needed her. Then taking up her father's letter she read it with a dimpled smile on her face. This was the first time her father had written to her so enthusiastically after his disappointment over that unobtained scholarship abroad. He had hoped that she would be as successful as Paul but her concept of success had to be different from her father's. He was devoted to his children, claiming that they had made his own meagre life as a government clerk worth living. Theirs had been the typical tradition-bound Catholic family in which the Sunday mass was the social highpoint in their family life revolving around meatless Fridays, confession, family rosaries and The Legion of Mary, of which her father was president. If her father had been disappointed, he was now very proud, joyous at being able to give to God his favourite child.

Marie excused herself from the recreation room and slipped into the chapel. Its semi-darkness gave her thoughts and pleasure the needed privacy.

'Thank you, Lord, for making the way so smooth for me. I'm glad that father is alright now. You alone know how much I love him and how terrible I felt in having to disappoint him. I'm glad he's feeling the honour of having a child chosen by you. You've been very patient with me, putting up with all my doubts and vacillations. Paul had been helpful too ...', but the moment thoughts of Paul came to mind she tried to push them away. 'No, why should I feel guilty about him? You, Lord, know all the ins and outs of my heart. I loved him but he has changed, he has changed. He is no longer the Paul who dreamed dreams. But I have found you, Lord. Give me the grace to do Your work. Take my eyes, they are Yours, my Lord. Take my ears they too are Yours. Take my hands, my heart, my all. They're Yours they're Yours, My Lord, take me, take me ...' Marie intoned in the manner she had been taught as a child, feeling herself filled with a love which wanted to give and give, which wanted to dedicate itself to something or someone who would embrace the whole of life, consume the whole of her being, the whole of everything and in whose centre was the mystery of Life itself. She bowed her head before the Blessed Sacrament with the altar lamp casting an orange glow about her head. At last she was happy. At last she could feel that she had done the right thing; that this was not an escape from the ignominy of failure as Paul had so cruelly suggested.

When Marie came out of the chapel, her Mother Superior saw the glow of happiness on her face and felt confident that here was one who would make it to permanent vows.

The Lord be praised.

Amen.

SER MEI

Bukit Temasek Road – straight, treelined and broad; capable of carrying eight lanes of traffic: four going up and four going down. An eight o'clock sun, serious about its business of shining bright and hot to remind Singaporeans below that the world did not owe them a living. Buses, cars and trucks speeding past each other to reach their destination on time. Independent Singapore always in a hurry. From the bus Marie looked beyond the cars at the monsoon drain on her right, straight and wide, running down the middle of the road with four lanes of traffic and a row of Rain Trees on each side. A huge drain, fifteen metres wide and fifteen metres deep, its concrete sides rising at a 70-degree angle and shining glaringly white in the morning sun. By international standards this was the cleanest monsoon drain in South-East Asia; almost devoid of man-made rubbish like soggy cardboard cartons, beer cans, broken bottles, foul-smelling carcasses of dogs, ducks and chickens. It was even devoid of Nature-made rubbish like rotting tree trunks, pieces of driftwood and fallen leaves. Ah, but this monsoon drain was not built to become a communal dustbin as most monsoon drains in South-East Asia inevitably become. This was built to remain a monsoon drain. Its function was to drain off excess water. This was a product of the kind of rational planning praised by Paul, aimed at straightening out all the irregularities and meanderings of Man and Nature to promote a comforting sense of orderliness and perhaps efficiency in a nation with little or no resources but which proudly and justifiably refused to bow to the poverty of such a condition.

Marie got down from the bus and joined the rest of the students walking up the slope of Temasek University which rose large, tall and white. Its 25-storey Science Tower stood out square, sharp-edged and proud of its effective utilization of space – a direct contrast to the sprawling complex of low-lying colonial buildings in the vicinity which housed the departments of History and Philosophy. This Science Tower and the adjacent 10-storey Administration Block sat atop a green slope; their harsh white outlines partially softened by the shady branches of the spreading umbrella-shaped Flame of the Forest. The road on which she was walking meandered up the slope with a hedge divider running down the middle with one lane for incoming traffic on the left and one for outgoing traffic on the right. This meandering would disturb the rational mind of someone like Paul. He would have wished that the engineer had straightened out the road by cutting through the slope instead of making the road go around it thereby lengthening the driving distance by another twenty metres. However, on reflection Paul would have comforted himself with the thought that his rational mind could afford to be more tolerant. Temasek University was the product of the old colonial days. National independence would rectify this defect in planning in time when the nation built a national university to reflect rational thought and cost-effective planning. Then it would be the centre to produce the men and women of top calibre capable of planning and building many more Bukit Temasek Roads and their monsoon drains. But for the time being the cream of the nation's brains would have to settle for something less than the best. Not for long. Things would change, Paul would have promised. At this, Marie was forced to agree, since nothing remains old in a dynamic nation.

The students streamed through the gates and up the path which ran parallel to the University Road, all moving on course as if propelled by a collective consciousness of goal and direction. Marie joined this stream of human traffic, not without a sense of reluctance, but although her heart was not glad on this bright morning she knew that the sight of this continuous multi-coloured stream of students filing up the slope into the portals of the University would have gladdened the hearts of many a policy maker.

Temasek University – the epicentre of learning and scholarship! The hopes and fears of all the years are met in thee today. They were the *crème de la crème* – these undergrads like herself, the survivors of a decade of keen competition. They were clearers of obstacles and hurdles and the passers of examinations – the P.S.L.E., the 'O' Level and the formidable 'A' Level. And now, after a decade or more of racing and chasing, they had learnt to gallop, to trot, to plod and to clop; always ready to change pace according to the requirements of the occasion for, as Paul had so earnestly asked, wasn't it true that the ability to change and adapt was the hallmark of those fittest to survive? And the ability to change according to the exigencies of the external condition was not an ability a developing nation could afford to sneer at; this he had always drummed into her head. Only those with an intelligence honed and sharpened to discern the needs of a situation; only those with the humility to bow to the demands of external forces; only those with the courage to rip off parts which had become useless could change, adapt and survive! He had always wanted her to agree with his point of view. The really absurd thing was that somehow he seemed afraid for her. Two million people living in a city state which perceived itself to be surrounded by hostile forces could never afford the luxury of thinking beyond the level of basic survival. Don't rock the boat whatever you do! The ocean is full of sharks. A few sharks are hidden in our midst and some may be in ourselves. In you.

Marie knew this was what the popular mind thought too. Selfish commonsense. Peasant mentality. Such caution was cowardice.

Cowardice? Paul had screamed. We are at the mercy of all the big powers! Surrounded by hostile forces, we have to make it on our own! Nobody will help us! But her reaction to such rhetoric had dumbfounded poor Paul. How they had argued! He had accused her of living in an ivory tower. Didn't she know that the popular mind demanded from its leadership that same discerning realism which could balance the nation's precarious independence, poised between the dark rage smashing out of gnawing stomachs and useless hands and the calm satisfaction exuding from filled bellies and busy hands? The popular will demanded that a tough realistic leadership keep the rice bowls full; keep their hands busy and forge a sense of purpose and direction in order to turn the wheels of commerce and industry. Yes, yes, yes, always concerned about full rice bowls and prosperity. As long as they can deliver these goods we submit to them, we bow to them, we tolerate their arrogance. But Paul had scoffed at her. Didn't she know that the first generation of such tough realistic leaders had been the lucky product of a system designed only to produce the white collar auxiliaries of the white administrators of a far-flung empire? But now in our new Republic, and she could still remember how his voice rose, such a vital element of our national life would never be left to chance again. This tough-minded leadership would be bred, cultivated, nurtured and moulded according to the requirements of our national condition. Our leaders would use the University to transform our society into a modern industrializing nation geared for the technological age! Paul, dear Paul, how wrong. How narrow. Once more, she was glad that she had not married him. His vision was too limited, both his feet were on the ground, while she, Marie-Therese, intended to take wing and fly.

*   *   *

Two hundred potential leaders of society opened the doors of Lecture Theatre 1 and entered, chatting merrily. This was lecture 4 of Sociology I, a course conducted by Dr Ramsey J. Jones. Marie, Yean, Ser Mei and the rest of their group looked up at the tiers of seats being filled quickly. The front seats had all been taken or reserved by diligent students who wanted to be near the lecturer so that they would be too embarrassed to fall asleep.

'They want to hear and take down every precious word!' said Aileen who obviously did not think highly of such diligence.

'Don't you know that in this institution the word is revered!' Marie explained. 'The learning of the authoritative word, written and published by a Ph.D. whose books are on the required reading lists is the shortest road to academic success.'

'Oooh! I can't stand them,' Aileen declared. 'Let's go to the back.'

This was their usual practice. They would always sit at the back of the lecture theatre with the foreign students who usually took a more *laissez-faire* attitude toward their work. Ten past nine and still no sign of Dr Jones. This was quite unusual. Some of the boys were already fidgeting and had started on their favourite pastime of folding and throwing paper planes. Presumably they were practising for this afternoon's E O G M of the 25th Executive Council of the University's Students' Union. Childish! was the word which flashed across Marie's mind, and her look of contempt was reflected in the faces of Yean, Ser Mei, Kim and Aileen while the boys just looked amused.

'Those buggers down there are sure to disrupt this afternoon's meeting, as usual,' Peter laughed but Marie did not find it amusing. She did not laugh and, taking the cue from her, neither did the others.

Then the door swung open and in strode Dr Jones armed with a cassette recorder and a huge roll of paper. As the buzz of voices died down Dr Jones greeted them and immediately turned and faced the blackboard. He unfurled a large sketch of himself caught in a blank-eyed stare behind his thick glasses. He pinned this up and turning round to the students again, stood with arms akimbo, eyeing the students, obviously relishing their surprised silence.

'Ladies and gentlemen, I've had four weeks of your silent adoration as you arduously tried your best to note down every pearl which dropped from my mouth. You adored my words. And so, to give up my pearls unadulterated by my presence I have here this morning a replacement (and he pointed to his portrait and tape recorder). Should you then miss any part of my lecture you may simply stop the tape, rewind and play it back again with no fear of insulting me. Good morning then, I leave you to your labour. I'll be in the canteen having my breakfast.'

He made a right-angled turn, strode out, and a loud buzz rose up and burst the momentary silence as the lecture theatre door swung close.

'What's going on?'

'Is he coming back?'

'Is this another of his jokes?'

'You bet! Must have missed his breakfast. His wife overslept, too much fun last night. Ha, ha, ha!'

No one seemed to know what to do but not for long. A Students' Union councillor came to the rescue. He leapt from his seat and gallantly went up to the front of the lecture theatre where, a little self-consciously, he raised his hands for silence. When the crowd quietened down he switched on the tape recorder. A loud cheer arose; his re-election that afternoon as councillor for another term was assured: he had acted decisively as all leaders should in a crisis. His friends and supporters were proud of him. As Dr Jones's voice came over the speakers loud and clear, Marie watched, amazed, for everyone else took up their pens and began to write. No question, no argument, simply acceptance!

Yean looked at Marie. She returned Yean's enquiring look and both shared a smile. The two of them looked down their row of seats. Aileen, Kim and Mei turned toward Marie. And so did Kenneth and Peter. Then as if a secret code had passed between them they stood up in one accord, scrambled over the other seats and got out. The two foreign students, looking highly amused, followed suit.

'Hey, what's he up to?' Kim asked the moment they were outside the lecture theatre.

'I don't know,' Marie answered. 'It's sheer stupidity! They don't even feel insulted. Look at them still writing in there.'

Only five other students had followed the group out. They went in the direction of the library, perhaps to catch up with their research work.

'Let's go to the canteen and ask Dr Jones,' Marie suggested.

Dr Jones who was there munching on a roti prata, waved and invited them to join him. The group sat around him, fascinated by this man who was bespectacled with a short black beard, often seen striding down the corridors of the campus with a gangly grace because of a short body placed on rather long legs. He was well liked by the students because he was always doing something or saying something to shock them out of their unquestioning acceptance of everything they heard during lectures. Once, to demonstrate that the limits of personal freedom were often self-imposed, he stood on his head for ten minutes, yoga-style, and lectured in that pose. He challenged the students to call him crazy but of course, none of them did.

'Well, didn't ya enjoy the lecture?' he asked with a twinkle in his eyes.

There was an immediate resounding 'No'.

'Why did you do it?' Marie asked.

'Guess.'

'To test our reactions.'

'To see whether we have learnt anything from your lectures on freedom and responsibility,' Peter said.

'Yes, yes,' Aileen joined in, eager not to be left out. 'You wanted to see whether we would exercise our freedom.'

'Or simply just saying you're bored because we treated you more like a tape recorder than a person,' said Kim who was always conscious of the feelings of others.

Dr Jones laughed, obviously pleased that at least one group had understood his lectures. The whole group was invited to a party at his house the next Saturday and Marie was happy with this recognition of her group. They were no blind followers like the others; they could discriminate, discern and make up their own minds.

'You must think us terrible to play such an awful trick on us,' Ken pointed out.

'Well ...' drawled Dr Jones, 'considering the present evidence, aren't you?'

'Ya, but we're not all like that.'

'Yes, how many of you are here? Seven. Seven out of ...'

'Five more. They've gone to the library,' said Kim, eager to defend the local student too.

'Very well, twelve out of two hundred. Not a high percentage is it?'

Yean thought that Dr Jones smiled almost triumphantly for like all pedagogues he wanted to be right. But Ken and Peter were not convinced. Ken still felt Dr Jones was being unfair.

'I mean, take his reaction when we didn't accept his challenge to call him crazy. From there he said we lack guts and are too conforming. He doesn't even know us. How can he make such a generalization?'

'I think it's just his way of being provocative. All these expats are like that. They like their students to question them and only respect those who challenge them,' Aileen tried to explain.

'Ah ah, but we're not brought up like this. It's good we didn't respond to his challenge, you know. It's just not right to call a lecturer crazy even though he is,' and the group laughed as Ken mimicked Dr Jones's gestures and facial expressions.

'If we had called him crazy to his face we would have allowed a single American lecturer to undermine two thousand years of Chinese civilization in which respect and decorum were one of the cornerstones,' Peter declared solemnly. He was proud of being a Chinese although as a Peranakan he spoke no Chinese at all.

'Wow! Listen to the guy!' Kim teased. 'He has really gone deep into Chinese Philosophy. Dr Li must have impressed you, Pete.'

Peter grinned and waved his copy of the *Analects*. It was only at this juncture that they noticed Ser Mei's absence.

'Hey, where's Mei?'

'Oh, she's with Sis. I think they've gone for a walk.'

Yean shrugged off her hurt at having been left out again. Why wasn't she ever asked for a walk? What was lacking in her? Must one always have to have a problem in order to get close to Sis? She resented Ser Mei's melodrama. That girl always looked as if she were at a funeral.

'What's wrong with her these days? She hangs around Sis all the time like a shadow,' Aileen observed.

'She looks depressed.'

'Ya, when she's with us she doesn't utter a word.'

'She doesn't say anything to Sis either. Just now in the canteen all she did was smile. She should speak up. I think Sis is getting quite fed up with her,' Peter declared bluntly for he had never learnt to mince his words and being the only one who had to work during the holidays to pay his university fees he often expected the others to accept his comments without question.

*   *   *

Saturday evening waned amidst the lengthening shadows of the trees along University Road, its soft light filtering through the canopy of leaves to rest upon the few bungalows set in spacious green gardens bright with the orange, gold and red of the cannas and hibiscus. The pink and white frangipanis added their scent to the evening air – a sure sign according to Kim that this area was inhabited by foreigners since only they would plant frangipanis in their gardens.

'We plant them in cemeteries.'

'That's how the Chinese regard them but the Indians wear them in their hair,' explained Peter.

'No, not the white type which are the flowers of the dead,' said Aileen in that superior tone so often assumed by the true-blue Peranakan.

'Hey, stop arguing you two,' Ken called. 'Sis and Mei are already at the gate and Yean is with them. She must have gone to fetch them.'

'Hi!' Marie called.

'Wowee!' the four of them shouted.

'What happened to the white robe, brown cross and

veil? Is this the result of Vatican II?' asked Aileen who prided herself on having kept up with the results of Pope John 23rd's attempt to drag the Church into the twentieth century.

'Wow wow wow! Look at our girl!' yelled Peter.

'Quiet, you people,' laughed Marie, pleased with their reaction. 'Our community has decided that it's more practical to shorten our skirts and do away with the veil.'

Without her veil, Marie looked boyishly attractive with her close-cropped curly hair, dressed in a slim A-line dark blue skirt and soft white blouse, with a thin gold cross pinned to the lapel of her collar. The whole group admired the new Marie-Therese look and approved. This air of admiration encircled them, clinging to them and spilling over to the rest of Dr Jones's guests so that the whole group found itself basking in the keen looks cast in their direction. It was obvious that they had made an impact on the people gathered there – a motley group of seniors, lecturers, journalists and missionaries.

Marie enjoyed the attention she was getting as leader of her delegation. Word had gone round that this group of first-year students had impressed Dr Jones by walking out of his recorded lecture and he had honoured them with an invitation to one of his well-known parties to which only the Honours students were normally invited. Dr Jones came forward to greet them. 'Hello, do make yourselves at home, the food and drinks are over there.' He pointed to a table near the balcony where some guests were handing round cups of fruit punch and plates of chips.

The huge living room, which opened on to another spacious balcony, was furnished colonial style, with large armchairs and settees made of Indonesian cane. Many of the guests had made themselves comfortable on cushions on the parquet floor and some were sprawled on the Indian rugs, thrown here and there for careless effect. It was a bachelor's room made for comfort rather than style. Sasi, an overweight Indian girl, was helping Dr Jones play host. Grotesque in a long flowing kaftan she was reclining on the settee next to the table of food, like a fat queen bee, doling out chips to the guests. Yean took one look at her and grimaced in a mix of disapproval, fascination and pain. Sasi was casually sipping a shared glass of whiskey and soda with one of the foreign journalists. She took a puff from his cigarette too, leaving a heavy trace of her scarlet lipstick on the tip. Yean, whose image of the demure Indian girl was smashed, how could she do this with an Ang Mo, looked round at her group busily chatting with Dr Jones. Only Ser Mei seemed to have seen what she saw but although she looked in Yean's direction Mei's face was, as usual, an impassive wall.

'And this is the Rev Dr James Smith and his assistant, Hans Kuhn,' Dr Jones was saying.

'Hello,' the two men spread their smiles around the group, but except for the silver crosses pinned to the lapels of their collars Rev James and Hans looked more like graduate students than a pastor and his assistant. The tall, handsome, blue-eyed Hans Kuhn with his wavy blond hair looked like an athlete with broad shoulders and strong arms accentuated by a well-cut sports shirt which gave him an air of sophistication and style, something so lacking in many local priests, Yean reflected.

'Hey, you there are birds of a feather,' hooted Kim and everybody laughed as they took in the gold and silver crosses of Sister Marie-Therese, Rev James and Hans.

'Here is someone from an entirely different nest – the venerable Institute of Asian and Pacific Studies – Mak Sean Loong,' announced Dr Jones.

A tall, bespectacled and slightly paunchy young man with a head of bristling hair trimmed so short that they stood up like the hair of a tough toilet brush, approached the group. He walked with an air of challenging arrogance, his high forehead coated with a perpetual sheen of sweat, so that the overall impression was of an angry young man locked in the aged body of an overgrown gnome. This jarring effect gave him impact, bringing a negative electric current with him wherever he went.

'So you're the new elite in the Soci department,' he said almost tauntingly so that Peter asked, 'I don't understand. What elite? We're just here to study.'

'Precisely, that's the trouble. Everybody including myself comes here to get our passport to wealth. There is no meaningful participation here. Merely isolated efforts – some hours of voluntary work in an institution, a rag and flag big-do, and a grand dinner and dance in which we gorge ourselves sick and we have all the organisers patting themselves on the back! That's all there is to it – patchwork charity. Nothing more! Nothing! The intellectuals here are irrelevant. Their theses are mostly crap written by petty bourgeois minds!'

Marie listened to all this with great interest. At last, here was something honest and sensible about the university.

'We must invite him to our group for a talk,' she whispered to Yean, at the same time turning away from

Ser Mei who seemed lost in her own thoughts again. Marie was exasperated to see how Mei never could or never would make any effort to join the group's discussions. She would be there but always hovering diffidently on the fringe. Ah, Yean was different. Yean could hold her own in any discussion and would be the leaven in the loaf.

Ser Mei sank deeper into a corner of her soul as the talk drifted on.

I so old already; how long more you want me to work? she kept hearing her mother's shrill pleading Cantonese in her head. *All this I do for you ... if you not born you think I have to work? ... but I want to give you good things, good life. I know, I know he old-lah but he can pay you know. Pay very well. A house! You want some more is it? And he only sometimes can come. You can do anything you want still. I no need to work.* Ser Mei pushed such thoughts from her head. Was she being selfish rejecting her mother's pleading? Yean was by this time as animated as the rest. All their faces showed that they were caught up in a lively discussion with Mr Mak and the two missionaries. Except for her, they were interested and interesting. They were the concerned students that Sis wanted them to be. Ser Mei felt tainted. She had none of the others' purity of concern. None of their disinterest. Her interests would always be centred on her own life. Yes, she was selfish. Her mother was right. She could not see beyond herself.

'It's imperative that Christian and Catholic students move out of the tiny world of individual concerns into the larger world of societal issues,' Hans Kuhn was saying.

'Yes, yes, the Christian whilst not of the world must

63

live in the world to transform it. The Kingdom of Heaven is at hand, so say the Gospels but how will we make it happen?' Marie, too, was swept away by the rhetoric of the party.

Dr Jones looked approvingly at Marie and was glad that he had discovered her. Hans was glad too. A common chord was sounding. Both perceived themselves as having the task to guide, to mould and to re-direct the Christian and Catholic students' movements.

★   ★   ★

That night as Hans drove Marie back to the convent, he looked appreciatively at the young novice beside him, attractively slim in her 'civvies' as she called her new outfit. Marie was staring dreamily ahead, pleased with the way things had turned out. Hers would not be that lonely a task after all, for tonight she sensed a strong ally in Hans Kuhn, this young, handsome and idealistic missionary. She stole a glance at him and was startled to find him staring at her. They laughed.

'Watch out for the car in front! You dangerous foreign driver!'

'It's not my fault if God puts such lovely creatures in my path. I have to stop and appreciate.'

Marie smiled and dismissed Hans's compliment with a wave of her hand. They had arrived at the convent gate and Marie got out.

'Thanks, see you next Monday then,' she called as Hans drove off.

They would meet next week for lunch to discuss how they should work together in the new spirit of ecumenism. She would introduce him to the rest of her group as part of her effort to open up the Catholic movement to people from other denominations. But now she must face the iron gate. It was already half past eleven as she pressed the bell gingerly, careful not to wake up the whole community. Facing the iron gate resolutely, as if the sheer force of her penetrating gaze could will Sister Beatrice to walk a little faster, she reminded herself to ask for a spare set of keys. At last she heard the key turning in the ancient lock. The heavy iron gate creaked open, and Sister Beatrice's wrinkled face peered out at her.

'Mana pergi? So late then come back. Berapa jam sekarang?' her querulous voice demanded an explanation.

'Pergi university lecturer's party,' Marie replied.

'Aa ha, party party tiap-tiap malam party.'

Marie winced and hurriedly planted a kiss on the aged sister's withered cheek before running off to her room feeling more like a disobedient teenager than a novice serious about her vocation. But vocation she had, she was certain about that, though it would, of course, be broader in scope than that of Sister Beatrice, the gate keeper.

Meeting Hans over lunch to discuss the affairs of their respective students' Christian movements was one thing. Going to a party at night with Hans was another. Marie was very clear on this point and had firmly refused his invitation to a dance on Saturday night at Raffles Hostel. But Hans was not a Catholic priest who had taken the vow of celibacy, neither was he your regular conservative pastor's assistant who would meet the female parishioners only on Sundays after the Church service. He was different. Athletically handsome, blue-eyed and blond, he believed that the workers of God need not behave like retarded eunuchs. They were no different from other men, he had said, they had the same capacity to enjoy a woman's company.

On this Saturday night Han's companion was Ser Mei. Her fashionable attire and quiet deportment fitted into his conception of the modern Oriental Chinese girl. He had noticed, too, that Ser Mei had stuck close to Marie during all their meetings and took this to mean that Mei was Marie's protegée.

'Wo! Wo! Weeeee!' the guys at the party hooted and whistled as Hans and Ser Mei, complete with crash helmets, zoomed up the driveway on a bright red motor bike. 'Hey, Hans, good show!' they shouted and raised their hands in the thumbs-up sign of victory.

Hans, his face creased in smiles, helped Ser Mei with her helmet, then led her up the steps of Raffles Hostel to the students' applause. Ser Mei looked gorgeous in flowing pale green silk pants, trimmed with tiny blossoms and flaring at the ankles. Her pale green silk and straight dark hair made her stand out in the ballroom like a delicate Chinese blossom among the hot tropical colours of reds, golds and sophisticated blacks. The other girls in their showy sequinned long gowns looked ordinary beside her. Hans, the small-town American felt proud.

'Shall we dance first and have a drink with Peter and Yean later?' he asked.

Ser Mei nodded, as she tried hard to swallow once again the lump of fear and repulsion which had become inexplicably stuck in her throat. No, this was different. Hans belonged to the Church. The others were crude sailors and soldiers with tattoos. Hans wore a cross. She smiled at him and allowed herself to be led into the dance hall, dimly lit by myriads of coloured bulbs strung across the room like Christmas night.

The band made the dancers thump their feet, beat their hands, sway and jerk their bodies. They were all doing the Shake, the Jerk and A-go-go Twist. As if one of her selves had stood apart, she watched herself stepping to the music with Hans, tapping feet and clapping hands, letting the music take over their bodies as they twisted and turned in rhythmic jerks and shakes forming beautiful jagged designs with their bodies. The crowd applauded and made room for them as they danced beautifully just as in a well executed jazz ballet number. They were like parts of a whole as they separated and came together again and again; their bodies instinctively responding like close friends. Again and again the crowd applauded as they twisted and turned through three numbers before thirst and exhaustion pushed them out of the dance hall.

From the verandah, Ken called over the heads of the crowd. 'Hi! Hans, we're over here.'

'Hey, didn't you two dance?' Hans asked.

'We did, but you two distracted us,' Yean complained. 'How can you take over the dance floor like this? It's undemocratic, you know.'

'I don't know,' Mei replied demurely, 'but Sis did say that superiority comes from authority and skill. Do you think ours fall into the latter category?' asked Mei with a rare twinkle flickering in her eyes.

'Gang way, gang way!' shouted Peter bringing four drinks and a Sikh with him. 'Hans, this is Santok Singh.'

'Just call me Tok,' he said. 'And how long have you been here?' he asked as he pulled up a chair to join them.

He was one of the newly elected Students' Union councillors, and wasted no time in trying to find out more about this foreigner. He sat down beside Hans.

'Have you been here long?' he asked again, eyes alight, and his angular nose twitching with interest.

'Oh, about a year or so,' shrugged Hans who felt a streak of dislike brush past him at the thought of being interrogated by this self-important student official.

'How do you find our clean and green city?' Tok asked, still trying to be friendly.

'Impressive and disturbing.' The party lights caught just the faint trace of a smile on Hans's lips.

'Eh? What do you mean?' Hans's comments arrested Tok's attention at once.

'Look at these trees,' said Hans as he pointed to the rows of naked angsana trees down the road, standing like embarrassed sentinels in the orange glow of the street lamps, their sawn-off branches pointing skywards bearing thin strands of sprouting green leaves.

'Instant trees, you call them. They disturb me. Aren't they a symbol of the new Singapore which advertises itself as "Instant Asia" in tourist brochures? Your clean and honest government said, Let there be trees, and overnight there are trees. And then, let there be a hardworking and efficient work force. Overnight, there are your P and E councils in each factory. Instant productivity and efficiency! Your modern Singapore is a hothouse where things are doctored to grow faster and faster all the time.'

'But we have no choice. We have to; we have no natural resources. Don't forget, we've just been kicked out of Malaysia. From now on we have no hinterland to depend on; and the world does not owe us a living. We have to look out for ourselves now with subversive enemies on all fronts,' said Tok, breathless with the rapid recital of an argument learnt by heart.

'No, no, no,' protested Hans, waving his hands to stop Tok's recital. 'I have nothing against your attempts to survive, improve and progress. I only hope you're not ditching something invaluable. Your pressure cooker country is the epitome of godlessness.' Hans allowed a slight dramatic pause for the last word to sink in before he continued. 'Structures, systems and networks are established for the sake of doing things faster and more efficiently. Man has to adapt to this pace of an impersonal system all the time. What do you, the citizen of a country which prides itself as multi-religious, value?' Hans paused again to look at Tok, pleased with the silence he had created, while Yean shifted uncomfortably feeling this was too much like a Bible lesson; and Hans

69

continued, 'What should we value? The creation of God or the creations of man? Eh?' In this audience of four Christians and a Sikh he had, he felt, clinched the argument.

Ken got up. 'I need a drink, anyone for another drink?' No one answered. So Ken turned to Yean. 'C'mon, Yean, let's dance.' He pulled Yean up while Hans smiled at them, a little puzzled. The expected applause had not come. He looked at Ser Mei but her head was bent, deep in thought. She had not heard a word of what was going on. Yet for Hans as he looked at her, she was the only one who had understood and he leaned back in his chair, satisfied.

'You always angry with me and Ang Mo; you now go and dance with this Ang Mo. Got meaning or not? Where got meaning I ask you? I cheap; I say you the cheap one! I go out I get paid, you go out you got nothing, you give him free service. I go to bring back money for you!' Ser Mei cringed at the memory of her mother flinging this at her when Hans rode up to the gate on his motorbike. 'Ser Mei!' She shook off her guilt, looked up and smiled into the blue eyes of Hans who was extending a hand to her. She took it and he led her back into the dance hall. The band was playing a slow sentimental number. 'Yesterday ... all ... my ... troubles ... were so far away.' Only the shadows moved. Slowly. Very slowly. Swaying a little to the music. Shadows huddling close; so very close together. Hans was taking her in his arms, encircling her tiny shape. His hands gliding down her back, smooth and silky. He liked the feel and coolness of silk as he bent his head, enjoying the fragrance of her Chinese hair while his other hand fingered the nape of her neck, cool and smooth as down. Hugging her closer and closer, he pressed against her small full breasts. Abruptly she pulled away to stand there in the middle of the dance floor. 'I'm not well. Please take me home,' she whispered and Hans led her out.

*   *   *

> Deck the halls with boughs of holly
> Tra la la la la la la la la
> 'Tis the season to be jolly
> Tra la la la la la la la la

Their voices rang out from the sitting room of the manse glowing with the light from tall red candles and the tungsten lamps hanging down from the ceiling.

Marie beamed as she looked round at all the students sitting on the floor, holding hands and singing in this new spirit of faith and love. She had broken new ground in this joint service with Hans and Rev James. A few months ago such a service bringing Catholics and Christians together would have been unthinkable. When the singing stopped Hans began, 'December is the season of vulnerability, not the month of good cheer as the commercials would have us believe. It is a month of pretence and defence. Sorry to disappoint you lah!' He imitated the students who looked at him uncomfortably.

Yean knew that Sis wanted this to be a Christmas service with a difference. She waited to see how different it would be. The twenty students gathered here liked Hans; his height and blue eyes which seemed to look straight into you, had scored high points with the girls.

'Your campus is alive with societies organising functions – that's the official name for such activities,

I hear,' Hans continued, enjoying the students' surprise, for they had expected him to say something traditional for the occasion.

'Your Students' Union has proudly proclaimed its presentation of a masked ball at the Malaysia Hotel. Let me read this to you – Going cheap! Cheap? $95 per couple. Hurry, hurry! Limited places. Prizes galore! The hostels offer humbler fare – for $20, I'm told, you get beer, chips and chicks.'

Yean saw too that Ser Mei winced at the mention of 'chicks' and carefully kept her eyes on the floor. Much too sensitive, Mei, for the others just laughed and relaxed. They did not mind his attack on campus activities. Like Yean herself, they agreed with him.

'This is the season of planned pretence. Union committees plan these functions as if they're serious affairs. Strangers attend these functions and pretend to enjoy themselves. This is canned fun, package tours for foreigners.'

The third foreigner in the group, Dr Jones, roared with laughter at this while the students smiled at the truth of it and Yean half-wished that such comments had come from themselves instead of from a Westerner.

Hans continued, 'Jim and I didn't spend very much on this meal for you and we both welcome you to share a moment in our lives as we break bread together. The pampered bourgeoisie need money for fun, we don't.'

They applauded enthusiastically for although it was not what Yean would call a sermon it had given them some food for thought. Then Rev James rose to continue the service, 'Lord, we are gathered here tonight to celebrate . . . '

'Wait,' Mak Sean Loong interrupted, breaking the

gathering solemnity, 'I'd like to read something here.' He did not pause for permission to go on and they were startled at the vehemence in his tone. 'Christianity has been practically identified with certain systems and has become an ideology, a cultural captive and apologist of either feudalism, colonialism or capitalism. As a reaction to such political absolutism many Christians have opted out, refusing to judge any socio-political system, pleading incompetence and worrying mainly about private wealth and morality when privileges are threatened.'

Mak stopped and looked at his audience, expecting some challenge, but none came. They did not understand what he had read. It seemed so out of place and unconnected with what was going on. Only the three foreigners looked unperturbed. Even Sis frowned although she must have known that it came from one of her favourite authors, de la Torre. Fortunately, Hans came to the rescue.

'The main point here is that though we are concerned with our private morality we are de-personalising many of our human activities. But the significance of Christmas is that Christ, our personal Saviour, should remind us that we are the children of God created with free will and are therefore responsible for our lives.'

With this reassurance they all felt better; Hans had placed the speech in a religious light which they could understand.

'Let us join hands now and pray that we may have the courage and conviction to live our lives responsibly,' Hans began.

'And the strength to live as free men and not slaves,' Sis concluded.

'Amen.'

As if awakened and released the circle of bowed heads broke up and strolled into the dining room in twos and threes, eager for Campbell's soup and garlic bread. The aroma of crisp French loaves and bowls of steaming chicken soup filled the cosy dining room. Two red candles surrounded by green leaves and brown casuarina cones at either end of the white table gave it an air of festive cheer. They gathered together passing food to one another.

'Was it alright for Mr Mak to interrupt the service and read that quotation?' Aileen asked Rev James. She had meant it as a private question but it was heard by all around the table. Tall and forthright, Aileen was merely reflecting the feelings of those Catholics who regarded such interruptions and readings from secular literature during a service as almost sacrilegious.

'Yes, do you have any objections?' Mak intervened from across the room, smacking his lips for he had been waiting for just such a question.

Hans joined him in saying, 'The church is still part of the establishment here and as long as it doesn't identify with the Asian masses it's doomed to failure, it has no future.'

Both Marie and Yean looked at him, with Marie nodding in agreement. She saw a courageous Christian speaking out frankly, unfettered by blind loyalty to his organization. Yean with the rest of the students did not know how to react to these new but exciting views.

'Yes, at the moment it is an arrogant church,' Hans continued, 'which sees itself as the genuine and true religion above all other misguided faiths in the East. It is so filled with its own brand of the truth that it has failed to dialogue with the Asians for the past five hundred years, listening only to its own establishment – particularly its middle class parishioners, its financiers who sponsor her rallies and her crusades. So busy with planning mission strategy and collecting statistics on the number of souls saved it has no time to listen to the people. They become merely the objects of evangelism to be gathered into a building every Sunday to proclaim to the world – we're saved! we're saved! And all those folks out there must be brought into the fold!'

The students clapped heartily at one of the best sermons they had ever heard. This was the first time they had heard someone not considered as a pagan or Satan's tool attacking the church.

Ser Mei stopped clapping and looked at Marie, hoping to catch her eye, but Marie's eye was busy elsewhere.

'Now that we're not at a religious service anymore,' Rev James winked teasingly at Aileen, 'may I read this to all of you? It's part of Rev Fukuda's sermon before he left Singapore last week,' and like Mak, he did not wait for an answer. 'I dislike this word, crusading, as much as I dislike the serpent. I don't think that crusading has a place in the house of God. It has a self-righteous, pharisaic, military tone. It does not belong to the followers of the Prince of Peace who died on the Cross. I refuse to sing, "We are soldiers in Christ's army" marching against the foe. It does not express the centre of the Gospels – God so loved us He sent His Only Son who died for us. This hymn is cheap and ugly to sing. There should be a difference between Jesus Christ and General Westmoreland.'

Here Rev James stopped and looked at his audience. Ser Mei saw that the Christians in the group looked a trifle embarrassed for clearly he was directing this message at them. The Catholics in the group smiled with just a touch of complacency at one another for they had not been urged to crusade at all. Neither Catholic nor Christian and faced with more basic issues, Ser Mei took no part in the exchange, but concentrated on trying to catch Marie's attention. She must talk to Sis tonight.

'When did Christianity become a cheap military campaign?' Rev James continued. 'I contend that a good hundred million American dollars, one hundred years of Christianity and high-powered salesmanship with one hundred thousand Billy Grahams will not make Asia Christian!' His audience applauded enthusiastically.

'Rev Fukuda is right. Christianity is becoming like the military campaign in Vietnam,' added Hans, and Marie, catching the mood of the moment, raised her fist in mock salute and shouted, 'American salesmanship! Religion packaged as an army marching to a glorious victory, Hail General Westmoreland!' When Hans smiled at her, she felt rewarded, and as if to share this unlooked-for bounty Marie turned and smiled at Ser Mei sitting at the far end of the table.

Ser Mei gave a start. She had almost given up hope of Sis noticing her. She returned Sis's smile but too late, she had turned back to the general discussion of the war in Vietnam.

Everyone round the table was agreeing that:

the war was immoral,

the peasants were suffering most,

the Buddhists were burning themselves in vain, that the Communists were only trying to unite the land, and the Americans were interfering.

Hans finished by declaring that faith and love had to

have the courage to oppose all oppressors, that the Church must not be afraid and that she must fight on the side of the poor and the oppressed and Marie followed his fingers as they moved in mid-air, emphasizing a point here and elaborating an idea there. Such square masculine fingers. Such big generous hands. With his arms pressed against his sides, only his hands moving: coming together and moving apart; coming together and moving apart. She was fascinated. His hands had a rhythm of their own. Yet she told herself she liked his views and found the evening a most pleasant occasion. Besides the students had decided that they didn't know much about Vietnam and would like to discuss it further. Mak had promptly agreed to provide the reading materials. Now things were moving according to his wish too, and Marie was happy for her group who had shown an interest beyond their usual concerns. Yean was deep in conversation with Dr Jones. Ken and Aileen were still arguing with Mak about the Church. Even Mei, despite her reticence, was following the discussion with interest. Yes, tonight she was proud of her group. The leaven of the loaf was not too far-fetched an ideal. She was certain her vision of things would prevail.

Glancing at her, Yean knew that Sis was proud of them all tonight although this both pleased and disturbed her. Sis's ardent feelings and buoyancy were carrying them on the crest of a wave and nobody bothered to find out what was beneath. All night Yean had been noticing Ser Mei's quiet desperation at each failure of her attempts to get Sis's attention, not that Mei had tried very hard, her attempts were obvious only to those who observed her. Ser 'Mei had been quiet all evening, speaking only when she was spoken to but mostly following the talk and the laughter like one suspended. That puzzled Yean. At times Mei had seemed so strong, needing no one, utterly self-sufficient. But tonight her eyes betrayed a painful dependency, a hunger and a need for Sis's attention. Having experienced the same thing, Yean could sympathise with her but she couldn't help feeling that Mei was being foolish if she thought Sis could satisfy this hunger.

Ser Mei's eyes followed Marie across the room, lighting up when Marie caught them and held them for a moment in a smile. A public smile. The benevolent smile of a kindly pope as he blessed millions of the faithful in St Peter's Square. A smile that was food to those who hunger; those who thirst and the poor in spirit. But tonight, Ser Mei behind her dark liquid eyes set beneath that straight fringe of hair needed more than a public smile. Marie tried to rope Ser Mei into the discussion raging round the dining table. But Ser Mei's heart was not in the state of the Asian Church nor the Vietnam War. She had hoped that Marie would listen to her.

Yean saw this demand in Ser Mei's eyes and shook her head. Mei must learn not to demand so much from others, least of all from Sis. After all this was Christmas Eve; Sis had many obligations to fulfil and Mei should not expect Sis to tear herself away from the discussion now.

It was almost midnight before the party finally broke up. Marie had to rush back to the convent for midnight mass with her community. In the hectic hustle and bustle of arranging who was to go home with whom, Marie said, 'Mei, Hans is sending me home with Dr Jones. I'll see you next week,' and she tripped down the path to where Hans and Dr Jones were waiting for her.

Ser Mei did not say a word, simply standing there for a moment and then turned away.

Yean, angry with Marie for deserting Mei, spoke up, addressing no one in particular, 'Hey you guys, how come no one is coming in my car?' Then she turned to Ser Mei, 'Will you come? I'll send you home. That's Sis. We'll just have to accept that she is always in a hurry, chasing time-tables and ideas.'

Ser Mei shrugged. Unlike Yean she did not feel free enough to criticise Sis; that would have been utterly disloyal.

Yean drove up Changi Road in a silence punctuated occasionally by the desultory remarks both girls felt obliged to make since this was after all Christmas Eve and they had been to a party together. But they had nothing in common. Yean kept her eyes on the road, regretting her own impulsiveness, while Ser Mei, looking pinched and pale, sat stiffly beside her. Yean turned left into Mountbatten Park, a housing estate of gardens and bungalows favoured by the British and American servicemen and their families. But a few locals had bought houses here too. Strains of 'wo wo, yea yea' floated down the road from the darkened house that was Ser Mei's home. Yean looked at her. Ser Mei had not mentioned any party at home. She was now staring straight ahead down the road. 'Drive on. Don't stop,' her hoarse voice commanded. Yean obeyed. She did not feel close enough to ask Ser Mei any questions. In silence they drove back to Yean's also darkened but silent house.

'My parents are out, they're attending some function or other at one of the hotels. Come, let's sit by the pool. Would you like a drink?'

Mei shook her head. She sank into the white garden seat, sitting as listlessly as an abandoned ragdoll. Yean took off her shoes and sat at the edge of the pool, dipping her toes in the water, waiting. Ser Mei sat immobile for a long time and Yean could see, out of the corner of her eye, the flashes of feeling crisscrossing her face. Almost in a confessional tone, tired, beaten, defeated, Mei said, 'I had wanted to spend Christmas with Sis.' She stopped and looked at Yean waiting for a response.

'Isn't it difficult? Since she's a nun she would have to spend Christmas with her community. You've got to be reasonable, she has so many duties and obligations now.'

Ser Mei was silent again; the dark pool glittering like a malevolent eye of the darkness pressing in upon them. It was a long while before she spoke again in a tone full of bitterness.

'It's alright for you to sound so utterly reasonable. I know I'm the demanding, the unreasonable one. But you people! Sis has a community, you have a family, what have I? Nothing! Nothing! Do you understand? Look at you! Look at your lovely house! Of course, you can afford to be reasonable. Me! I've an ugly house. Not a home at all. It's a brothel. I've a mother who's not a mother. She's a mummy to all those who can pay her.'

Ser Mei stopped. The years of suppression, and it had all burst. Strains of 'wo wo, yea yea[1] interweaved with vivid images of hairy tattooed arms stroking white breasts and thighs thinly clad in scarlet and black negligees. A child peeped through the slightly parted curtains. A huge hairy hand was grasping her mother's breast. Its thick fingers and thumb gave the dark brown nipples a tight squeeze. A squeal of delight rang out. Ser Mei shrank. Not painful? She looked down at her own fore-finger. It was bleeding. She had bitten it. She peeped again through the parted curtains careful not to make a sound, watching, mesmerised. That huge hairy hand. Each hair standing up and curling on its own. That same hand with the anchor tattoo moving downwards stroking the bare breast, the belly and then the thighs. Then with a sudden movement it plunged into the dark patch of hair. A loud grunt of pain and her mother's body heaved, bare bottom rearing toward her. She squealed with fright and ran back into her room. Breath-less, she crouched near the door listening. Bastard! Get lost! said the angry American voice. The little child whimpered in her corner.

Now Yean looked at Ser Mei sitting there lost in thought. Innocent and protected, Yean did not know what Mei was talking about. What did it matter what one called one's mother? But she did want to be sym-pathetic.

'Nothing to be ashamed of, Mei, she's still your mother.'

'She's not my mother! You don't understand! Not my mother!' Mei flashed; anger breaking through her por-celain surface.

'I have no mother – do you understand? No mother! I'm an orphan.'

She glared at Yean who seemed at that moment to represent all the well-brought-up students in the convent who had never understood her.

'I'm not her daughter. I'm a crutch, something she can lean on in her old age. Do you know why I was allowed to be born? She couldn't abort me. I survived three abortions. You know why I was allowed to go to school? Because I can study and qualifications would bring money and a well-paid husband. I'm my mummy's road to respectability and security.'

If Yean was shocked by Mei's bitter voice she hid it well. She stared into the water and stopped kicking her legs. She could not understand.

'Aren't we all others' security blankets? I'm sure that I'm my parents' status symbol,' she declared, quite secure in that bit of knowledge.

'Oh you just don't understand. How can you? So rich, so protected! So pure! I grew up when a tattooed arm squeezed my breast. You and Sis are the same. I wish you people had left me alone. Then at least I could have endured, survived, existed! But you people asked me to live. Live fully. Be alive! Fine! But in living I see, I hear, I question, I yearn, I desire! And then you tell me to be reasonable. I wish I had been left in my shell!' Almost spitting the words out so that Yean recoiled from her attack.

'Now that Sis has drawn me out what do I do? Tell me, tell me when you're in need,' she mimicked. 'Well, I'm in need now. Where is she?'

Yean closed her eyes tightly, wishing she could close her ears as well. She had never heard anything so painful. But Mei, once started, was not about to spare her.

'You know what my mummy wants? She's not satisfied with a crutch, she wants a crotch. She wants to sell me – my sex, my virginity! Do you know how much a virgin costs? Ten thou, twenty thou! Even a house if he is an old man and a millionaire and doesn't die upon the first fuck!'

Yean was repelled by the ugly sneer across Mei's face. She had wanted to hug Mei but now she couldn't.

Instead, she got up and sat on the grass beside Mei's seat consoling herself with the thought that Mei was not the sort of person whose shoulders one could squeeze sympathetically. Sis was most probably the only one who would have been granted that right. But she was not there! Yean sat, silent, waiting as she watched Mei sobbing soundlessly. Only her body shook. When it was over, Yean said, 'Stay here tonight.' It was the least she could do.

'Charity!' said Ser Mei, spitting the word out. 'But damn it, I suppose I'll accept. After all, it's Christmas Eve.'

Yean ignored her jibe and led the way into the house. 'C'mon, it's getting chilly.'

They walked down the shady path brightened by the purple blooms of the saga trees. Yean glanced at Ser Mei who seemed to be listening very attentively to Dr Jones who was delivering a long discourse on the history of America's involvement in Vietnam. Sis was just a little ahead walking between Hans and Rev James, discussing what the Church's stand on the war should be. They had just emerged from Mak Sean Loong's study where they had planned to call for a moratorium on the Vietnam war to be held next term.

Ser Mei had not wanted to come at all but she knew how important this planning session was to Sis. Besides, she had not seen her since Christmas Eve. Neither had she seen Yean who had not called for her since that night when she had stripped herself to reveal her terrible scars and Yean had turned away, horrified.

Yean concentrated on the lilac blooms of the saga trees whose red seeds brightened the dry brown grass beneath her feet. She hadn't even had the guts to ring Ser Mei. Was it lack of courage or was it repulsion? She recoiled from probing deeper and saw this reluctance as an attempt to hide her own guilt. This made her feel even worse. But the bitterness of that acid voice had shocked her more than she cared to admit.

Ser Mei.

Quiet.

Delicately beautiful as a tragic heroine in a

Chinese opera.

But such crudity of language, such crass worldliness. She had never associated Ser Mei with anything sordid. It had never occurred to her that Ser Mei knew such ugliness or was capable of saying such ugly things. A shudder of disgust shook her but she struggled to be kind. God had been good to her. She had been very fortunate to have been born into an educated wealthy family. Yes, she had to be kinder to Ser Mei, so she quickened her pace, and reached them just as Dr Jones was saying, 'Saigon is the most corrupt and degenerate city in Asia. According to the latest figures from the U N it has more women, girls and even children selling their sexual favours than any other city in Asia.'

'Many are peasants who had fled from the war in the countryside,' said Rev James, shaking his head. 'It's often their only means of survival. For them prostitution is an act of self-sacrifice.'

'No, not all of them are self-sacrificing peasants. Many of these prostitutes are from well-to-do families, who succumbed to the materialistic culture of Saigon. These are high-class professionals who service the wealthy mercantile and diplomatic communities,' Hans laughed, pleased that he had destroyed Rev James's sociological stereotype of the hapless prostitute.

'They are the parasites of parasites then. The lap dogs of the rich,' exclaimed Marie.

Hans nodded with the authority of a foreigner who had spent a fortnight there and Marie, to show that like Hans, she had no romantic notions of the helpless prostitute either continued, 'The immorality of the war and the immorality of this thing posing as love will taint Saigon forever. The scarlet woman cheapens life and love.'

Somewhere inside Ser Mei something imploded. It caved in, causing a dark gaping wound which like a Black Hole in space sucked everything inwards to bleak nothingness: in the dim light, flashes of a red negligee and a tattooed hand stroking her mother's thigh. Yean saw Ser Mei's downcast eyes redden and brim with tears which threatened to spill, her facial muscles contorting and fighting in vain for mastery over those tears. Yean turning away quickly said, 'I don't think we can so easily dismiss prostitutes as cheap.'

Marie turned round. 'I'm not saying that they all are. Those women who form the peasant class can't be. They were forced by war and hunger. I was referring to those with some education who willingly became the lap dogs of the rich. These are the ones who cheapen life around them, tainting their vicinity by masquerading as the real thing . . . like, like the harlot Life-in-Death in *The Ancient Mariner* . . . and . . . ' Catching Yean's look and glancing then at Ser Mei, she did not finish her sentence.

The three men stopped too, standing in the shade of the saga trees. Hans turned to Marie; his eyes seeking an explanation but she looked just as nonplussed. He recalled Ser Mei's strange behaviour at Raffles Hostel. Ah, a sensitive girl's reaction to the tragedy of the Vietnamese peasants. A noble feeling, and bending down he put an arm round Ser Mei's shoulders to show his sympathy and approval.

'Hey, what's wrong girl,' his stage whisper clearly audible to the rest of the group.

Ser Mei shrank from the easy intimacy of his touch. She broke away, turned and ran down the path.

Hans straightened himself. Another overly sensitive Chinese girl. Dr Jones and Rev James had turned to

Marie and Yean, questions in their eyes. 'Did we say something wrong?'

Marie shook her head. 'I was the one speaking,' was her curt reply.

'Look, you two go after her. We'll see you sometime, okay?' Dr Jones left with Rev James.

Just before Hans followed them, he turned to Marie and gave her a light pat on the shoulders. 'Good luck,' he said, 'you've got a sensitive case on your hands.'

Marie acknowledged his sympathy with a smile. Yes, she could see that she had a sensitive case on her hands but Dr Jones and Rev James had recognised her counselling abilities; she should be able to handle this and get to the bottom of the matter. She turned to see Yean's look of guilt.

'Alright, Yean, let me know the truth.'

'I can't.'

'But why?'

'I just can't. It's not my right.'

'You've got to tell me what's wrong. Did I say something wrong?'

Yean remained silent but Marie was not one to give up so easily.

'Look, Yean, you know that I've been trying all this while to encourage Mei to come out of her shell. Tell me what's wrong.'

'I thought she had told you.'

'What?'

'You mean you really don't know?' Yean was truly surprised.

'Know what for goodness' sake!' Marie was getting impatient. She had always been the confidante of everyone in the group and the first to know. She turned to Yean with all the authority she was used to wielding, her eyes demanding an answer. So Yean took the plunge. She could not see what else she could do.

'Her mother is a prostitute.'

Marie remained silent. How could she not have known so basic a fact? Why didn't Mei tell her? All this while she had been kept in the dark, yet she had been encouraging Mei to speak up, to trust more, to move out of herself, to be more involved with the group; and all this while Mei had kept quiet. She had Yean as her confidante. Ashes, ashes, all ashes.

Ser Mei was walking toward them now. She must have gone to clean up. Yean marvelled again at her demure beauty. A weeping willow, she mused, and felt a strong protective urge. But she held back, knowing that she had no right. Sis was here.

Ser Mei glanced at the two of them waiting for her. She did not hurry. Her mother's words from last night were still ringing in her ears. *Ya, you think you so high class. You think just because you go to university you so good. I got go to school last time also you know. I stop all because I born you. No one want you. You got no father. I keep you and look after you.* Ser Mei wiped away the last traces of her tears. No one, no one, she felt, would understand her. Her mother was a cheap harlot. Harlot! Harlot! She wished she had been abandoned at the convent instead of suffering this canker in her life. Ser Mei looked up at Sis and Yean uncertainly. Yean's face told her that Sis knew.

'Ser Mei, I'm sorry. I apologise,' Sis's words shot out like the opening of a salvo.

'It's alright, Sis . . . I . . . I was too emotional, I guess . . . it's not your fault . . . you didn't know . . . '

'Yes, I was kept in the dark.' This second salvo shot out in immediate response.

'No, no, it's not like this at all,' Mei protested; her face crumbling again at Sis's disapproval. Yean too had caught that look of censure and anger which flashed across Sis's face despite herself. She wanted to speak up for Mei but the words got stuck in her throat.

'No, no, it's alright,' Sis protested as she gazed directly into Mei's half-appealing, half-hesitant eyes. Ser Mei was twisting her wet handkerchief round and round. 'Really, it's alright,' she continued. 'As I've always said, no strings attached. You're not bound to reveal everything to me. You're free to trust whom you like; I understand,' Sis said, looking at Yean who knew she was included in this third salvo. She cringed a little but thought it politic to remain silent, acknowledging her wrongdoing and receiving her due punishment. Mei, however, began again.

'Sis, please, Sis, I'm sorry.'

'Look, please, don't make things worse by appealing like this. It's spineless. Stand up for what you've chosen to do. It's alright,' Sis insisted, 'I should be the one to apologise. Let's go home. No, I think I shall go to the library. Yean, don't wait for me, I'll go home on my own.'

Yean could not bear to see the look on Ser Mei's face. She turned away and walked toward the car park in the opposite direction, a little impatient with Ser Mei. Why did she have to go on and on? Mei need not have apologised so profusely. She should have remained silent like herself or stood her ground or defended her own action. Then Sis would have respected her, however grudgingly.

Ser Mei found herself alone in the shade of the saga

trees, the indifferent witnesses. Abandoned. Her mother was right. She did not know how to love. Like mouse's shit you don't kill, you wrench my guts out, her mother would have said, and her mother was right, she knew only how to hurt others, utterly selfish, unthinkably so. She had hurt Sis, the only one who had tried to pay attention to her. *Yes, you selfish! You see my white hair, and you do what? You still want me to bitch. You think I never mind I cheap already? You think I enjoy is it? I only do for you what, my own daughter. Now I so old already I still sell my body. For what? I ask you for what? So you can go to university and come back only think your mother cheap and useless. I sacrifice for you so much you don't know. I ask you this once only; one time only and no more. He old but he nice man. Once only you do this for me and you say don't want. Why? High class university student what! My heaven ah show some justice ah, see my white hair see and show pity ahhhh!* And her mother had collapsed on her bed in a mass of dishevelled hair. Ser Mei had shrunk in horror at the sight of her mother's undyed hair. She had never realized how old her mother was. Her dyes, her powders and her negligees had hidden her tired face and her worn-out body. Now that head of grey hair reared up in accusation. Having made her decision, Ser Mei ran down the path. She must get home before she changed her mind.

*   *   *

The air-conditioner in the room hummed softly. The bedroom was hushed, cool and new. Thick maroon velvet curtains blocked out the street lights and muffled all sounds coming from the outside. The brand new formica of the imported bedroom suite gleamed white and gold in the yellow light of the bedside lamp. The metallic gleam of its gold trimmings gave the room an air of newly bought luxury. Two red electric bridal candles cast a warm red glow upon the walls. The bright pink satin bedspread shone just a shade too bright so that despite the soft yellow light, its bright pink almost hurt her eyes.

Beneath the satin bedspread Ser Mei lay spread-eagled. Her arms and legs were tied to the four corners of the bed with red strands of velvet for good luck. The lower part of her body was raised by a hard kapok pillow. She was chewing a ginseng root slowly as she waited, her eyes closed. She had drunk a full glass of brandy straight off, she was determined to shut out everything, close her eyes and her ears. Her soul should fly to the stars and remain there forever; then she need not care about what happened to her body. Her body, mere clay, let him have it, this old man. Let her mother have it. It's the least she could do after all these years.

'Fifty thousand dollars is a lot of money what!'

'Very good price,' her mother's friends had exclaimed and they had advised her not to haggle. She must accept it quickly before he changed his mind. You never could tell with these rich old men.

'Rich but so stingy lah!'

'Why in Saigon or Hongkong, price not so high, only one-tenth this; so cheap over there; those girls cheap like dirt.'

'Ah then no guarantee,' smiled another of her mother's friends.

'They all say they young and innocent; they all say they real chicks; where got? Most of them old hens lah!' And the older women had laughed, wise to the ways of the world. Her mother, glad of their sanction, had agreed then to fifty thousand dollars with twenty thousand dollars as downpayment and thirty thousand to be paid the morning after.

'That's fair,' everyone had exclaimed, pleased with their part in the negotiations.

Ser Mei bit hard into the ginseng root; allowing its bitter-sweet juice to trickle slowly down her gullet. The ginseng would strengthen her, her mother had said. It would also prevent her from biting her tongue should she be unable to tolerate the pain. She must relax, her mother had said, then it would not be so bad. Hovering between dream and stupor, Ser Mei struggled to keep in front of her her mother's worn wrinkled face and dishevelled grey hair. Slowly she fell asleep.

The door opened and shut with a soft click. The old man entered. His florid face and balding head was so flushed with drink that his sparse silvery hair appeared even whiter than it was. He felt warm after the bowl of chicken brandy soup, and taking off his shirt he carefully hung it on the back of the chair, deciding that his long-sleeved undershirt was warm enough for the air-conditioned room. He looked round the room with its brand new bridal suite and smiled approvingly. It was just like his newly married son's room. The huge jade ring on his left hand gleamed in the yellow light of the bedside lamp. He unzipped his black pants and they slipped on to the floor.

White hair.
White singlet.
White knee-length cotton pants.
And a gleaming jade ring

on a withered hand
rubbing a withered pouch.
His hand moved upward, rubbing his
protruding belly – his 'fook' – the
Cantonese would say.

He smiled. Tonight he was pleased with his 'fook' and his eyes rested on the face of the girl sleeping beneath the pink satin cover. Her youth moved him. Something reared between his groins. He moved to the table. Ah, it was ready for him. He picked up the cup of steaming ginseng chicken soup and gulped down the contents. It should work for him, this aphrodisiac. It should give him back his vitality.

He slipped off the satin cover and pulled down his knee-length underpants. The girl, spread-eagled, lay like an offering before him.

Fair body,
That wisp of curly black hair
excited him.
He could feel himself throbbing.
In happiness burst into song –
a bawdy Teochew refrain:
'The rider has far to go
The mare is waiting
To be mounted, ho!'
And he fell on top of her.
Ser Mei bit hard into her ginseng root.
Spasm after spasm of pain seared
through her.
She bit harder.
Her eyes closed tight.
Her fists clenched as load after load
came crushing upon her.

A hard rod shoved and thrust itself
into her;
grating harshly against her dry virginal walls.
A sudden squirt of hot liquid.
The deadweight sprawled limp.
The tears rolled down Ser Mei's cheeks.
She stifled a sob.
The air-conditioner hummed.

'The rider has far to go
"His steed is rearing
The mare is impatient
to be mounted, ho!'
And again he fell on top of her.
Fifty thousand dollars!
He would get his money's worth.
Ser Mei bit hard into the ginseng root
as again and again
the deadweight fell crushing upon her.
Harder and harder, she was pushed and shoved.
Harder and harder, faster and faster.
She screamed.
He shook convulsively.
Again and again he shook,
clutching her.
His hands tore wildly into her.
She fought him.
She could not breathe.
A ton weight pushed her down,
crushing her.
Suddenly, the deadweight went limp again.
Like a sack of rice it lay on top of her.
She tried to push the weight off.
She opened her eyes.

She swallowed her scream.

His face was frozen in a glassy stare,

in a grimace of pain.

'Ahhhhhhhh!' her voice returned.

And with that scream the door flung open. Her mother, pale with fright, ran in with two other women. They pulled the old man off her. He was already dead. They covered him with the satin bedspread.

'Quick, quick, call the police!'

'Call the ambulance!'

'No, no, close his eyes first, close his eyes first!'

'And push that thing down! Choy! Choy! This bad luck, very bad luck!' Mei's mother moaned as she hurried to and fro about the room.

'Why this happen to me hah? Why? And in my own house! Surely bad luck forever!'

'And he not old; only about sixty.' The women shook their heads and clucked sympathetically.

'The ginseng lah,' theorised another woman.

'Ginseng and black chicken too strong ah!'

'Don't talk, don't talk,

See to the girl, see the girl!

She's fainting!'

'Untie her, dress her up

and cut away the ropes,' ordered another.

'Quick, quick, go to altar downstairs,

bring up goddess Kwan Yin's glass of water,

and two pomelo leaves from garden at the back,

quick, quick,' the distraught mother shouted again. Her good fortune was at stake. The woman returned with water and pomelo leaves in hand.

'Yes, yes, now sprinkle her, sprinkle her

with holy water.

Use the leaves, use the leaves;
O Mi Toh Fu, O Mi Toh Fu,'
Ser Mei's mother chanted.

She felt the wet and the cold. She opened her eyes
and let out another scream. She got up and rushed out.
She ran down the stairs, out of the house and down the
road just as the ambulance and police car came screeching
round the corner, their orange lights blinking hot and
fast.

I didn't do it!
I didn't do it!
a voice in her screamed;
tears streaming down her face.
I'm only a hole;
a rotten hole;
a black hole of death!
I didn't do it,
I didn't do it!
battling for the last shred
of self-respect.
But I killed him,
I killed him,
and she ran aimlessly away from the house.
I killed him,
a hole of death,
I killed him!
Nothing, nothing but rot;
I KILLED HIM!

The phrase exploded in her head as she ran down the
road, running toward the new blocks of flats as heedlessly
as the cars whizzing past her in the night.

★   ★   ★

Kwan Koong Road, narrow, congested and alive with human chatter and clamour, the clashing of colours and the glare of the electric light from powerful lamps hanging from crowded stalls. Near the entrance to the street, stalls heaped high with oranges, apples and water melons jostled for the crowd's attention. The hawkers cried their wares in loud strident voices: 'Lai, lai, lai; ngo kat, ngo kat; Fifty cents only, very good melons, sister, very cheap.' Their Hokkien voices rising higher in pitch than the metallic mix of electrical sounds coming from the radio cassette stalls – A-go-go music vying with Mandarin pop all belting out lyrics proclaiming a lover's undying devotion.

Siew Yean walked through this sea of buying and selling Chinese crowding the verandahs of the shophouses which had closed for the night and spilling on to the road. All down the street were food stalls selling mee, porridge, turtle soup, cheap shirts and gaudy dresses. Passing those stalls busy with people at their evening meal she turned into Kwan Yin Lane away from the bright lights, and the hustle and bustle of shoppers and diners. An invisible barrier snuffed out the noise and gaiety of Kwan Koong Road. Kwan Yin Lane had the sombre air of decrepit age waiting for death to make his claim. Old men and women sat on the verandahs among abandoned boxes and cartons, fanning away the evening heat with palm leaf fans. Were those grasping hawkers and these dying old men the proletariat of Chinatown so extolled by Mr Mak? Yean did not know. Chinatown was so different from Kensington Park and Orchard Road. And this was an unfamiliar part of Chinatown. She walked past the old people quickly till she reached a rickety stairway marked by a pole upon which a piece of white cloth was hung as a sign of mourning. She went up the stairs lighted by a single electric bulb whose dim yellow light was absorbed by the thick grime on the walls.

As she reached the landing she saw that Sis, Aileen, Kim, Peter, Hans and Mak Sean Loong were already there, looking solemn and ill at ease. Sis led her into a cavernous dimly lit room which was above the front of the shop. It looked huge and high because it had no ceiling. Great black beams arched across the room, laid bare like a crude declaration that Death had to be faced squarely, barren and harsh. Yean stole a glance at the two sides of the room. Along the walls in the semi-darkness were rows of beds upon which lay the shadows of the dying – old men and women – wheezing out the breath of slow decay in the twilight world of Chinatown's death houses. Yean and Marie watched spellbound as an emaciated old man struggled to sit up. He got up, coughing a dry racking cough, cleared his throat loudly and spat into the spittoon by his bed. Then he leaned back and lay on his bed staring vacantly into space. Each of them had the look of one waiting, waiting for life to ebb out of their bodies; the hollow containers of souls no longer there.

Yean turned away and studied the black coffin squatting in the centre of this room where the dead and the dying met. Ser Mei's photograph was propped against the head of the coffin. Her impassive unsmiling face was staring out of eternity now. Yean found herself staring back, her mind blank. She did not know what to say to the dead neither did she knew what to say to the living.

Marie who had followed Yean's glance along the walls shrank from such unadorned reality. She averted her look and nudged Yean. 'Ser Mei's mum.'

Yean raised her eyes and saw a tragic mask – the mask of one who had lost a daughter. There was nothing else to say. So Yean nodded and she acknowledged it by silently motioning them to take a seat by the door.

As Marie and Yean rejoined their group, Peter asked, 'May we say a prayer for her? Are they following Buddhist rites?' His voice was edged with irritation at the superstition of Ser Mei's family. A Catholic brought up to believe that 'God is Love' he felt that by placing Mei's body in the death house, her family had rejected her because of the nature of her death and their selfish concern for their own 'luck'.

'Let's not disrupt anything. We'll say a prayer for her in our hearts,' said Hans with professional caution.

The whole group bowed their heads and prayed that God in His Infinite Mercy would forgive Mei who had lost the courage to live.

'Come, come, take a drink.' And a woman came over and placed some bottled drinks on the table for them. She bustled off and brought back two plates of sweets and peanuts. Hans' shocked expression at this unseemly custom made Kim giggle.

'Hans, we Chinese eat on every occasion. Now we eat to keep the dead company. Some people even play mahjong. You Ang Mo look stiff and solemn at a funeral wake. For us Chinese a wake is an occasion of high drama. Priests chant prayers banging loudly on drums and gongs as they lead the dead man's soul through the various layers of Hell. And in order to prove to the judges in Hell that the dead man had been good and therefore sorely missed by kith and kin we wail near his coffin. We even hire professional criers for this job.'

'Then why is it so quiet here?' asked Hans who had

been listening with interest to Kim's store of exotica.

'This is because Mei committed suicide,' Kim whispered. 'It's considered a great misfortune to have an unhappy spirit in the family. Besides, Mei is young. The white-haired must not bemoan the black-haired, say the Cantonese; we Peranakans are also like this. The older person must not cry for the young. Tomorrow, Ser Mei's mother, if she follows tradition, and it looks as if she would, will not accompany the coffin to the cemetery. It's to avoid bad luck and misfortune. The living must be protected. Her unhappy spirit may drag her mother to the nether world too,' Kim smiled. Her amusement over the last sentence was obviously for Hans's benefit. He must not suppose that all Chinese believed in this.

The woman who had brought the drinks sat down among them. 'You all Ser Mei's classmates hah?' she asked in Hokkien.

Hans looked to Marie for a translation who was no help since she spoke no dialect herself. Still she answered the old woman in English. 'Yes, auntie,' for she felt that she had to be the spokesman of the group. After all she was supposed to have known Ser Mei better than the rest.

Since the old woman had come to talk, not to enquire and listen, Marie's friendly smile and short reply was enough for her to begin her story.

'Very good, you come,' she began in peasant Hokkien. 'Mei Mei very sad. Her mother very sad too. She, very very small, I look after her. That high only she was.' She held out her hand to show them her Mei Mei's height. She sighed and wiped her tears, obviously waiting for them to ask questions.

Aileen, in her usual mix of kindness and curiosity, obliged. 'Auntie, what happened? Why did Ser Mei die like that?' she asked in her best Hokkien.

'Aiya, hard to say, hard to say! Mei Mei she good girl, always study so hard. She, too good, too good. They say good people always die first,' and she shook her head while the group waited for her to continue.

Marie took a closer look at Ser Mei's nanny. Again she realized this was another aspect of Ser Mei she did not know and she wondered whether Yean knew. She glanced at her but Yean was busy translating what had been said to Mak and Hans.

The nanny, dressed in a sombre blue and black samfoo, glanced round the room. Seeing Ser Mei's mother in the other corner, she drew her stool closer to the group and began again in a low conspiratorial tone.

'My Mei Mei ah very pitiful girl. Her mother, she very greedy. Never satisfied; always greedy for money. Always she want more money to buy big house. Every day she cried and cried to my Mei Mei and she so soft hearted she cannot stand it and agreed to be old man's wife for one night and then mistress. He very old already but want to be young again. Aiya all men are like that. Pay very high price for virgin. And my Mei Mei she not cheap girl; always very good. Never got boy friend. And he not stupid; he knew good thing when he see it. That old man paid,' and she lowered her voice dramatically and held out five fingers to impress upon them the worth of her Mei Mei, 'fifty thousand dollars!' she said with deliberate slowness.

The group gasped and the nanny smiled satisfied with the success of her dramatic pause. Then just as dramatically her smile disappeared.

'But she had bad luck, very bad luck. The old one died that night – right on top of her. So Mei Mei frightened ran away. I think the old man's spirit not satisfied, follow and pull her down the block.'

Marie stared wide-eyed at her. She could not believe what she had just heard – such horror spewing out of this woman's mouth; flowing out in such a matter-of-fact manner. Was she talking about Ser Mei? Yean too was horrified, not by the nurse but by her own turning away from Ser Mei at the point when she most needed a friend. She had failed Ser Mei. The rest of the group were also struggling to understand Ser Mei's death. Hans felt Ser Mei must be the truly genuine Chinese girl whose filial duty was as yet undiluted by exposure to the values of the West. Mak Sean Loong was trying to place this suicide case within an ideological framework he could understand.

Death and Revolution!

Death and Exploitation!

He was still trying when a loud commotion near the coffin made all of them turn round.

Ser Mei's mother was knocking her head against the coffin, howling as if in great pain. Five or six women were trying to pull her away.

'Aiya, aiya, don't do this, let her spirit go! Don't do this!'

'Oh my Mei Mei ahhh; my Mei Mei ahhh! Your life so cheap hah! Ten months I bore you in pain. Then I born you and bring you up all these nineteen years and now you want to go away from your mother so suddenly. Leave me all alone. Because of him you die ahhh! Other people kill you and other people treat you cheap. Now they cheat me. You die and what I get?'

Ser Mei's mother looked up and gave the young man standing beside her a dark angry look. He cringed a little and held out a hand as if to console her. She refused it and turned away. She looked at her daughter's photograph and wailed again; her Cantonese voice rising and falling in tragic cadenza.

'Yes, you die and what I get for you? Two thousand dollars only. They think very big money. They think can buy life with just two thousand dollars is it? They think we poor people's life so cheap. You know, my daughter she very clever, gone to university,' she said, appealing to her audience.

Mak listened intently. Here was a member of the proletariat attacking a member of the degenerate bourgeoisie. He marvelled at her innate political astuteness. Ah, this was the class struggle!

'Nineteen years I care for my daughter and they think two thousand dollars enough! You think this fair hah? You say this fair or not?' she asked all the women gathered around her.

The man dressed in mourning black looked embarrassed and disconsolate.

'I born daughter. I gave her to your father and what I get? Two thousand dollars eh? He promised me fifty thousand dollars hah! You want to do honourable thing? Do properly. You want honour for your family? Then you, the eldest son, you settle his debts. I honest, I no cheat. Yes, he gave me deposit, twenty thousand dollars. Still owe me thirty thousand. This money – this my daughter's blood money – her money, for me! Oh my Mei Mei, my filial Mei Mei, come back come back to your old mother. Come back, I don't want their dirty money, come back ahhhh!' and collapsed beside her daughter's coffin.

The man, obviously unprepared for such a display of

grief, did not know what to do. He looked around help-lessly, but none of the women were his allies. His honour and the honour of his family were at stake.

'Don't cry, Ah Soh, don't cry. I'll try my best. I'll talk to my mother when everything is over. She is now very sick. This cheque is just for the funeral expenses. Later I will ask my lawyer to contact you.' And with this he hurriedly deposited a cheque with her.

Marie looked askance at the group of women who were trying to comfort Ser Mei's mother. She kept moaning in a low voice; crying over her financial loss. Marie motioned toward the staircase and the whole group shuffled out. The nanny, their sole point of contact with the situation, had deserted them for the drama around the coffin.

Such crass materialism!

Such brazen calculation!

Marie reeled off phrases angrily in her head. It was all too sordid. Hans understood Marie's indignation. He placed his hand lightly on Marie's shoulder as they went down the stairs, a touch suggesting so much warmth and affection that Marie felt comforted and even found the touch pleasurable. But that instantaneous realization of pleasure made her skip two steps down the stairs away from Hans's hand. She was grateful for the dim light on the ancient stairway which hid her flushed face.

The group stood at the foot of the stairs, grim with helpless anger at the mother's calculative ways. In life and in death Ser Mei had been so unloved. Marie broke the silence.

'It's not worth it! It's just not worth it at all! She has died for a worthless cause!'

'It's so obvious her mother was using her,' said Kim.

'I must say the mother is a damm good actress, boy,'

said Peter. 'Let's not stand around here, I'm starved, I haven't had my dinner yet.'

They followed Peter's suggestion and sat down at one of the hawker stalls.

'I took a look at Ser Mei. She had a pearl between her lips. Isn't this a sign of her mother's love?' Aileen asked naively as usual in her perennial quest for some good in others.

'No, silly,' answered Kim who prided herself on being the voice of reality. Kim acknowledging goodness only if it were made obvious. 'The pearl in her mouth is to prevent the breath of death from contaminating the breath of life. It's the usual selfish Chinese custom to protect the living.'

'In that room death and life looked the same. Those poor old people lying on their beds might as well be dead. No one seemed to care,' observed Peter.

'It's amazing,' said Hans. 'Your culture upholds filial duty but you have such pretty death houses and even cite them as tourist attractions.'

The truth of Hans's flippant observation could not be denied, Yean felt, but she had to clarify the situation for him. 'These people have no families. They left their families in China when they came over here to work long ago. By right their employers should look after them.'

'And why aren't these employers doing that? They squeeze them dry and abandon them here. All are exploiters like the old man. Ser Mei's mother is his running dog; that's why she's paid.' Mak was angry again and looked ready to launch into one of his readings from his favourite authors. After all every opportunity must be used to demonstrate the evil of capitalism and materialism in bourgeois society. Aloud he said, 'I never thought I would meet an actual case of parental exploitation but now I believe Mao when he said that one should rebel to retain one's rights even as children. Look, let me read this to all of you.'

And before they could protest, Mak opened his *Red Star Over China* and read from it.

'The dialectical struggle in our family was constantly developing. One incident I especially remember. When I was thirteen my father invited many guests to his home, and while they were present a dispute arose between the two of us. My father denounced me in front of the whole group, calling me lazy and useless. This infuriated me. I cursed him and left the house. My mother ran after me and tried to persuade me to return. My father also pursued me, cursing at the same time he commanded me to come back. I reached the edge of a pond and threatened to jump in if he came any nearer. In this situation demands and counter-demands were presented for the cessation of the civil war. My father insisted that I apologise and *k'ou t'ou* as a sign of submission. I agreed to give a one knee *k'ou t'ou* if he would promise not to beat me. Thus the war ended, and from it I learnt that when I defended my rights by open rebellion, my father relented, but when I remained weak and submissive he only cursed and beat me the more. There, you see the meek do not inherit the earth. The oppressed must rise and destroy their oppressors.'

Mak closed his book, hoping that his reading would launch them into a discussion of the class struggle in Chinese families. He looked expectantly at everybody without realizing that this was neither the right time nor the right place. He was, therefore, disappointed when Aileen commented. 'How come Mao talked about his quarrel with his father as if it were an international conflict? Isn't his vocabulary a bit bloated?'

Yean looked down at her bowl of mee, too angry even to smile. Serve him right. How could he be so unfeeling. She knew that Aileen's questions had offended Mak for whom Ser Mei's death was an excellent example of the dialectics of the class struggle.

'Why didn't she rebel?' asked Marie as if posing the question more to herself. 'Why didn't she see that her mother was exploiting her? Why didn't she consult us?'

She could not understand how Ser Mei could have remained so weak and submissive. Hadn't she always encouraged Mei to be strong and to stand up for her rights? What had gone wrong? Where had she, Marie, failed? She was upset tonight partly because she did not know the answer and partly because of what she felt on the stairway a moment ago.

Hans stole a glance at her. She looked so beautifully vulnerable when she was upset on someone's behalf, her lips quivering as she sought to control her feelings.

But Yean who was also watching Marie did not see that beauty. Instead she saw useless tears of remorse.

'Where were you when she needed you?' she almost shouted but instead she swallowed a mouthful of mee and was immediately sick. Tonight she could not eat. She stood condemned by Ser Mei's death.

*   *   *

Marie hurried down the corridor toward the convent's chapel. She needed to pray for Ser Mei's soul, ask God to forgive Ser Mei for taking her own life. What had gone wrong? Where had she failed? Why hadn't Ser Mei consulted her? Hadn't she done her best to draw Mei out of her shell? She was in no mood yet to join the other sisters in their evening prayers, but instead lingered in the evening light along the ancient arched corridor, its greyness matching her mood. Arch upon arch followed one another, a pattern in human life – of rising expectations, the achievement of happiness and then a fall into disillusionment. She must, she thought, be in the last third of this journey. As she climbed the steps into the chapel, the roar of the traffic grew distant and the candle-lit interior swallowed up her white figure embracing her with the comfort woven by a hundred years of prayers offered to a God so mysterious to those who had dedicated their lives to Him; a God who bled and who was as vulnerable as those who adored Him.

She genuflected, slipped into her pew and knelt, concentrating on the Blessed Sacrament, trying to conjure Christ's presence in the tabernacle. Row upon row of white-clad sisters, heads reverently bowed, murmured their prayers in unison; their chants rising like wreaths of incense woven jointly by so many loving hearts throbbing in unison. The evening light streamed through the red and blue stained glass windows high above the heads of the community, bathing them in a soft ethereal light. Marie watched and listened, lulled by the melody of the chanting. She was not one of its contributors. Occasionally she broke into their spiritual wreath-making but she had none of the others' capacity for sustained prayer. She tried instead to centre her thoughts on prayer for the repose of Ser Mei's soul but that dim stairway kept creeping into her consciousness, that warm touch of the hand, those blue eyes . . . she shook off the image and turned her thoughts toward Ser Mei again. Had she failed her? Why didn't Ser Mei confide in her? Hadn't she always encouraged her to do so? She felt betrayed. Ser Mei had chosen to confide in Yean. Ser Mei had held back while she, Marie, had reached out and now, even after her death Marie still felt exposed and vulnerable. Her invitation had been rejected, but so silently that she had failed to sense it; interpreting it instead as hesitation, shyness and timidity. Marie looked steadily at the flickering candles. A warm flush stole over her, its heat increasing in intensity as it concentrated on the region of her heart till like a red hot brand the word, Rejected, was firmly imprinted there. She had been a fool! For a long time she knelt with her head bowed, letting the humiliation cauterize her once proud spirit. What a fool she had been! Looking up the huge silhouette of Christ hanging on the Cross startled her. It seemed to say: I am the greatest fool in history. She paused. Alleluia, why didn't she see it earlier? This was alright then. She had only been a fool for Christ. Was that not her calling and her vocation? Christ too had been betrayed by His apostles. Like Him, hers was a commitment to a journey of passion – a human journey. Hadn't Paul Tan said that in each of us was either a journey of passion because of involvement with others or a journey of emptiness because of non-involvement with others. According to him, either way, man was trapped. No exit. Man could never win. It was either the painfulness of being human or the painlessness of being a zombie. Perhaps if she were a zombie she would not feel the warmth of that hand so intensely. Vexed by the dark humour of her Creator she looked up at the Cross again. Was this the life she was committed to? Of heightened awareness? She was flesh and blood and each drop which oozed out had its own sensations, she thought, as the humiliation of rejection and the universal yearning for affection washed over her once again. The pain while it lasted told her that she had feelings, was indeed vulnerable and alive. This awareness was its own reward, releasing her from the intimate slumber of the dull earth. Although pleased with her own facility with words she was not sure whether this was a prayer or an insight she had gained. By the end of vespers she had accepted Ser Mei's case as her failure. But she must not love her failures more than her God. Life was to be lived in the here and the now, Mother Superior had said. The important thing was not the fact of failing but what she had learnt from it. Her mission still lay in living life fully, embracing the world's pain and suffering.

Prayerful reflection reassured Marie that her vocation was still intact with a goal and a meaning.

*   *   *

The spacious garden still wet with dew shimmered green and blue in the early morning sunshine. The sparkling reflection of the clear blue sky in the swimming pool gave the garden its air of cheerful serenity. But Siew Yean, coming out of the pool, was neither cheerful nor serene. She grabbed a towel and began to rub herself vigorously, grimly determined not to spare herself any pain. For the past few days she had stayed at home, keeping away from the others. She was angry, very angry; mainly with herself but partly with Sis. A hot wave of shame still overwhelmed her whenever she recalled how she had very nearly shouted at Sis about Ser Mei. She should have; and not only that, she ought to have directed the same question at herself. Where was she when Ser Mei needed her? Why hadn't she telephoned Mei herself? Why did she recoil from Mei, preferring her own romance to Mei's reality? She too had rejected Mei – careful to preserve the marble polish of her own life's surface.

For days Yean sat in judgement over her own failures, remembering all her sins. All the 'ifs' and the 'could haves' piled on her soul like so many sodden mattresses. She could hardly breathe. If she had only been more sensitive . . . if she had possessed more courage she could have helped Mei think through her problems. She could have helped Mei see through her mother's drama . . . She could have prevented Mei from jumping to her death! Coward and betrayer. She wished she could have disowned everything – her sprawling home and spacious garden, all the advantages she obviously had. She had taken her parents' wealth for granted, with little or no thought for anybody else. Kim had every right to be sarcastic when she had failed to fetch the crippled Yin Peng. And where was Yin Peng now? Abandoned by them all since she had decided against coming to varsity. Was this her own circle now – mere varsity acquaintances? Children of the rich? All those who had made it to the top?

She went into her room and changed quickly. She would go for a walk, say good-bye to Mei once and for all, and get on with her own life. She would not waste Ser Mei's death in mere self-pity. Wealth had cocooned her: she would break free.

UNIVERSITY

Marie and Yean continued their agitated walk round the upper quadrangle of the Temasek campus. The grey green needles and dark branches of the casuarina trees which lined the sides of the quadrangle gave it an air of sagacious age in a university barely a hundred years old. But then, as Marie wryly observed, in a progressive and dynamic country fuelling a massive rebuilding programme, a hundred years did seem to be very old. They looked at their watches again, wishing the others would hurry up as they would like the rally to begin on time. It was already ten past six and except for about thirty students seated on the grass near the platform the quadrangle was still empty. Where were the students? In a student population of more than three thousand only about thirty had responded to the invitation to pray for peace in Vietnam. Marie was disgusted. She felt she should call it off.

Hans, who had planted himself next to her, sensed her disappointment.

'It's to be expected. The Singapore student is generally known to be apathetic. He's indifferent to things not directly linked to getting a degree.'

Hans could accept the student apathy matter-of-factly but Marie was angry. She would never accept this as a mere fact to live with. These were her people; she would have to do something about it. What it was that she would do she had only the vaguest idea but she felt that somehow with God and Right on her side she would succeed.

Dr Tamney Jones, the guest speaker for the rally arrived, and Marie signalled to her group of helpers. As planned, Kim and Yean distributed song sheets and candles while Peter and Ken took up their positions behind the slide projector. Marie, seeing that everything was ready, nodded to Mak Sean Loong to begin the rally.

Mak stood on the raised platform, hands in pockets, thick glasses gleaming in the brief tropical twilight.

'Welcome everyone! It's good to see some of you still alive and willing to learn of things not directly related to exams!' Mak's voice boomed across the quadrangle. 'I welcome you to this evening's attempt to call for a moratorium on the war raging in Vietnam – a war which had sapped the energy and youth not only of the United States but also of many Asian states like Laos, Cambodia and Vietnam. Many atrocities were committed and are still being committed. But of course, since in this part of the world we are dominated by the so-called free press we read only of the atrocities committed by the Communists. Tonight we have some slides made by a neutral group called Peace International which reveal atrocities committed by the United States. Before we begin, we have Dr Tamney Jones here who will give you a short history of his country's shameful involvement in Vietnam. Dr Jones,' and Mak stepped down amid loud applause for Dr Jones who climbed on to the platform and stood there, feet apart, facing his audience. In fifteen minutes, he awed the students with an account of how the United States had become a bullying imperialist denying the

113

Vietnamese the right to choose their destiny. His government, he was ashamed to confess, had generally supported puppets and military junta which subjugated their peoples. The military-industrial complex of the United States needed the support of such local dictatorships to ensure a supply of cheap raw materials and labour for its capitalist empire.

Like the other students Yean marvelled at his analysis and fiery eloquence. Such courage! Such clarity! Then just as Ken switched on the projector and the slide show began with Yean reading the commentary with the aid of a torch light, Marie noticed three officials from the Students' Union beckoning to three Chinese students – two boys and a girl – who were sitting on the fringe of the crowd under the trees. After conferring for a few minutes the three Chinese students left the quadrangle while the three officials remained, more as observers of the rally than as participants since they did not join in the singing at all.

'Now everybody, please light your candles!'shouted Ken.

The candles were lit, dispelling the darkness which had descended upon them. And in the flickering candle light, the crowd, led by Marie's group, burst into song:

> Lord we pray for golden peace
> Peace all over the land.
> May all men dwell in liberty
> Walking hand in hand . . .

The faces of the thirty or so students took on the look of fervent hope, trust and faith. Marie standing on the platform facing the crowd was moved and inspired. This was it, the students were not indifferent. Given the opportunity and the push to open themselves up to new experience they could respond positively. Yean, standing beside Marie, felt the same too. What this university needed were events like this to thrust the students out into a world wider than Singapore and a full rice bowl.

The whole group adjourned then to the sarabat stalls to celebrate for it was agreed that although the turn-out was small the event had been a success. Many students had agreed to meet again for more discussions and this was a good sign. They sat around three wooden tables joined together, each with a glass of steaming *kopi susu*. The switch to *kopi susu* had been deliberate. Following the compelling arguments of Mak, the group had decided to support this local drink and reject the alluring advertisements of Nescafé and Maxwell House. Marie, looking down the row, beamed with pleasure at this symbol of unity – two rows of steaming *kopi susu* glasses.

'Hey, what were Santok and company doing tonight?' she asked Peter who was on one of the union committees. 'I saw them talking to three Chinese students who seemed to be from the Chinese department.'

'Ah, they were throwing their weight around. I had invited those three. They're from Yuan Tung University,' Mak said.

'Hey, they look communistic, boy!' exclaimed Kim.

'What do you mean?' Mak barked angrily, almost as if he had been caught out.

'Aiya, look at their hair!'

'What? What's wrong with their hair?'

'Short and stiff-lah like a toilet brush,' Kim laughed.

She was joined by the others except Mak who took such matters seriously.

'Hey, you people hah, have simplistic notions; and no bloody idea of ideology. Short hair equals communist; long hair equals bum. Brainwashed lah! See I wear white

115

shirt and dark pants you think I government supporter ah?' Mak asked, impatient with this group of students. 'And your student officials were giving the Yuan Tung students the boot tonight claiming that they were recruiting,' he continued; his voice filled with disgust.

'Why would they want to do a thing like that?' asked Yean, shocked at the police tactics of these elected officers.

'Hah! They're probably members of the Alpha Club. You know; these people in the Union see themselves as the guardian of the political purity of this campus. Like our political leaders, they believe that the students here in Temasek are gentle fishes of the aquariums while the students in Yuan Tung are the prowling sharks of the oceans. The moment we let them in ahh, they would swallow all of us. The Alpha Club members will join the ruling party so they have been appointed to keep an eye on us,' Mak answered, proud to show that, unlike the other lecturers, he was in touch with students from both campuses.

'But not so long ago didn't Yuan Tung students help the Chinese students of Nan Hai organise a demo outside City Hall?' asked Ken, who felt that there was some truth in the belief of the political leadership.

Mak nodded and said with some pride in his voice, 'These three were among the organisers.'

Ken who had always been cautious made no comment but he began to see Mak in a more critical light than Marie and Yean.

Marie was pleased to know that there were students in Yuan Tung willing to stick their necks out for others. 'We should meet more of such committed students and work with them instead of setting ourselves apart from them because they speak Mandarin.'

'Difficult,' said Hans, speaking for the first time. 'The Bukit Temasek students are apathetic and self-centred. The Yuan Tung students are committed and communalistic. The English stream student works only for himself and he's happy with the status quo as long as he is assured of a secure future.'

Peter and Ken rose in defence. 'Hey, surely we're not as bad as you make us out to be. How can you be sure that yours is not a surface judgement? Have you done a comparative survey? Or at least a sampling?' challenged Ken who had attended Dr Jones's sociology lectures.

'No, I don't have to do a large-scale survey. I look at the turn-out tonight and the hundreds that mug in the library each day and I draw my own conclusions,' replied Hans, keeping his voice even because he did not want to be drawn into an argument with Ken and Peter with whom he wished to work later, on a project he had already discussed with Marie.

'That's not fair! I know many of them are the kia-su type. They will mug and mug in the library but you can't call the whole student body muggers and rats,' added Kim.

'And if we live in a rat society you have to act like a rat to survive. Boy! do we have to rat to gain a little respect in this world!' Peter was very conscious that he had to come to Ken's aid. Loyalty to his friend and his campus somehow demanded it. In this, reason took second place. After all they were arguing with someone who did not belong to the group.

'And what's wrong with wanting a little respect? Everybody wants to be respected. Where would you be if nobody respects you?' asked Ken triumphantly.

'But people only respect your paper qualifications and money,' Yean protested, so anxious to strip off her protective layer of wealth that she was unaware of the undercurrent of group loyalty against Hans.

'That's it,' said Ken excitedly as he put his empty glass down with a thump, 'that's why we have to mug and mug,' pleased that he could point out the obvious.

'But exam results aren't everything,' Yean persisted.

'That's how people think. Can't be helped,' Ken shrugged. He was used to acting according to the reality of the situation rather than what ought to be.

'But surely life is more than just gaining respect?' Yean asked.

Marie was pleased with Yean's persistence. Here at least was someone who shared her beliefs and she felt she would be able to work closely with her. She would invite Yean to her next meeting with Hans and Mak but she ought to keep out of the debate now. She did not want to be seen siding with Hans. It would be awkward. She was so aware of his presence.

'Look, we have no time. It's not a matter of going all out to gain respect, we just have to study and pass,' Kim was saying, exasperated that the idealistic Yean was refusing to see reality again.

'Don't we care a damn for the underprivileged, the refugees and the victims of senseless wars?' Yean was persistent.

'Yes, but we can't do anything. You want us to march around in demos like the Americans?' Peter asked, peeved that Yean had managed to appeal to Kim's and Aileen's sentiments. 'Boycotts and revolts are negative. Our care and concern must be constructive, what! Running around carrying placards fun lah but can't help anybody except the media.'

'Peter Pang! I wasn't suggesting that!' Yean almost shouted at him but this time Peter did not respond.

Marie, however, could no longer contain herself. She was not going to let him maintain this victorious silence after such an altercation. She ought to come to Yean's aid and let the rest know where she stood on the issue. 'Are you seriously telling me that you're satisfied with life according to lecture, lunch and library; lecture, library and lunch?' she asked, looking down the table. 'Are you satisfied with being digits and manpower potential to be slotted into a pigeon-hole; have a four-figure salary, a flat, a car and colour TV? You would rather be a rat than a human being? A digit rejecting your right to protest? All in the name of stability and prosperity? For whose sake? Yours or the foreign investors? Look at us now. You do this you'll be fined; you do that you'll be rewarded. Is this what you want? A carrot and stick society? Is this the level of your morality?'

Five heads bowed a little in shame. The teacher in Sis had surfaced and they felt that somehow she was right though they resented her authority.

The discussion had come to an end. The group broke up and went home in different directions. That early appearance of unity had vanished. The present line-up seemed to be Marie and Yean with Hans on one side as the advocates of the higher life while Ken, Peter, Kim and Aileen were on the other side clinging to the ordinary and the mortal. Mak seemed somehow to stand alone; his hair cut stiff and short, his eyes squinting behind thick ringed glasses framing a face coated with oily perspiration.

*   *   *

119

Clad in a pair of jeans and a T-shirt Marie was walking to the university to meet Hans, Mak and Yean. Her lithe body moved with the grace and ease of one used to long walks without being bothered by the heat of the day. The cloudless sky still shimmered a pale blue as the early morning sun spread a light golden sheen on the leaves of the tall angsana trees swaying in the breeze. It was still a beautiful world, and the leaves of the bushes along the canal nodded in agreement with her. Singapore was still beautiful if one were to cut off from one's view all the new concrete structures beginning to dominate the skyline and the constant roar and dust of the traffic. With every few steps her heart wanted to leap into song and soon, unable to resist this delightful impulse, she hummed 'a gift of song is a gift of love . . . '. The pink feathery blossoms floating on the tops of the Rain Trees joined her in song while the branches of the bushes reached out to touch her. The blades of the grass lifted their heads in homage and invited her feet to step on them for that was their singular purpose in life. Creation was delightful. As everything served a higher purpose, so she had no qualms trampling on the grass for that was what grass was made for. But she was not grass. She was a Flame of the Forest in bloom whose shade and beauty served to remind the world of the Father's love and benevolence despite the hate and suffering which at times overwhelmed all life. She did not deserve it, of course, but He had been good. He had been so good. Such warmth in those eloquent hands. Such warmth whenever he had rested them on her shoulders. Such a contrast to his blue eyes which remained still suggesting the tranquillity of great depth while his hands moved constantly in rhythm to his voice; a low deep voice charged with controlled excitement whenever he was sharing some of his convictions. At such times the hands moved but not his eyes which were still, gazing at her. Enthusiasm and caution held in counterpoise. A disciplined person, she concluded with a little smile playing on her lips. He was a fortress into which she had gained access. No, she had been invited, persuaded and implored to enter. It was very flattering indeed; but she must stop dreaming of him. Bashful though there was no one else with her, she quickened her pace. This was bad. She had caught herself daydreaming again and looking forward to being with him. Where was her discipline? Where was her commitment to her vocation? The first attractive male, a foreigner and a church worker at that, and she was feeling like a dizzy sixteen-year-old. She should check this weakness, although it was a very common human failing; this appreciation of warm affection, this yearning to be special to someone and that highly pleasurable feeling of finding someone attractive attracted to her. She had sometimes caught him looking at her in a way that was different, and she had been secretly pleased. Secretly! that was it! This must remain a secret. No one should know of it, least of all him. What would Mother Superior say? She must take a firmer hold over her feelings. It was vanity to enjoy Hans's attention. From now on she would stick to work. Everything should be for the project in hand and nothing else.

Marie entered the library and went up behind Yean. 'Hi, sorry I'm late,' she whispered.

'Yes, I'm hungry. Where's Mak and Hans?'

'They're waiting for us in the canteen,' said Marie, walking quickly toward the exit.

'Hey, no need to hurry, the canteen is still crowded.'

Marie arrested her walk and slowed down, reminded of her promise to stick strictly to business as far as Hans was concerned. She strolled across the field with Yean in companionable silence, their saunter a direct contrast to the hurried pace of the other students.

'Students here make a bee-line for everything – food, studies, even love. Each goal achieved in due course, as scheduled but by the shortest route. So very sensible and rational.'

Yean smiled at the contempt in Marie's voice, as they halted at the entrance to let those in a hurry overtake them. The canteen was crowded, grimy and noisy. Char kway tiao, garlic and curry filled the air, thick with pungent smoke. The char siew rice stall was surrounded by a throng of undergrads jostling each other. It was each man for himself at lunch-time in the university. Push to the front or be pushed to the back.

'How like the tactics of survival Singapore style,' commented Marie.

She wouldn't push. When it came to the crunch it was Yean who had to push for the both of them. In such a situation Marie needed help. She had yet to master the intricacies of the Chinese dialects to communicate easily with the hawkers and taxi-drivers. With such people she had often felt helpless. And now it was left to Yean to shout out their orders to the fat hawker manning the char siew rice stall who didn't blink an eye to indicate he had even heard the order as he continued to cut and chop the meat. Yean watched, mesmerised by his oily grace, sweating like a horse as he cut, chopped, cut, chopped with his rapid flashing blade, the sweat pouring off his forehead and rollig down his short neck to be absorbed by his once white singlet. There was an almost hypnotic grace in his rhythm of cut, chop, cut, chop. Next! and the operation was repeated. A human conveyor belt, Yean thought. Was this a meaningful existence? Or was the search for meaning confined only to the educated rich like herself? Why couldn't this rhythm of cut chop cut chop be her rhythm too? But as the man handed her her order Yean knew the answer was that she would never choose such a life. Her educational successes and her parents' wealth had given her other options to choose from.

They joined Mak and Hans at the table with their plates of rice. Mak with characteristic abruptness welcomed them by pointing to the inherent inequality of the canteen system.

'Note that the academics because of higher pay and status sit in air-conditioned comfort in the building designated Academic Staff canteen from which by edict all the social riff-raff are excluded.'

Yean squirmed for she certainly preferred to sit in air-conditioned comfort too rather than sweat like the hawkers out here but Mak turned his attention back to his *nasi biryani* and ignored them. Marie looked at Hans for an explanation but he merely shrugged his shoulders; it was one of those things one had to accept in Mak. Marie coloured a little for she had turned to Hans again for reassurance and explanation despite her earlier promise. However a glance in Hans's direction comforted her with the thought that he had not noticed anything so she looked up and smiled.

'You weren't happy with last night's meeting,' observed Hans.

'No, it was terrible. What worries me is that the students are not aware of anything wrong in wanting a good image,

123

respect and security,' she replied. 'There was no questioning of society's values or their own values. What they want are just good results and security.'

The two men smiled, pleased with an analysis from a woman which tallied with their own.

'True, true. Selfish! Bourgeois!' and Mak suddenly banged the table with his spoon to show his approval.

Marie in turn was pleased with the effect she had created. She darted another look at Hans who was thoughtful when he said, 'I agree with you. This university is not producing people who think, who question and who are critical. There seems to be little understanding of the real issues involved.'

Marie once again felt less isolated in the presence of these two men for they understood and agreed where Paul Tan would have argued with her. Strange, how Paul Tan came into her mind. And, of course they were right. Hans was just as logical as Paul, and in fact far more agreeably so.

'Is the university producing leaders who think? Who are concerned with the country's future? Are they willing to sacrifice personal interests for the good of the whole?' Hans's logic was just as beautiful as her own intuitive spontaneity.

'I'm not surprised you're depressed by this batch of students,' Hans continued. 'Most of them come from solid middle-class backgrounds. They have a stake in the status quo. These students realise that they are separate, special and privileged; the top ten per cent. It's in their interest to preserve things as they were. As your leaders put it, they should not rock the boat.'

'I should think not,' growled Mak in between mouthfuls of *nasi biryani*, 'and they will heed such excellent advice. Those spoiled bourgeois brats will conform; it's easy to make people conform. Our educational system domesticates rather than liberates!' Mak's voice rang with such authority that the students at the next table looked up, surprised. He gave them a disdainful glare and turned his back on them; and Yean found this immature trait of Mak's rather irritating.

'Acceptance, agreement and accommodation are the keys to survival and success here,' declared Marie, pleased with her own slogan, but by this stage Yean was refusing to join in the game, while Hans and Mak were nodding their heads. And such agreement was sweet to Marie for Paul Tan had always argued against her. As a successful 'returned scholar' Marie felt that he would naturally side with the establishment whatever the issue.

'We must do something about our educational system and its products,' Marie urged, looking at the three of them.

'I'm certain that your elite are totally ignorant of working conditions in factories and hawkers such as these,' said Hans as he pointed to the hawker stalls in the canteen. 'And yet this elite will, no doubt, be formulating policies affecting the lives of all these people.'

Yean shifted in her seat apologetically for she belonged to this ignorant elite, and so did Hans although he spoke as if he knew more about the plight of the Singapore masses than any local person.

'These establishment kids are not only ignorant, they're odious!' exclaimed Mak. 'Those Union guys, luckily not the brightest, actually swallowed hook line and sinker the official line about Yuan Tung University students planning a take-over of our campus here. They told me, and they were dead serious – those buggers –

that Yuan Tung Students' Union was a communist front and therefore must be watched and controlled. Rampant paranoia. They know their days are numbered.'

'Perhaps some of them are strong advocates of Maoism,' Yean ventured, remembering what Mak had told them about the three student organisers of the Nan Hai College demonstration.

'But not all of them are Communist sympathisers,' Marie hastened to add, for she was keen to work with such committed people. 'You can't lump everyone who is critical of the system as Communist supporters.'

Hans smiled at her but Marie was too upset to acknowledge his supportive gesture. She was convinced that such branding had snuffed out critical opinion on campus.

'No,' said an emphatic Mak. 'But one of those idiots doing P. S. or Soci must have snitched to the dean. The old man called me into his office this morning, and very politely asked me about the Peace International slides, how I got them, why I was showing them. And I replied, very politely of course, that I wanted to correct the imbalance in the flow of information from a U.S. dominated world press. You should have seen his face. I know he wasn't pleased. He told me to get clearance from the department first and to concentrate on my thesis. He sounded vague and said the higher ups were concerned about my activities, but I was too fed up to pay much attention to his dribble,' Mak snorted. 'Leaders? Timid rabbits!! Now a man like Chin Peng, that was a real leader. Committed unto death. No surrender even in defeat.'

But Yean knew that Mak had conveniently forgotten that many Communist leaders had died ignominious deaths in the Malaysian jungles, betrayed and deserted by their followers.

'Your dean seems worried about your academic initiative,' laughed Hans, a little baffled by Marie's indifference to him.

'That old bugger is constantly worried about this and that. He's a snitch, keeping an eye on everyone. Politically he's wishy-washy like the rest. Supporting U.S. agression in Vietnam because it's important to Singapore's survival. Doesn't care a damn, as long as it benefits us and the industries here let's support it!' mimicked Mak.

Yean laughed, for Mak was like a teenager giving an account of a fight with an authoritarian father.

'The spirit of protest and critical enquiry will not be allowed at a time when your authorities see the nation as an Israel of the East,' Hans remarked.

'Hah, you want to know what the V C said? Individual liberty is only the concern of ivory tower academics and our old man had agreed with him wholeheartedly,' Mak continued as if Hans had not spoken.

'But these people are sincere; they only want to preserve our independence,' Yean was insistent again.

'Nah, they're paranoid. These lackeys of the imperialist powers are scared. They know they may not last out,' and Yean caught the flash of determination behind Mak's steel-rimmed glasses.

'Hey, what about this other rumour which many people believe? Your government is so anxious to keep out sinister interests it has now employed spies on campus. They have even infiltrated the Legion of Mary,' Hans laughed as he imitated the local accent. 'Remember Operation Cold Storage? Don't talk too loud if you don't want to end up in Moon Crescent-lah!'

Mak gazed at the smiling Hans and to Yean's observant eyes he seemed a shade paler. Apparently he took such rumours seriously for as he said, there was no smoke without fire. It was difficult to make out why he believed in such rumours. Yean admired Mak's sharp critiques of capitalist society. And yet something that Mak said worried her without her quite knowing why.

'Time now,' he said, 'for protest and to tear down the whole system. Time later for strict control when we have what we want, when the people have been given back their dignity and the running dogs of imperialism have been whipped back into their kennels.'

'Wait, Mak, calm down, calm down, don't get carried away. We've got to discuss our project now so that I can write it up over the weekend. Yean doesn't know much about it yet.' Marie was now more conscious of her role as director of the group, determined to stick strictly to business and overrule the whisperings of her heart.

'Yean, are you ready?' smiled Hans as he took a sip of his lime juice. He too was determined not to let his discomfiture affect him unduly. 'This is a bold attempt to supplement what had been neglected by the university here. A gap which the churches should have filled had they been courageous enough. As we see it, university education is more domesticating than liberating. A hierarchical structure exists limiting students' participation in decisions affecting their lives. Everyone is subjected to heavy pressure from a rigid exam system to which he either conforms or loses out.'

'Ya, our university system is thus a "conformistic" rather than a learning process.' Marie concluded, a triumphant glint in her eyes as she looked at Yean, waiting for her applause. Almost unconsciously she had joined forces with Hans to convince Yean.

Although Yean did not as yet share the enthusiasm of the other three she could not deny the truth of what Hans had said. She nodded to signify agreement and Mak immediately took over.

'The present political leadership had decided that this university's role is to produce top managerial elites who will work in close alignment with industry. In this merito-cratic society the university has isolated the individual from the real social and political problems in the country today. Education here is merely the means to prepare for minority rule over the majority. It supports the capitalist structure by producing vast numbers of managers and specialists to execute the will of a still smaller group of monopoly capitalists.'

Yean admired the way Mak could speak so clearly and simply on his favourite topic.

'If you all agree with this analysis we can work on a project which Hans and I have tentatively planned. It could bring about great changes in our educational sys-tem.' Marie's voice was tinged with hope and enthusiasm for Yean's endorsement.

Yean agreed to join the group in its weekly discussions on 'the contradictions in Singapore's society' as Mak had chosen to term it after one of Mao's famous essays. But for Yean this meant that Ser Mei's death would not go to waste. She was determined to move out of her nar-row circle in the university.

'Alright then, we'll meet at James's place on Friday night. I have to rush off now,' Mak gulped down the remainder of his drink.

'Me too,' and Yean stood up.

Marie stood up too, slightly disappointed that the meeting ended so soon. Still faithful to her promise she did not want to linger in the canteen with Hans. 'I have to go too,' she said. 'I have to see Dr Jones about my assignment.'

'I'll walk with you,' said Hans. 'I have to see him too.'

Checkmate! He had gotten himself a bit of time to be alone with Marie. She had been keeping him at arms length; not as open as before. Something was bothering her and he wanted to know what it was.

It must be something to do with him and if that was the case he wanted to clarify a few things. He was not one to run away from difficult situations. Being frank and open was the best strategy. He got up and followed Marie out of the canteen and they strolled across the quadrangle under the shady casuarina trees, Marie enjoying the springy feel of their brown needles under her feet. Hugging her files to her chest she walked slowly, concentrating on the rough texture of the tree trunks.

'Marie, are you afraid of life?

She gave a start at this unexpected question, and stole a glance at him before replying, 'No, why?'

'You're afraid to let people come too near you,' Hans said it as if he were making a clinical observation.

Marie remained silent. It would be an insult to lie to him when he had been so open with her. If only she could say she was afraid of him – no, afraid of her feelings for him, but since she could not she kept quiet and began to walk again.

Hans came quite close to her before asking:

'Are you afraid of me?'

After more than three months of discussion Marie's new group of four was now ready to unveil their plan of action. The setting was the lounge in Rev James's manse. The chairs and the tables were pushed back against the wall leaving a large carpet in the middle on which the group of fifteen or so sat cross-legged in a circle. With heads bent, they were reading the pink stencilled sheets just distributed by Marie. Dr Jones, sitting among the students, put on his glasses, leaned against the wall and stretched his legs into the middle of the circle in order to read in a more comfortable position. Egalitarianism was to be the hallmark of this group which proclaimed that it would not differentiate on the basis of wealth, status, age or experience as commonly found in bourgeois groups. In theory a student's words weighed as much as a lecturer's but in practice most students deferred to Dr Jones and Mr Mak.

Marie sat next to Hans, leaning against the red leather armchair, as she waited for the group's reaction. She had spent many weekends writing up this project and wanted it to be accepted. Hans smiled reassuringly and his eyes said that he was proud of her, causing a warm glow to seep through her and the light to shine out of her dark eyes. She was free. Whatever fears she had had of him had largely disappeared; he had been kind, warm and understanding, he would not push her into anything, and they would be very good friends without allowing fear of their own feelings to hamper the development of trust, honesty, and the sharing of a deep commitment to the community. She reached out and touched Hans's fingers. Their eyes met, locked for a fleeting moment and they turned their attention back to the group.

Paul Tan, sitting in the circle, jerked to attention, stung by the meeting of those eyes. Once again cut by the pain of rejection. He had not come to witness this and was not prepared for it. He sat up stiffly, examined his usurper, as he recalled what he had read in the confidential files in his office. Hans Kuhn used to be called Chuck before he decided to reclaim his German roots. As Hans he seemed somehow more serious and committed than as Chuck who tried to be as American as apple pie. Confused American. Paul tried to dismiss him as Marie smiled across the room, pleased that she had managed to persuade Paul Tan, an Assistant Superintendent of Police, to attend today's meeting. She was to be congratulated on her foresight; it would be good for everyone to hear a different point of view after months of supporting each other's gripes against the alienating forces of modern society. Paul would provide the perfect balance. Besides, being an outsider, he would be in a better position to point out the weaknesses, if any, in her proposal. And, of course, she was glad to see him again after his two years' sojourn in the United States.

Paul shifted his position and tried to cross his legs into a less uncomfortable position. Why didn't they use the armchairs, he thought irritably. Yean, sitting next to him, sensed his discomfort and was sympathetic. He had come straight from work and his office attire gave him an air of awkward formality, a contrast to the casual dressing of the academics and students who worked in the more genial atmosphere of the Bukit Temasek campus. Paul flicked through the pink stencilled sheets in his hand.

'What a lot of waffle.'

THE STUDENT-WORKER ALLIANCE PROJECT

Statement of belief

We believe that students will be confronted with the problems of rapid industrialization, changes, progress and dehumanization when they join the managerial elite upon graduation.

The industrial process so vital to our economy has undoubtedly created a higher standard of living and provided more jobs for the people. The economy boasts of a leap in its GNP over the past few years. But industrialization has also meant:

1. an expanding but miserably paid proletariat – 200,000 workers in the pioneer industries

2. miserable working conditions – many in the electronics industry suffer from poor eyesight and girls in the textile sector are paid a low daily wage of $2.40

3. exploitation of immigrant workers – many live in over-crowded rooms in the industrial estates without CPF, medical benefits and insurance

4. rising foreign investments with the inevitable attendant increase in foreign control of consumer and labour markets

5. implementation of anti-labour laws – strikes are banned and the centralized union leadership is no longer aware of the feelings and needs of workers.

Under these circumstances of strict governmental control there is little or no opportunity for the rectification of these serious defects which are the results of rapid industrialization within a meritocratic system. It is therefore imperative that a project like the Student–Worker Alliance be implemented here to fill the widening gap left by the ritualistic and conformistic education. It will provide a framework for meaningful Christian involvement in the context of economic oppression in Singapore.

Paul stopped reading after the first page. Such short-sightedness, why couldn't they just be patient and let things evolve? Singapore is still barely four years old. He was resolved not to comment aloud on the proposal but would listen to what the others had to say. Folding his arms and leaning against the wall, he stared straight ahead for he knew that Marie would eventually try to catch his eye and get him to say something. He was not going to give her that opportunity.

'Well, any reaction?' Marie asked tentatively as she looked round the room. The circle of people did not look up, and in the silence, Hans gave her a look of encouragement so she asked again, 'Well? Still no reaction?'

Papers rustled as people shifted and changed their positions. Then the shuffling subsided and the silence in the room solidified. Disappointment was beginning to show on her face; the group seemed reluctant to comment on the proposal.

'Fantastic!' Dr Jones exclaimed. 'If accepted and implemented it could change the face of education in Singapore. I like your Phase 1, Phase 2 strategy; it's very methodical.'

Mak saw his chance to intervene. 'Phase 1 is devoted to the conscientization of students from Temasek, Yuan Tung and the Ramakrishna Poly who will form the core group and broaden the student base in these campuses. In Phase 2 the students will establish contact with the workers in Jurong and establish a power base for the Student–Worker Alliance.' The idea of applying Mao's writings to Singapore gave Mak a heady feeling. He would be the first Singaporean to achieve this, nothing would be beyond him. He would be the Alliance's ideologue and strategist.

'Fantastic!' Robin Fox, a foreign journalist invited to the meeting by Hans who wanted to show him something exciting, added his praise. 'I never thought Singaporeans would dare come up with such an adventurous proposal. Your government is in for a rude shock!'

The group of four smiled and Marie was glad that the foreigners realised that they were not as submissive as the international press made them out to be. Paul watched as the pleasure of being bold and daring subsided and caution returned.

'Are you all aiming for a Communist revolution?' Ken asked.

This blunt question cut through the general chatter. Everyone stopped talking. Mak turned to take a good look at Ken. Marie was too trusting. This boy could be one of the Administration's spies. Mak checked his rising anger but one more provocation from that boy and he, Mak, would throw him out. This kind of questioning could ruin everything.

'No, no, this has nothing to do with revolution but everything to do with education,' Hans replied hastily. 'What Mak said about a power base is something in the far-off future. In the immediate future, the workers and students in Phase 2 would develop a mutual education programme which would sharpen their awareness of the harsh realities of their society. What they intend to do after being made aware is entirely up to them.'

Hans sounded reassuring but as Paul noted with satisfaction, Ken was unconvinced. Not wanting to meet Marie's eyes, Paul continued to stare into space. He was determined to stick strictly to business; his heart was not as strong as he had thought.

'Hey, what about all our names here?' Peter almost shouted. 'This is the first time we've heard of our involvement in this project,' and the others were glad that the question had been raised, so Marie hastened to explain.

'I naturally trusted all of you to support this project after going through so many discussions on the defects of the system here.'

'Yes, but you didn't consult us,' Kim pointed out.

'I'm consulting you now ... but I knew somehow you would agree since we all share the same values. And besides this is not the final version, you're free to change any part of it.'

Marie was sounding a little defensive and Paul Tan, sitting ramrod in his corner, suppressed a smile. She had taught them well and the students were being discriminating. Paul was also pleased that he was getting his feelings under control.

'What if we don't want any part of this project?' Ken asked, almost wickedly as if to test Sis's patience.

'There's nothing I can do, you're free to leave.'

136

Again there was a forced casualness in the way she shrugged her shoulders. Hans patted her lightly to remind her not to lose her cool. Yean, watching, knew that she wanted the group's support very badly; her face had become a mask and her eyes no longer twinkled. She had always had difficulty handling opposition. So Yean felt obliged to support Sis since she herself was also part of the new group of four.

'Look, you guys, what are you quibbling about? Do you think this is a worthwhile project or not? Do you want to support it?'

Ken and Peter kept quiet. Her questioning attack was a good defence. Aileen spoke up. 'Yes, we do, but it's so sudden.'

'I agree,' said another student who had been dragged to the meeting by Marie. 'We haven't had time to think about this. Once committed we've got to put in a lot of time and work. What about our studies?'

This last question was almost apologetic since worrying about one's studies was already considered a selfish bourgeois trait.

'Don't worry, these details can be worked out later. Most of the activities will be during the vacation anyway,' Hans was reassuring.

Paul however viewed him with some suspicion; this foreigner trying to be the harmonizer of differences in the group! Someone with nothing to lose! If things go wrong he would just pack up and leave.

'Do you think the Admin and the Temasek Students' Union would approve? I'm sure the Union chaps would want a piece of the action,' quipped Peter.

'We don't need their approval!' Mak was adamant. 'We're independent of the Admin's lackeys. Those sycophants are not to be trusted!'

'It's a fact of life; whether we like it or not the Admin has its eyes and ears everywhere to keep tab on us,' Ken pointed out.

This admission convinced Mak that Ken was indeed a student spy. Mak glared at him for he wanted this face imprinted in his memory.

'But if we're in the clear and in good conscience, doing what we believe is right, what do we have to fear?' Marie clung to her belief that the rightness of one's actions would eventually shine through and Paul smiled. She was still so naive, assuming that motives could never be misconstrued.

'What you think is right, they may not think so,' someone else pointed out.

'Ya, isn't this the eternal tension in any community?' Marie answered. Here she was raising again the eternal questions of life and living, Paul reminisced, before he reminded himself sharply that he should stick to the issue under discussion.

'Forget about the realm of philosophy. Let's get back to the facts.' Yean, too, was impatient with Marie. 'You guys, do you or do you not think this project is worth supporting?' she interrogated the group as her eyes travelled round the circle to rest on Kim.

'Yes, yes, yes,' Kim gave in, 'but we can't commit ourselves fully to it yet. You people have had months of discussion while the rest of us have only come to the meetings on and off. How do you expect us to give an answer right now?'

'It's alright,' Hans said soothingly. 'We only want to use your names in this proposal. We need some local names for our sponsors abroad to convince them that we already have a student base.'

The students were silent. This was something new again. Paul watched them; this tussle between loyalty and natural suspicion interested him.

'Why not?' Kim asked, full of bravado as usual and perhaps of loyalty too. The rest of the group followed Kim. If Sis needed some names for her project she could use their names. It was the least they could do after what she had done for them.

Marie was pleased again. Her trust in her students had not been misplaced. Her eyes shone. She knew she could win them over when they adjourned for tea in the dining room. Everyone was talking happily except for Paul and Mak who eyed each other with dark suspicion. Paul glanced round the rest of the room. Marie was closeted in the corner with Hans and Dr Jones. Her chief supporters would be these foreigners. They would be the ones to support this kind of foolhardy thing in the name of liberty and progress. But Paul's presence was disturbing Mak. He did not trust anyone from the police force. He would convey his caution to Marie. Suddenly he burst out, 'Government spies are everywhere! Everywhere! Everywhere!' and stormed out of the room leaving everyone astonished. He would report the night's proceedings to his own group in Jurong.

Paul too left the manse. That guy was sick in the head and the rest of these people were fools! Did they really think they could change things with a three-year programme? And such bombast in their language! He was surprised it had been written by Marie. What had happened to the clear-headed girl he had once known? This proposal sounded like any other government project written by bureaucrats, forever thinking of 3-year plans and 5-year plans as if man could be changed by plans! He was disgusted with the whole thing. Power was what was at stake, and of course Marie did not realise it. She trusted the workers and the students; as if the mere act of bringing them together would lead to a better society! Idealistic fool and dangerously naive! She was ripe for the Communists! This whole project smacked of subversion. He would call Marie on the phone and arrange a private meeting with her. He felt a duty to warn her about her companions. Meddling foreigners were bad enough but that guy with the spectacles was not to be trusted on any account. He glanced back through the window at Marie, still talking animatedly with her American. She had forgotten him. Paul got into his car, slammed the door and drove away gunning the engine savagely.

* * *

It was the coffee lounge of an exclusive club. Its soft dim lights soothed her eyes after the hot glare of the afternoon sun. The dulcet notes of an organ floated round the room, hovering above the murmur of voices and lingering in the air; its tender tones assuaging the frayed nerves and tired feet of members exhausted by a day of flurried shopping in exclusive stores. Marie wrinkled up her nose at the luxurious decor of this indoor garden aimed at pleasing such pampered bourgeoisie as Paul. She felt out of place amidst the gilded glass tables, brass lamps, potted plants and plush green velvet seats. Better the camaraderie of the sarabat stalls for a *kopi susu*. Paul and Marie turned aside to make way for the waiter who brought them tea in a silver teapot and thinly sliced ham and cucumber sandwiches on a blue and white porcelain plate edged with delicate English flowers.

Yean, invited by Marie to give moral support, sat opposite these polite adversaries and knew that she, too, would not enjoy this tea despite their splendid surroundings. She viewed Paul admiringly in his light blue shirt, dark pin-stripe pants and dark blue tie brightened by a strip of red, sitting with the ease and geniality of a host offering a good meal. And Yean who was no stranger to exclusive clubs knew that it was his generosity which marked Paul as a member of Singapore's rich young set to whom money was not going to be a problem. Marie, however, the advocate of those to whom money would always be a problem, attempted to look like a factory girl. Her pair of black pants and blouse with a floral print was the outward sign of her inward faith in the proletarian lifestyle, as she was fond of saying. Yean sympathised with her discomfort now just as she had sympathised with Paul a few nights before. She sat very still and hoped the two of them would forget about her presence.

Marie turned away. She did not like this conversation any more. Same old Paul. America had not changed him one bit. He had been there but was so tightly cocooned in Singaporean fibres that the student protest and anti-war movement had left him untouched.

'Look, Marie,' he was saying, 'you have to be realistic. You can't go through life looking through rose-tinted glasses. Grow up, this is the real world, not the convent.'

In answer, Marie looked straight at him but he avoided her and concentrated on pouring out the tea into those delicate porcelain cups. With great deliberation she said, 'I refuse to grow up if by growing up you mean walking down the broad straight road to goals set in concrete. This is your way – always so practical, accepting and

141

prudent. I refuse to be practical like you,' and she waved her hands in final dismissal, then leaning slightly forward she asked, 'What's wrong with being idealistic? To dream and look at the stars? I refuse to accept the cruel and the ugly. And as for your prudence,' she whispered, 'it's a euphemism for lack of courage. You're afraid to act against anything and you call it prudence and patience.'

The impact of this made Paul push back his seat. It had hit him where it hurt. He realized he had advanced himself because he had accepted as facts a lot of things he could not change. Only the slight quiver of his mouth betrayed his wound for his lips had drawn into an almost straight line and his mobile face had set into a mask of hard logic. He was determined not to show his feelings again.

Yean, watching, noted with dismay that there would be no attempt at dialogue now.

'Yes, yours is reality,' and Marie's voice rose almost an octave higher. She was excited, scenting victory. 'For you life is competing, striving and accumulating; and living within such a framework you seek only to adapt yourself to it, never to change it.' Then leaning back, she looked at him and said caressingly almost tauntingly, 'Life can be changed, you know, into one that is warm, tender and loving. But of course,' and her voice hardened, 'being a practical man, you have no time for such stuff. I am not a practical man of the world and so, will refuse to live life as it is while I have a vision of what it could be!' and from her point of view she had won.

Yean continued to sip her tea, lukewarm and bland but it comforted her.

Paul surveyed Marie's graceful profile, trying to determine the cause of her hardness. Was it just cruelty? There she was, sitting opposite him full of composure, mocking him with the warmth and love of life, the very tenderness she had denied him while he had to wrestle with the cold reality of a love denied. Whoever said that life could be changed? He could not change the fact that she had refused his love. He could not change the fact that she had chosen someone else.

Yean glanced up. These two were caught in some absurd drama and they were very serious about their parts.

Marie recalled with satisfaction her experience in the chapel where she had gone to pray for Ser Mei and unable to resist another burst of eloquence continued, 'Yes, in your eyes I'm a fool but I'll gladly continue to be a fool for the one whom I call Lord is the greatest fool in history!'

'Don't be a martyr,' Paul growled. 'You're not called to such greatness; at least not yet; and you must admit that was a pretty melodramatic speech. You make it all seem so noble – living life as it might be – it just shows that it's you who can't adapt. If this disability is serious, it's not far from a psychotic condition!' he spoke in his usual matter-of-fact clinical tone which Marie had always resented.

Yean marvelled at their outward calm as Sis leaned backwards and crossed her legs waiting for Paul to finish. Sis seemed determined to practise patience in the face of this provocation. How dare he imply that all those who disagree with the establishment are psychotic! But quite oblivious to Marie's and Yean's feelings, Paul continued, pleased now with his self-control and common sense.

'Look, I'm not trying to put you down,' unconsciously adopting the old patronising tone he used when they were in their teens and in love. 'What I'm trying to tell you is that whether you like it or not people do value their rice bowls. They want flats, they want houses, they want cars, they want money in the banks and they're getting them under this system!'

'Yes, yes, yes,' Marie was exasperated with his common sense, 'but who are the people who would eventually get these goods? Not the ordinary worker in the factory. Only people like you! But at what cost to your souls!'

'Don't be idealistic, Marie,' and his voice had a harder cutting edge as he continued, 'reality will soon catch up with you. If this project involves you and you alone I would not have bothered but you're leading quite a few idealistic young souls astray too,' and he glanced at Yean and was all the more determined to say what he had to say. 'You're using them for your own discontent. Are you being responsible for them?'

To Yean he sounded as if he were the president back in Katong Church conducting the weekly Christian Youth meeting and asking his members difficult questions again.

'No, I'm not responsible for them,' Marie shot back angrily. 'They must decide for themselves. I didn't ask them to follow me. They must follow their own conscience.'

'That's not fair. They've been with you far too long. They're young and they are your group.'

'No longer.'

Yean was surprised and hurt. Why was Sis disavowing them? She had not expected to hear this at all. She was here to support Sis and now it seemed she did not need her any more. Neither did she need the group.

'So you've abandoned them for a more exciting group

of Ang Mo is it?' and Yean was not sure if she detected a note of malice in Paul's question. But she waited eagerly to hear Sis's reply.

Sis's voice became softer, sharper, a little angry. 'Must you sink so low in order to win an argument?' looking straight at Paul. She was conscious of having made a mistake in Yean's eyes. Was she now trying to regain lost ground?

Still Paul was silenced and for a moment, embarrassed, before he returned with, 'Who is this Hans anyway? Why is he so involved in this project? Why is he using the students' names and not his own? Is he using them as a front? I bet these questions never even entered your head.'

Sis was silent now and Yean realized that she had not thought of asking such questions. Sensing his advantage Paul pressed home with, 'He is an expat. Expats have no right to get involved. And as far as I'm concerned they are all still neo-colonialists. They still think of themselves as our great saviours. Ask him to go home. The U.S. is also in a mess.'

Sinking deeper into his seat, Paul looked at Yean for the first time. He had voiced a general feeling about these Westerners out here eager to help Singapore. He had worked with them and he hated their feeling of superiority under that veneer of helpfulness. But Yean had been taught by some highly competent expatriate lecturers and was a little disappointed by that defensive note in Paul's voice.

Marie, as oblivious of anyone else's feelings as Paul had been, made it worse with her counter-attack.

'Must you see a subversive in every critical intelligence and a colonialist in every white man? Can't you see we use students' names because the sponsors of this project wanted the names of local people? That's all there is to it!' She was angry with him for thinking so lowly of Hans who was no coward and need not hide behind anybody. Hans was a concerned church worker like herself. The community was his vocation too, and the issues of human rights and human dignity affected everybody and should transcend national boundaries. 'Aren't we being jingoistic to be threatened by their presence? Don't you have any faith in our ability and our powers?'

'I don't like these Ang Mo strutting around pretending that they know Asia's problems better than we do; that they have all the answers. After their adventurism here they go home; glorified as heroes thrown out of Asia by despotic governments. They spoil our good image abroad!'

'Image! Who cares about image? Why are you so caught up with appearances! The important thing is that we are people – human beings, children of God, working out our common destiny. Don't you remember?'

There! Another bulls-eye! Yean thought. Sis had made another hit! As president of Christian Youth Paul had always stressed that the human community shared a common destiny; that Man's ultimate love and loyalty belonged not to the state but to God and that they should see, judge and act not according to Man's laws but according to God's laws. Now he looked as if he would rather forget what he had said earlier when he was young and idealistic.

'But you know you can't change anything so why waste the effort?' he asked almost lamely. Her ardour and faith in the goodness of humanity had never failed to move him. He kept his eyes down and remained silent.

'Oh Paul, what's the matter with you?' Sis looked at

him with eyes full of pity. Paul concentrated on stirring his cup of tea.

'Has the commercial world changed you so much? Where's your faith and C Y spirit? Right now, yours is the voice of despair. If we don't try or believe enough to try how can we succeed?'

Paul bowed his head. Yean sat up. Sis had caught him this time.

'Someone must be the first to fling a pebble into the lake to test its depth. I'm just throwing a pebble in. How the ripples might go I don't know, that I can't control.'

'Ah! That's it,' Paul jumped back into the fight. He seemed determined never to accept defeat at her hands again. 'This is the height of folly and irresponsibility! If you're not sure of your goal and strategy you've no right to stir up anything. You haven't an iota of right to lead these students on.'

And he looked to Yean again, this time as if for support. Yean did not look at him; instead she reached out for the pot of tea and proceeded to refill her cup.

'These students are young and impressionable and they look up to you. You're their demi-god. In their eyes you can do no wrong.'

Yean smiled into her cup at this. How little Paul knew about her group and its relations with Sis. Not all of them would simply follow Sis, least of all herself.

'They look up to you and you're exploiting them. They're fodder for your battles with the establishment – the "in" word now.'

'That's not fair! You sound like big brother now. You're the patronising one in case you don't know. You are looking down on them. They can think for themselves, they're already second-year students and it's high time we decide for ourselves and be responsible for our actions. I'm not their demi-god and they're not as stupid as you think.'

Yean was pleased, oh, so pleased with Sis's spirited defence. She knew her group had never required Paul's protection. Thank goodness Sis believed in them.

'Still, you can't run away from the fact that your discussion groups are destructive. All of your talks are negative criticism. If you want to criticise you must offer alternatives and suggestions for improvement. Do you have any constructive alternative to offer?'

For a moment the image of the typical bureaucrat in white shirt and dark pants flashed across the mind of Yean. She and Sis exchanged a smile for they knew that this was the most effective clamp on the critics of any administration. Don't criticise if you have nothing constructive to offer!

'Your project will create trouble,' Paul would not let up. 'It's the perfect front for the Communists and you'll be putty in their hands. Do you really think you can succeed?'

'Paul, what's wrong with trying and failing? And even if we can't offer an alternative, is it so terrible to point out the defects of society? Must every critic have an answer to everything? Why can't we be brave enough to ask the honest question and perhaps the honest answer will meet us along the way?'

Paul looked unimpressed. Her eloquence no longer moved him.

'Don't lull me into acceptance with your pretty images. Your phrases hang in mid-air. You're still being irresponsible. You stir things up but you have no means of ensuring success. You don't even know what will happen.'

'You want to be in control. Success is all you care for! You're the one playing the demi-god,' Marie retaliated; her voice as harsh as Paul's. 'Haven't you realised that life is uncontrollable most of the time? Creation is chaotic. To build anew you must first destroy. People like you cling to the old structures because you don't believe enough in man that he can rebuild.'

Yean wanted to applaud this speech. This was the old Sis who used to rouse her whole class and give them the courage to dream the impossible dream. Paul was the voice of cautious age. Morality figures, the both of them.

'You're playing with fire. You want power and you don't even realise it. You and the students will be burnt. Our authorities are not yet that tolerant.'

Angered by Paul's ominous warning Sis launched into her favourite diatribe against the government. 'You and your kind are full of contradictions! You want a people who are intelligent, critical and analytical, discriminating blah, blah, blah and then you say, that's enough don't rock the boat. Any false move and we sink. Enemies are lurking in the corners ready to jump on us and jealous foreign powers will exploit us. This is rule by fear, Paul. This garrison mentality will soon rob us of our vitality. We build our walls higher and higher, eating our rice in fear. Don't you think that one day we will choke?'

No answer. Paul looked at his watch and said he would have to go to keep an appointment. He signalled to the waiter, showed his membership card and signed the bill. The waiter bowed respectfully and withdrew. Organ music continued to play softly. Yean stood up, excused herself and left. She did not want to witness this last moment.

Marie and Paul stood up too. They exchanged a brief smile. Both knew the truth. They would never meet as friends again. Outside the clubhouse, night had fallen. They faced each other for a moment, and shook hands, sealing their differences.

The touch of her hand shocked him into remembrance of things he would rather forget. He let go, nodded and walked toward his car.

His business with her was finished. Finished. Finished. Finished.

* * *

Marie walked home alone down Orchard Road. She would never see him again, unless it was for something official. She turned round the corner and walked past C.K. Tang's, crowded with night shoppers, bargain hunters, past Orchard Motor's showroom, Fitzpatrick's, the Prince's Hotel and the Moon Gate Antiques Shop. Playthings of the rich, she thought, as she stopped to examine a pair of blue glazed lions in the window case and huge porcelain vases of the Ching period. Once she had shared Paul's dream of owning such things. But that was a long time ago. Strange how she had changed and he had remained the same. However, her breathing was still regular; her hands and feet moved as they should; her heart beat just a little faster but otherwise it was normal. The medical check-up over, she was a little surprised that she was not as heartbroken as she had expected to be. She had dreaded meeting him alone but it had not been such an ordeal after all. Just a little hurt like a sharp razor cutting a thin line across her heart. Melodramatic image! Just a surface cut, no bleeding. It was a pity that Paul could never see eye to eye with her on the most important issues in their lives. She was relieved she had not married him to become eventually the wife of a prosperous member of exclusive clubs, the mother of two cute little children spending most of her time chauffeuring them to ballet classes, swimming and music lessons in a second family car. Well, God bless you, Paul Tan, walking down your safe and narrow path, and she turned to walk toward Cold Storage.

Mak Sean Loong standing just behind the glass doors of Cold Storage, peered out into the night through his thick steel-rimmed glasses. The car-park opposite was ablaze with the gas lamps and electric bulbs of the hawker stalls, stalls with crowds of diners, shops still selling fresh flowers and groceries. The barber's and the tailor's still doing business. And that man in the checked shirt still standing there, looking up and down the road as if waiting impatiently for someone to turn up. Ah, he had to be careful. Relax; relax, just relax. They must never know that Mak could be this sharp. Act nonchalant! O U C H! He wheeled round expecting to look into some mirthless face but no one was there. What had hit him? A cry made him look down. What's this? A toddler must have bumped into him and hurt himself. Its anxious mother hurried over from the ice-cream counter, gave him a glare and picked up her precious bundle who bawled at the top of his voice to announce his pain to the rest of the world. Mak shrugged off the incident and followed the mother and child to the ice-cream counter. He bought a cone and licked it absentmindedly. Aah, he must be inconspicuous; a fish in water as Mao had advised. This task should steel his nerves and he gave his cone another lick.

He peered through the glass doors again. What? The man was still there, looking up and down the road. He must be looking for me, and Mak sliding behind a pillar peeped at the man again. Ah! Now he was pretending to check his watch but Mak wasn't fooled. He must be signalling his partner or reporting to his chief. That watch must be a small radio. Damn it, he could not stay in Cold Storage forever. His ice-cream was melting. He would have to make a dash for it. He gave his ice-cream cone a hurried lick and bit into the wafer. Perspiring despite the air-conditioning, he pulled out a handkerchief and dabbed his forehead, pushed his handkerchief back into his pocket and peered through the glass doors again. Wait a minute, wasn't that Marie out there? Mak dashed out of Cold Storage leaving the glass doors swinging violently.

'Marie, look casual. Say hi to me,' Mak enjoyed his melodramatic whisper. Surprised, Marie complied. Mak had jumped out of nowhere. She could not see his eyes because his glasses reflected only the light of the street lamps, but she could see the rest of him bathed in perspiration, his forehead wet and oily.

'What on earth's the matter?'

'I'm being followed. No! don't look round,' he hissed and dragged her along with him. 'Come, come, walk with me while I throw them off.'

They hurried past the shops toward the Hongkong and Shanghai Bank.

'Don't look round, pretend to be my girlfriend and hold my arm. There's a guy in a checked shirt who's been tailing me since I came out of Michael's bookshop.'

'How can you be so sure? He could have been going in the same direction,' but she took his proffered arm all the same, a trifle amused at the urgency in his voice.

'No, no, no,' Mak shook his head emphatically. She had never taken him seriously. None of them ever had. One day he would show them, but now he must be patient. Damn it, he must not get angry with her. 'I tried to shake him off. I went into Cold Storage and bought an . . . ' He looked at the ice-cream cone still in his hand and flung it away. 'The guy was standing outside checking his radio.'

Marie smiled, her eyes bright with amusement. Mak could be so funny when he was not discussing politics and ideology.

'Wait a few minutes and look behind you if you don't believe. You'll see this guy in the checked shirt following us,' Mak said proudly.

They walked on, past the entrance to the Istana where two young guards stood stiff and bored. The shops along this stretch of road had closed for the night. The crowd had thinned.

'Now look back,' ordered Mak. Marie turned but there was no one. She looked again.

'Don't turn round too many times, you may rouse his suspicion,' and Mak stared straight ahead at the darkened bank as if his life depended on it.

'But there's nobody there,' Marie whispered.

'What?' and Mak made a hundred and eighty degree turn on his heels and stood still for a moment staring at the two Istana guards suspiciously. Nothing moved. He turned back and walked briskly toward the bank. 'We must have shaken him off or he has given up,' Mak was disappointed as he continued to walk beside Marie, past Cathay and the darkened bookshops of Bras Basah Road, peering into the shadows cast by the broad pillars of these old shophouses, still anxious about being followed, convinced that he was a marked man.

'Are you worried about getting into trouble?' asked Marie.

Mak shook his head. Fear of trouble? Ignorant woman! She did not know him well enough, paying all her attention to that American. Why, in the States he had marched with the likes of Norman Mailer and Angela Davis! Did she think he was a nobody? She used to think him great; had she begun to doubt him? Must be that American's influence! Afraid? Didn't she think him man enough to handle things? If they had not died so early and abandoned him to relatives his parents would be proud of their First Dragon now. Those higher-ups must have taken note of his involvements in the States. He was no stranger to government agents infiltrating consciousness-raising groups. He an activist! Wait till she found out about his connections, then she would not be so smug!

'Are you getting worried?' Marie asked again since Mak had remained silent. He had been acting strangely these past few weeks – gruff and morose. Perhaps there was some truth to what he had been saying specially in the light of Paul's ominous warning this afternoon. However, she still thought that they were not important enough to be kept watch over. Mak was obsessed, forever pulling her aside to tell her about his involvements in the States, interesting, but only when he discussed political ideas with her. Other than that he was irritating to the point of being odious. Still, one must work with all kinds of people for commitment to the project was more important; and she was proud that she could balance resignation and resolve.

'Mak, perhaps you're right; let's get the project off

the ground soon before anybody stops us.'

Mak grinned. At last she was beginning to see him in his true light. His plan was beginning to work.

JURONG

Their bus sped along the broad straight road to Jurong, the new industrial estate. Marie shut her eyes; its newness was painful to see. Its mantle of green had been stripped off leaving the raw wound of red brown laterite. The land had been dug up, churned over and bulldozed so that piles of earth rose like painful boils all along the sides of the road, stretching inland as far as the new blocks of twenty-storey flats – the only landmark for miles around. Stretching toward the new town were these great heaps of red brown earth placed almost equidistant from each other. Their bus passed mound upon mound of such porous red soil on which nothing edible grew, only tough coarse bullgrass, lallang and those tropical trees, shrubs and creepers which thrived in harsh sunlight and torrential rains. These had been the secondary jungles and swamps of Jurong, Paul would say, urging her to be realistic.

This was their land.
No lush green fields of padi would grow here.
No plantations of rubber and swaying palms
would thrive here.
It had been mile upon mile
of lallang, jungle and swamp.
This was their land.
Nothing much.

Nothing to be proud of.

Their land, poor in natural resources.

In the distance, out of the levelled laterite rose block upon block of flats and factories. As her bus entered the new town, Marie was greeted by broad straight roads designed to facilitate vehicular traffic to speed the movement of goods and people from one point to another. But she saw only a too neat division into squares and oblongs even though the planners had tried to soften such hard uniformity by planting trees along every roadside. Ah, Paul, can't you see?

This was the new land.

Jurong New Town the product of your kind of planning.

No wild green things allowed to grow here.

No jungle and its ever-present creepers

allowed to thrive here.

Mile upon mile of concrete and asphalt

fending them off.

Jurong New Town was aesthetically dead, boring.

Where was the variety?

Where was the beauty?

Where was the memory of human spontaneity?

And she could imagine how Paul would soberly listen to her and then earnestly argue that Jurong was nonetheless something to be proud of, wrestled out of their sterile land. This town, square blocks of factories, oblong blocks of flats; bulldozers, pile-drivers, cranes. And trucks and lorries travelling down straight broad roads, and trees planted at mathematical intervals. And even these mounds of red brown earth – these are but testimony to the proud spirit of those who worked in steel-clad determination mastering Nature and controlling the vicissitudes of Life. Here was our strange mixture of faith, arrogance and ruthlessness. Surely, there was a dignity here in our refusal to accept the poverty of our land; our refusal to bow to its harshness and our rejection of defeat. No, Marie, we have every right to be proud of Jurong.

But at this moment its dignity escaped Marie as the bus carried her through it. That relentless energy was lost on her. She saw only regimentation and exploitation.

'Note the monotony,' she called to the students, sitting around her. 'Who suffers from all this?' her hand sweeping across the landscape. 'Not you, not me but the workers. All those with little or no education. People of our class prosper on the backs of their suffering and sweat.'

The students grinned uncomfortably, feeling pangs of guilt, so Marie continued.

'You will graduate to work in air-con offices. They will work in these conditions on a miserable starting pay of less than three dollars a day. Our starting pay will be nine hundred and ninety a month. Can we in all honesty allow such conditions to prevail?'

No one answered. Each student studying the landscape trying to extract an answer.

At the terminus, they got off the bus and walked down Street 16, like a band of zealous missionaries bringing the Good News to the poor; lead by a white-clad nun straight out of *The Sound of Music*. In the still bright light of a cloudless five o'clock tropical sunset Marie's habit shone luminously but not as brightly as the lustre in her eyes. Today, she was happy. The Student-Worker Alliance was off the ground at last and she and Yean had managed to organise a meeting between this group of students and workers. So she was at her winsome best, uplifting flagging spirits after the long bus ride and now faced with a long walk up Street 18, down Street 21 and into Street 23.

At the end of Street 23 stood the Young Workers' Hostel, a grey, squat five-storey block, not luxurious, but at least less crowded than some of the company-run hostels which sometimes had as many as eight cramped into four bunk beds to a room and not even a wardrobe. Marie delighted in pointing out such facts of life to her group, casting her critical eye over everything, seeing only what she wanted to see. Where others saw slums cleared to provide adequate housing for a fast multiplying population, she saw only space cramped with families sleeping six to a tiny room. Where others saw the provision of light and water, she saw higher rents, higher utilities bills and unnecessary financial hardship for those used to living cheaply in attap houses. Instead of adequately clothed and well-paid workers acquiring new skills, she saw a floating, alienated, youthful population, exploited, bored and frustrated. For her the whole system of international trade and commerce where the many were controlled by creations of the powerful few was a terrible sin. She had to respond. There had to be a strong commitment to the liberation of man. Commitment was sacred to her, the gift a man made of himself to his brothers. 'For you give nothing unless you give of yourself,' she told her students quoting the Palestinian poet, Kahlil Gibran. 'And the greatest gift is the dedication of oneself to the struggle for a more humane and just society which would give man his rightful sense of pride and dignity. To that end,' she declared with great emphasis, 'it is not enough to convert the individual, we must struggle to change the institutions which govern our society.'

But as she finished Marie remembered how disturbed she had been that time when Mak had echoed her, declaring: 'Before anything can be built, we must first destroy!'

By this time they had reached the Young Workers' Hostel where Alice Wong, the superintendent, met them to show them around, pointing out with pride the new table-tennis tables donated by M E C, a foreign-owned company employing more than a thousand workers in Jurong, and the basketball court built by the Lee San Bank. Hearing this Yean beamed with pride herself and, relieved not to have come from a grasping family, whispered to Sis that her father was one of the bank's managers.

'But donating basketball courts is peanuts to such banks,' said Sis so Yean kept quiet for the burden of her parents' wealth was beginning to trouble her.

Alice Wong, walking briskly now and with efficient grace, was busy opening and closing doors, pointing out all the workers' facilities.

'This is the TV lounge for all the residents, and here's the sewing room for the girls.'

Yean saw that Marie's interest was only polite. She had expected Alice Wong to be eager to discuss the hardships and problems faced by the workers, especially those who were foreign. Yet whenever Sis or Yean tried to raise such questions Alice merely smiled and pointed out instead the advantages of living in the Young Workers' Hostel where 'we're like one big happy family'. Sis was eager to expose university undergrads to the hardship of a worker's life but Alice Wong adroitly turned the occasion into a public relations opportunity, showing off the excellent facilities provided by the Young Workers' Hostel.

'Ah, here's Pei Lan,' Alice introduced a member of the Hostel Committee. 'She is one of our most responsible residents,' and with her arm resting on the girl's shoulder, Alice showed off her favourite specimen to the group of visitors. 'Pei Lan, this is Sister Marie-Therese, please, bring her round to meet the rest of our family.'

Pei Lan, dressed in a pair of black slacks and a pink floral blouse, had the mien of someone who wanted to please, her face constantly creasing in a smile. She was a little surprised to meet a sister of the convent for, coming from a small Malaysian town, she had never seen one before much less talked to one.

'Why, you're like one of us,' genuinely pleased with the honour of being chosen to introduce 'this very nice and pretty sister' to her friends; a comment which amused the undergraduates and delighted Sister Marie-Therese. Pei Lan opened one of the bedroom doors.

'Hey, come, come, come. Come and meet this sister from the convent. She want to talk you lah.'

Yean watched as six young girls in their late teens popped out of the room and looked at the group with surprise.

'Talk to us for what? We all Buddhists, not Christian. Not interested,' said one of the girls in shorts and curlers. She seemed to be some kind of group leader, and her defensive tone worried the students as they crowded round Marie and Yean. They were apprehensive now for they had been told that factory workers were often rough and uncouth in speech and they did not want any unpleasantness.

'No, no, don't worry. We're not here to convert you,'

laughed Sister Marie-Therese, putting everyone at ease. 'We're here because we want to meet you, get to know you and find out about conditions of your work.'

The six girls relaxed too; they had obviously been cornered far too many times by earnest missionaries anxious for the salvation of their souls.

'Nothing interesting lah, our work. Very boring! Everyday sit and sit and put in wires,' answered another girl with an impish grin.

'Where do you work?' asked Yean.

'Mata Hari Electronics.'

'And you?' asked Yean again looking at the other five.

'Same – all same company,' answered their leader, the girl with her hair in curlers.

'And the company pays for your accommodation here?' asked Marie.

'Ya,' they answered in chorus.

The undergraduates were amused for they sounded like primary school children answering their teacher.

'So your company is good,' Marie wondered.

'So-so lah. But supervisor very fussy,' answered the impish girl.

'Ya, he very bad. Everything also he want to be right. Fed up. I answer back only he scold. Now I can't be bothered. He say do this I do this. He say do that I do that. What for I do some more? Same pay what. Why so foolish hah? Right?'

Marie nodded, pleased that here was a worker, as she interpreted to the students later, who was aware of the need to struggle against the existing power structure.

'All supervisors like that lah. Push their way around like they are the manager. Act tough only!'

'Some worse boy! They want to date us and we say

don't want – they give us dirty work to do and sometimes won't let us go to toilet ah! Say we waste time.'

Like the rest of the students, Yean was shocked. She had never realised that such conditions existed in the factories, and she noticed, too, that the six girls were pleased with the effect their words had on the students. Marie grasped the opportunity to continue with her questions.

'Ya, but life like this,' they answered, 'no schooling and we got to work like cows and horses like my mother say.'

'But life can be changed,' Yean pointed out.

'Ya, how? Everyday work, work, work and overtime some more. We all not like you, so lucky, got brains to study,' said Pei Lan who told the rest of the girls that this group was from the university.

The six girls gasped in admiration and the undergraduates laughed.

'You can try to study again. We'll help you,' one of the students impulsively volunteered, and Yean registered how Sis had immediately seen the value of the spontaneity of one student offering to teach the young workers English. It was a thrust in the right direction.

Sis had seized the opportunity to pin the students and workers down to a long-term commitment. There would be regular English classes for workers conducted by the Bukit Temasek University students led by Sis herself. These classes would provide a point of contact between the students and the workers which could be developed. The students would reflect on their experience and the SWA core group would deepen their insights into the contradictions of a capitalist society.

* * *

Hans went straight into his study the moment the meeting ended. Standing at his desk, irresolutely he took out his conference papers, flicked through them, sat down, re-arranged his papers and generally tried to be busy, all the while knowing what a fraud he was! He was not busy. He had nothing to do but could not do anything even if he had wanted to. All he wanted was to be with Marie and make her his. But how could he tell her? She was so committed to what she was doing and being. A nun in a convent! No, not quite a nun yet, and he smiled, twirling a pencil in his fingers. She hadn't taken her permanent vows. A postulant? Catholic jargon. Still his case was not all that discouraging. But this was Asia not the States or Europe where priests and nuns could leave their orders to get married. It was acceptable. But here? What chance did he have? The despondency of his situation seemed to weigh him down and he hunched over his desk vainly seeking for a solution among his papers. She lived within the rigidity of her Catholic traditions and values. He was crazy to have fallen in love with her. Madness incarnate! Out here in Asia, cut off from friends and family and faced with this wall! He stuck his pencil into a piece of rubber eraser and angrily proceeded to dig a hole in it. The hard wall of her commitment. All these months he could not even make a dent in it! Should he leave? After all he had never planned to stay. He had wanted to go to Vietnam and if it had not been for the corruption there he would have got his visa long ago. Now he was stuck with this girl in a nun's habit. He should have gone away sooner. Now it was too late. His face had lost its boyish expressions which used to criss-cross his face like the light and shadows of flying clouds. Yet, he did not regret leaving his parish in the States. Upper middle class. Sterile. Ministering to those who found meaning only in a financially secure future. The church matrons had mothered and smothered him with their tea and cakes; the dolled-up girls had sickened him. Dolls stuffed with straw! Hollow men of a decaying civilization. The East had offered hope and he had seized the opportunity to escape from the land of the living dead only to find in Singapore a society struggling to become exactly what he had left. It was crazy! And this girl, novice, postulant or whatever, was she aware of him?

A light knock on the door made him turn around. Marie, who had stayed behind after the meeting to tidy up the manse for Rev James, had noticed Hans's listlessness and now she came to find out the cause of his lack of enthusiasm for the SWA project.

'Hi, how was your conference?'

'Okay, just the usual pontifications of the bishops and church bureaucrats.' Hans had no patience for pretentious authority.

'Hmm,' nodded Marie, sharing his sentiments.

Then, silence. She, standing by the door, looking bright and cheerful, waiting for a confession she knew would come soon. And he, sitting at his desk absorbedly digging a hole in his eraser, stealing a look at her. Her slight figure in a T-shirt and pair of jeans looked lithe and alive, light and motion pulsing through her. He stopped his digging, took a deep breath and said, 'I'll be leaving for Vietnam soon.'

She remained standing by the door. Motionless. The light gone out of her eyes. Only one sound escaped her: 'oh'. Hans watched her with all the keenness of a bird-watcher careful lest the bird fly away.

'The S W A still needs your presence and skills as an organiser,' she finally said; her tone a deadpan neutral.

'Someone will take my place.'

It did not seem all that hopeless now. Still, he had to be sure. She looked small and vulnerable talking about the difficulties of getting the S W A project off the ground although a moment ago she, in her enthusiasm, had already declared it off the ground. Hans smiled at her rationalizations.

'I know the project needs me. Aren't you going to ask me to stay?'

'I would if I could! If I had the power and means!' She did not like his teasing tone, smacking of complacency and enjoyment of this situation. She was angry with herself for feeling angry that he was leaving.

'If anyone has the power and means to make me stay, it's you.'

'Huh? Sorry, I didn't hear that.' But she had. It was just that she could not believe what she had heard.

Hans repeated his words again with slow deliberation while all the time he kept his eyes on her face. She felt naked standing before his penetrating gaze. 'I said, if anyone has the power and means to make me stay, you're the one.'

She kept her eyes on the floor. The silence in the room flowed all round it, closed in upon them and wrapped them in its cocoon. Hans got up and moved toward her. How like a quivering sparrow she looked. For the first time in his life he felt lost and clumsy. His hands, too big and awkward as he put them round her shoulders now. So soft, warm and small as his arms encircled her and drew her to him, yielding, not resisting and for one heavenly moment resting her head on his broad chest content to remain there forever. Then, she pulled away. Rudely awakened, the spell was broken. The clouds evaporated and the hard edge of reality in the form of a desk touched him. He sat on its sharp edge perching there, waiting.

'You musn't do that again,' she whispered hoarsely, not looking at him. Her eyes were fixed on his hands, clasped against his knees. She was vulnerable. So vulnerable; so that there was hope. That was all he was aware of. Hope. Help me, Lord, he whispered and moved toward her.

'No, Hans, please, no,' putting out her arms in defence. 'You promised that we would be friends and remain friends. My life in the convent is messy enough without you adding to it.'

That stopped him. The wall again. But no, this time he was cruelly determined not to give in. He would strike down that wall. He would. And it was not as hard as it appeared.

Marie gave up and closing her eyes, let that warm breath carrying the whispers of 'I love you, I love you,' envelop her. Such gentle hands enfolding her softness firmly.

Lips touching her hair, brushing her ears before meeting hers in a kiss and she yielded flowing down the stream of feelings dammed up so many many months ago. He held her hand still, reluctant to let her go. But she must. She had to think things over. Caught between joy and anxiety she would only feel safe back in the convent's chapel.

She fled from the manse and drove home in a daze, keeping her eyes fixed on the road. That continuous stream of cars droning like a bulldozer in a faraway field on a hot lazy afternoon; droning till with a sudden screech of brakes she became aware of fickle pedestrians criss-crossing the road. Sounds and movements floating in and out at the edge of her mind, swimming in a dark sea of confused feelings, tangled weeds whose dark spreading roots she did not care to trace. Her soul shrank from the question. And yet it was ready to take flight. Poised like a butterfly afraid to spread its wings; afraid of that jet of soaring happiness shooting out of that dark pool of guilt.

'Hey, hurry, hurry, slow coach! The bus is coming! We'll be late.'

'Okay, okay!' And the whole group clambered up the bus to Jurong for yet another meeting with the workers. The ten boys and girls settled noisily into their seats.

'Hey, you saw Mr Mak today? We nearly died of shock. He was bald!' All the girls in the group screamed with laughter.

'He sure is turning communistic.'

'Ah, ah, you're forgetting what Mr Mak said about hair and ideology."

'Ooooh, he was so cute! You should have seen his face when we stared at him,' shouted one of the girls. Another peal of laughter.

The bus driver and conductor frowned. The bus conductor came up to them and knocked his ticket clipper on the back of the seats.

'Ten tickets to Jurong, please,' said Yean.

'Hah?' shouted the bus conductor, his voice rising above the roar of the engine. 'Kong-sa-me?' he demanded in Hokkien.

Flustered, Yean put up ten fingers and said, 'Jurong.'

He gave her the tickets and flung a look of disgust at the whole group.

'Ang Mo Kau ah! Deng Lang buay hiau kong deng lang wuay! Chinese not know how speak Chinese,' he shouted his English translation to the bus driver for the benefit of the students who'd not understand otherwise.

The bus driver laughed good-humouredly and answered him in Cantonese: 'Chap choong! These people! These fat fat yau can only say I see, you see, I no see. Forgotten ancestors already. Study ang mo, speak ang mo, act like ang mo,' and he guffawed at the stupidity of such English-educated Chinese.

Yean and her group remained angrily silent, ignoring the rude comments although Yean knew Cantonese for there was nothing much they could do without it turning into an ugly confrontation in the crowded bus. The rest of the passengers, used to multi-lingual life in the city, were keen but uninvolved observers. Most were glad to keep out of this 'sensitive issue' as the media would have termed it.

The bus screeched to a stop and about twenty people tried to get in. An Indian boy clambered up through the rear door meant for exit.

'Hey, hey, you! Get down, get down!' the bus conductor shouted in his best English. 'Come up front lah you people. Got front door don't want to use front door. Make life susah-lah! Don't move!' he commanded the bus driver, 'he still there. Get down, get down!' he shouted and glared at the Indian schoolboy till embarrassed and angry, the boy got off the bus. 'Ya, move now,' and as the bus moved off the bus conductor turned to the passengers to vindicate himself.

'Basket he! Ask him to get down don't get down. Still stand there. Wah! Grandfather own the bus or what? Come up front like everybody else lah! You go back I not see you, I ring bell and door close susah-lah, right?'

The passengers averted their faces and no one answered him. Yean too ignored the rising anger in her heart. She couldn't defend the boy. Like the others, she had been helplessly glued to her seat, afraid of ugly scenes. She hated this small tyrant and was determined to report the incident to the Jurong group later. With this in mind she forced herself to register what the imbecile was raving about.

'Ya, some passengers like this. They make life difficult – this complain, that complain. They write letters to *Straits Times* – show off only that they know a few words. I also can speak English,' and he turned to the bus driver and laughed raucously at some private joke. 'Some women farny too – so fussy – say we conductors cheeko. What man? I married. I want cheeko I go to my wife, yiok song! I can go Johore Road too, why I want cheeko on bus? This my work. Not my fault – bus crowded and women still want to come up, sure get touch touch here and there lah. Farny women and not good looking some more!'

Yean turned away and concentrated on the long dreary drive to Jurong.

'But you can't blame him. This is his only way to let off steam. He has been oppressed all his life and you're the elite. You can think. You can write. You have the power of articulation. He's one of the silent oppressed.'

'He sure was silent, boy,' Peter remarked but his sarcasm was lost on Marie, bent as she always was on judging individuals in terms of class background which was in line with the SWA's current theory developed under Mak's direction. This particular bus conductor, however, did not seem to belong to the silent oppressed while the elite in this case were not as articulate as they were reputed to be. But Yean had discovered that Sis

171

was now more interested in strategising their moves, having adopted the language of the liberal left, than in discussing issues which questioned the validity of the S W A's assumptions. Nevertheless, the S W A was dealing with human hardship and Yean, so aware of her own good fortunes, was eager to help. She would never repeat what she had done in Ser Mei's case – avoid ugliness and withdraw.

At the Workers' Hostel Pei Lan reported that one of the girls at the textile factory had had half her hair torn off by the machine.

'There, now you see how the proletariat is exploited and yet remain silent,' Mak said triumphantly.

'You should all visit the girl tomorrow and ask the union to fight for compensation even though she is an illegal worker,' Marie directed, much to Mak's satisfaction.

'We would follow up on the story and write an article on industrial safety and employers' responsibility,' Hans added.

'This is the result of allowing the multi-nationals to dump their third-rate machines here to exploit our workers,' declared Mak angrily. 'Do you know that according to the latest figures, not released of course, two-thirds of all the girls in electronics change jobs because of poor eyesight? They spend eight hours a day threading those tiny wires.'

'Ya lah, and they complain we work here, work there, never want to stay long in one place,' Pei Lan added bitterly. 'Then also corruption, people eat money. If supervisor like you and you give him sex you get easy job ah; if he hate you die lah.'

The students, especially the girls, were shocked. 'What

about the men hah?' they asked.

'Don't know ah, ask Ah Huat lah.' Ah Huat, a construction worker looked up, his dark sunburnt face glowering. 'They suck our blood,' he spluttered; fists clenched.

Marie gave him a warm smile as a reward and Ah Huat muttered, 'Nothing but low pay and dangerous work.'

'But if they're getting low pay, how come I see so many of them going for tim sum? My father says they're fairly well-paid nowadays,' one of the girls asked Marie; directing the question to her as though Ah Huat was not capable of answering for himself.

Ah Huat kept quiet and studied their faces while Marie rose to his defence.

'You like to live well; workers like to live well too. Ah Huat here is in construction, dangerous work. He lives from day to day and if he doesn't live it up now and then, he will have gained nothing when he dies. While he is alive he wants to give his best to his family so he brings them out for tim sum, like your father. Isn't this a natural human aspiration?'

Hans smiled approval as the students looked a little shame-faced at Ah Huat who eyed them without a trace of emotion on his face. Marie returned Hans's smile with a grateful almost shy glance and looked away almost immediately. But Hans continued to admire her profile. Soft rich lips. Her face mirror-smooth like the surface of a lake, depths holding the promise of feelings yet to emerge, feelings asleep waiting for him to waken them. He would open her hard encrusted shell, pry it open and roll lustrous pearls in his hand. Hans was absorbed by his own fantasies.

Marie got up and walked out of the meeting room. No, she should not. She should not. She should not let herself be fascinated by his hands. Such big generous hands. Strong yet sensitive hands. Hands that make a cat purr. Hands that say beautiful things to a woman. Hands . . . she stopped. The Lord would have to forgive her again and again and again.

'Mak, don't you think the workers tonight are fantastic? They were so analytical and perceptive, especially just now when they were describing the local power structures in the factories,' said Marie as she sat down beside Mak to wait for the others to come out of the meeting, not wanting to go in and be distracted by Hans again. 'I wish the students could be like this.'

'What do you expect?' Mak growled, for she had not even noticed that he had followed her out of the room. 'The bourgeoisie is a dying race. The proletariat will take over soon. Upon their backs rest the future.' He knew she liked the ideologue in him so he continued: 'In the Philippines and Indonesia, the students are more radical. They work very closely with the workers. Here!' and Mak ended his speech with a snort of disgust just as Hans came out of the meeting room with the rest of them.

Marie rushed off. She was sending the students home in the convent's car and had to be back at the convent before ten o'clock.

'Those sisters don't like it if I'm back too late. They don't understand what I am doing up here. They probably think I drive students up and down Jurong for fun.'

That edge of irritation in her voice which the others recognised as time to be silent and not probe.

Less than a year's work in Jurong and already Marie could see some results. The young workers were responding to the English classes and to the informal discussions on working conditions in Singapore and the political situation in South-East Asia. She was especially pleased with the way Mak had organised the workers and students into study groups. He had churned out numerous papers for their discussions and he always made himself available to drive her home whenever Hans was held up with church work. Poor Mak was nice, as she confessed to Yean once, but sometimes it was difficult to take him seriously. He was always harping on the coming revolution and the conspiracy of power. 'You never can tell,' he would say, his eyes staring out of his thick glasses to prepare you for his prophetic statement, 'they keep an eye on everything. Everything that goes on. They don't give scholarships for nothing, you know, and these buggers spy for them in return.' And she had tried not to smile. She was glad she could talk with Yean. She had not lost her capacity to develop deep loving relationships. Despite some disagreements, Peter, Ken, Aileen and Kim were still loyal to her. The workers adored her and many of the girls had poured out their problems to her. She felt honoured and grateful. She knew she had the gift to overcome barriers of race, age and status. She was conscious that people liked her and she believed more firmly than ever now that they would always do what she asked of them. She prayed that she would use this gift responsibly 'to guard each man's dignity and save each man's pride' so that people like Pei Lan and Ah Huat might be directed to their rightful place in the sun.

Pei Lan returned to the hostel. She had just said good-bye to Sister Marie-Therese, her best friend, as she told everyone in the hostel.

'She very nice, you know, so sweet lah. Like a chatter-box lah, I, talk and talk and talk; complain, complain about my supervisor – that stupid man; and she listen, so patient, you know,' said the girl with the impish grin.

Pei Lan smiled and nodded. No one could help liking Sister Marie-Therese who always looked so fresh and sweet especially in her habit.

'Hey, don't forget hah tomorrow night got meeting downstairs seven o'clock,' Pei Lan reminded the girl.

She was enthusiastic about her role as group co-ordinator. Sister had singled her out and she was pleased and proud that she had been chosen above all others. She did not consider herself pretty nor skilled in work except in threading tiny wires at the factory. In a loud Hokkien voice her mother had always boomed out to all and sundry that her Ah Lan was 'bor lor yong!' 'Use-less!' her mother had screamed even in front of friends and relatives. But these past six months had been dif-ferent. As she had confessed to Sister, at last she felt able to do something positive, wasn't just useless wood as her mother had labelled her. She wanted to be of use and was glad Sister Marie-Therese was using her. And in this group she was even offering these people from the university, advice, especially that Mr Mak – 'and he, a lecturer some more' – as she proudly told the other girls. And Sister had been so good, so good to her. If she were not already Buddhist, she would become a Christian and not care what her mother would say. She would do anything for Sister. Anything!

'Why she not wear her white robe anymore hah?'

Pei Lan turned to her friend again. She saw herself as the best person to explain Sister Marie-Therese to the others.

'Why she want to look like us hah?' asked her friend, eager for a bit of gossip after a hard day's work. 'Maybe she want to marry that Father Hans right?'

'What father? He not father lah! He not a Catholic priest,' answered Pei Lan, not very pleased with her friend's view of the Sister.

But her friend had eagerly responded with, 'Better what, can marry.'

'How you know? As if! Kay poh only!'

'Can see what! Everytime come together; go home also together.'

'Now alright what! In America, now very modern – priests and nuns can marry. You people hah, sometimes too narrow minded.'

'Ya, ya, clever lah,' said her friend, irritated with Pei Lan's accusation that she had been narrow minded. 'Last night you talk like you know so much. You think you American hah?'

'What I say true what, all these big shots talk like they know so much, say we go here go there got no loyalty, don't know hardship and must tighten our belts. See lah my belt so tight already,' laughed Pei Lan, showing her belly to her friend.

'Farny,' answered her friend who was not amused. 'One day you end up back across the Causeway then you know. They say in Jurong, walls have ears.'

'Why I can't talk ah? I speak true. Why cannot even say the truth ah?' Pei Lan tried to appeal to her friend's common sense.

'Not say you can't speak true,' her friend responded just as sensibly, 'but your voice small small lah; other people's voice bigger than yours, stoopeed!'

'Ya lah, that's why Sister Marie-Therese so good, she speak for us,' Pei Lan was glad she could point this out to her friend. Sister was her best friend and she would defend her anytime, just as she knew Sister would defend her in turn.

*   *   *

Hans glanced at his watch. Nine forty-five. Forty-five minutes late. Marie was getting worse. So many people to see and she could not say No. Hans switched off the overhead light in the car and was plunged into darkness. He sank back into the driver's seat. Eyes adjusted, he watched couples strolling in and out of the Young Workers' Hostel. Dark moving figures against the fluorescent glow of the neighbouring blocks of flats. Almost ghostly under the yellow arc of the street lamps. No privacy. No labyrinth of winding lanes and shady avenues. Merely long straight roads cutting at right angles, efficiently lit with bright neon lights driving away the shadows of romance and mystery. These factory workers will have to hold each other's hands along fluorescent lit corridors – love and desire in full view and his own Western soul cringed at the lack of privacy. He would take Marie to where they could be by themselves. That woman was driving him crazy. He hoped she would make up her mind soon about their relation-ship but she was clearly not a woman to be pushed. So all these months he had waited. Had he any alternatives? He simply had to wait. Patience. He must have patience if he did not want to lose her. At the murmur of approaching voices, Hans sat up, ready to start the car.

'Sorry Mak, another night I'll have supper with you. Bye, Yean.'

Yean and Mak stood on the kerb, waved, watching her drive off with Hans. Mak took off his glasses and wiped the oily sheen from his high forehead.

Hah! Busy woman! She has commitments. Don't take up too much of her time. How come he can take up her time? Spare tyre, that was what he was – a spare tyre – whenever the damned American was too busy to fetch her. No matter. Mak Sean Loong was a fighter and he would show her how much more powerful than Hans he could be. But first he must lay his foundations and build his house upon rock. He smiled. He was getting better at the Bible these days. His watch told him it was still early. He would drive over to Yuan Tung Hostel and meet his other gang there. Aah, his day would come. No one knew yet, not even a Marie-Therese, the extent of his connections. He wasn't named Sean Loong for nothing. He would be great yet.

Yean watched Mak get into his car, sullen and sulky as he slammed the door, turned the ignition key with a single twist and ground into first gear. His car, a battered grey Datsun, coughed into life belching smoke. But not fire, thought Yean. Could Mak be in love with Sis too? What a mess! With Mak rumbling like an awakening volcano these days, this situation of the eternal triangle would be too much for Sis.

Hans's V/W purred as it sped down the broad avenue away from the bright metallic glow of Jurong. A burst of gasoline fumes made Marie wind up the window pane. Hans sounded his horn impatiently. A glare of headlights; a flash of red and their Volks had overtaken the city bus.

'Hey, what's the big hurry?' Marie asked softly.

'To get us out of here to some place quiet. I want more time with you and the convent has strict bedtime rules.' Hans's throat felt a little tight as he glanced at the demure figure beside him.

'Don't worry, no curfew hours tonight. I'm back at my parents' home for a few days.'

'Great! Let's celebrate your release.'

'Don't tease, Hans, I want to be able to tell them about us. My parents are of the old school. Mother Superior may understand and accept but not my parents, especially not my father.'

How was she to explain? Where to begin? How was she to pinpoint that moment when he was no longer Hans – just Hans. When did he quiver into life in her? All this while when she thought he was a beautiful person to whom she wanted to reach out, he was already inside her waiting for her to see him. Inside. He was there, waiting. How was she to put into words all those waves and ripples in whose rhythm she had drowsed all these months. These years they seemed. So her father would never understand. And she realized that beneath all his pious Legion-of-Mary softness was a hard man, driving himself with a businessman's relentlessness to the gates of heaven. Did he expect her to be devoid of human feelings and desires? Did he want a fleshless saint for a daughter, white and pure, smiling like a lily of the valley, an Asian madonna? Why couldn't he accept her as she was? God did. And here she was encountering great men and women whose ideas she shared: Karl Marx, Mao Tse-tung, Max Weber, Marcuse, Germaine Greer, Hannah Arendt. Hans explaining the significance of The Banality of Evil – first in relation to Nazism and second, in the context of military-industrial societies. Hans – the lover of peace was the greater analyst. Where Paul Tan would have analysed her shortcomings and pointed out how airy-fairy her ideas were, Hans had explained the modern world and opened up areas so that her ideas did not seem airy-fairy, a phrase coined by Paul to reduce her. Hans respected her intelligence and she was his partner dedicated to the common task of making this world a better and safer place; she was his equal-in-love – Hans's phrase.

'Hey, wake up dreamer, we're here.'

Hans parked the car and walked up to one of the stone benches beside the reservoir. Tuesday night. The place was deserted. Globes of yellow light pushed back the darkness creating spaces of soft half-light between them. Marie sat on the stone bench and bent down toward her ankles busily pulling out thorns from her jeans.

'Look, love grass,' she said as she held out her palm to Hans sitting beside her. He blew away the tiny thorns and held her hand. She breathed in deeply, stretched out her legs, and leaned back against the stone bench letting the cool semi-darkness enfold her. Tonight she would forget about her father. A light breeze played among the soft folds of her thin voile blouse, suggesting small firm breasts. Hans could not take his eyes off her. But Marie concentrated on the lake enjoying its beauty.

181

'I like this kind of cloudy night with everything dark and mysterious, shimmering, soft shadows, no definite shapes. I dislike shapes which are too defined, you know what I mean?' and she turned to face him.

Unable to speak, he nodded, and pleased that he had understood, she laid her head on his shoulder. His arms went round her, careful to be gentle and he held her in his arms, breathing in her presence. The tiny hairs curling at the nape of her neck fascinated him and he bent to kiss them gently. His exploring fingers told him things about her. She was so different from all the American girls he had held back home. Her sandalwood skin was fine and smooth, her earlobes cool. Brushing away strands of hair from her forehead and half-closed eyes he bent down, his lips brushing against those tiny eyelashes; then the tip of her nose and next, her lips, so full and soft – just there for him. He pulled back a little, and looked at her, then conscious only of those lips he gathered her into his arms and kissed her deeply as her lips parted slightly to receive him. Their tongues met, warm and mobile; now darting eagerly, now stroking each other gently, gently, exploring inner space. In an outburst of all the feelings he had suppressed for long months, loving and working with her on issues, issues, issues he pressed her closer and closer. If only he could squeeze her heart out and know for sure what lies there. Then she was gone. So abruptly that Hans was left looking at her as she stood beside the lake adjusting her blouse and smoothing her hair.

'Marie . . .'

She turned, 'I'm sorry. Please take me home.'

'Marie . . .'

Again she said, 'Please take me home,' and walked down

the path to the car park.

'Wait!' he jumped up and held her by the shoulder.

'Don't touch me!'

He recoiled immediately, hit by three rocks. 'Marie,' and he stayed his hand in mid-air, from where it fell back, helpless, by his side.

'Don't touch me, please, don't touch me,' she whispered, her eyes downcast.

'Marie,' Hans began again, and when she remained silent, he whispered, 'Darling, I love you.'

'Yes,' she turned to look him full in the face, fierce as a Chinese woman warrior, 'and that gave you the right to paw me, maul me and cheapen me, right? Right? I'm not American you know!' and her eyes flashed angry lightning. Then, tired and spent, she bowed her head. 'I'm disgusted with myself. Just don't come near me.' She held up her hand as Hans moved closer.

'I'm disgusted with you too. You always asked me to relax in your presence. How can I? The moment I relax you take advantage of me. I can't put my head on your shoulders for five minutes without you reading all kinds of meanings into it. I've got to be on my guard against you and I hate it. I know I'm supposed to ask for permission to leave the convent soon but I haven't done it yet and I feel stained, impure. Oh! I don't know what to feel now.'

Hans looked at her, standing there with her back toward him. He was hopelessly confused.

'Stained? Impure to be touched by someone who loves you and whom you love?'

'I don't know.' She almost stamped her feet with impatience. 'I don't know what I'm feeling. I'm just not ready, I think,' and walked toward the car.

Hans followed, defeated. Damn it! Why couldn't he do anything right? In the vast empty tarmac space of the car park she turned to face him. She was crying.

'Can't you wait for me? Till I'm ready?' Hans nodded silently. 'I realise you love me very much,' her voice trembling with the admission.

Hans held himself in rein, tight and taut, only permitting himself to hold her hands.

'Will you forgive me?' his voice was hoarse with the effort.

She smiled and nodded too. Seeing the shame and apology on his face, she relented and walked beside him, his hands now hanging awkwardly at his sides. She stole a glance at him. How could she explain any of this? She was not even sure of her own feelings.

Brides of Christ
All chaste and pure
All thoughts and desires
Centre on Him
The Lover of us all.

Mere refrains, mere refrains. And yet, she was a novice in a convent. She had let all of them down, and this second disappointment was yet to strike her father. What could she say? And during all her growing years didn't her mother and grandmother warn her about men? Don't trust them. Never. In the dark they're beasts. No good girl will let a man touch her before marriage, her grandma had said firmly. And no well brought up young man would touch a girl. Chieh! Boys and girls, hah, never never ... she stopped. They had reached the car. He looked so miserable.

'Darling, I love you,' she whispered and her lips caressed his cheek. 'You know,' she said brightly, pushing away the tension, 'I've always believed that marriage ought to be what Gibran said – I can't remember the exact words – two pillars holding up a roof and there's something about two trees growing apart but with their roots intertwined.' She squeezed his hand, full of affection now that he was not asserting his will. 'But I have my own symbol – mine is the three-quarter circle; not the complete circle which is enclosing and imprisoning. Marriage ought to be joined at one end and opened at the other end allowing for the rest of the world. Marriage ought to be all-embracing, right?' She looked up into his face expecting praise and approval.

But Hans's face was dark and immobile. His nose now appeared sharper than it was, between eyes that were cold and unseeing.

'Marie, you love with your head! No feelings! Don't you sense my vibes!' His words were like hot sparks. 'Your ought-to marriage is selfish. You're afraid of total commitment. You always want to give yourself to a whole community! That's faceless giving! Can't you give yourself to a single person – me; and give in a more concrete, more fulfilling way?' and there was a glint of steel in his eyes. 'Can't you sense that I need you? Can't you feel it? I want you. I want to touch you, hold you. Why come here in the first place if you didn't want us to do this?'

He shouldn't have said that. The look in her face made him turn away. How could he make her understand? She looked as if she had just been stabbed. These things had never occurred to her. She was so frustratingly naive! Yet so like a woman. Had he come all this way to meet her? Had he?

'Hans!' A cricket chirped. He turned and she clung to

him, hiding her face in his chest, dissolving into tears. He held her tightly; her breasts heaving against him so he waited.

Leaves rustled in the breeze, shadows in the car park merging into each other. Closing his eyes he kissed her soft lips again, invitingly wet. He pressed against her harder and harder, passionately now, straining to be one with her; the blood rushing full and hot in his veins, pulsing through his arteries with an urgency he could no longer control. For one supreme moment he felt himself pouring into her.

O Marie, Marie.

In the enclosed garden behind the grey walls of the convent the night slowly solidified into a dark heavy mass. Two white figures emerged from the chapel, walking slowly round the school field while beyond the convent's grey walls, the neon lights of the cinema blinked a red and green hollow gaiety to the sombre walls which enclosed a joy known only to those who had suffered and come out whole. Mother Superior sighed inwardly as she looked down at Marie-Therese, this small Chinese girl beside her ample Irish girth; this bright-eyed sparrow, restless and alert. She would have liked to offer her her wisdom and her patience, so much of which Mother Superior had garnered during all her thirty years in Singapore. She wanted to say: my pet, you're a bird. You'll fly. This nest here is too small for you. You will want the freedom of the skies. You will not be able to accept the obedience we require of you. You will want to go beyond us, to extend yourself; to do great things – what they are I do not know but you will need to discover your limits – what they are you do not know. Still you will want to go ahead with your living and eventually leave us, my child; and we will have to let you go. Someone else will claim you and you will have to decide. But go where your heart pulls. Fickle though our hearts are at times, they are stronger than our brains.

Mother Superior would have said all these things if Marie had allowed silence to rest between them, to create that space of emptiness into which Mother Superior could pour her thoughts for her thoughts and feelings as yet undefined but only vaguely felt, needed that silence to give them birth. But Marie's thoughts tonight needed to be born out of words. Restless words since speech was the medium which bore her thoughts. She had so much to tell, to share as she put it. And so her sparkling stream flowed on and on into the deep calm of the older woman beside her. Looking up at Mother Superior's face, calm as a desert traveller who had learnt to sit still in the shadow of a rock waiting in the dry heat, for a few drops of rain, Marie knew that she had no such patience. Theory and practice; faith and deed – these went hand in hand. She had to live out her faith. She had to change the desert into a garden even if she had to drag the icebergs down from the North Pole. And in the ardour and fire of such faith she had to push aside her private feelings and affairs. Hans would have to wait. It was the right thing to do. She could wait therefore he should wait. So, not tonight. Some other night. Tonight was for the S W A project and she must convince Mother Superior.

'So I told the students in my group that it's our responsibility to educate the workers. The need to learn is there so it's our responsibility to meet that need. I said that the capitalist student only works for himself, his grades and degree.'

Mother Superior nodded and that was enough for Marie. 'So I told them that we owe the taxpayers something; and that it's fallacy to think that the academic success we achieve is all our own. Our family, our community and the Lord had a hand in it too.' Again Mother Superior nodded for how could she not agree?

'Then you'll allow me to present the case to the community?'

Mother Superior nodded.

Mak, too, would be pleased. He had been urging her to involve the convent for it would increase the impact of their student-worker demonstration against the warmongers in Vietnam. For centuries, Mak would say, the Church and clergy had worked on the side of the establishment as the instrument of colonial oppression. And we had never been involved except out of selfish interest, she would reply. So she had urged the students to think beyond themselves.

'We can't,' Peter had protested. 'We'll be jailed.'

'No one can speak except the three hundred who run this country,' said Ken.

'Not true, have you tried?' she had challenged. 'I agree that we have been locked out of the nation-making process but we have to regain our proper place and dignity. Are we going to allow a mere three hundred to decide our fate?' And she could not help but give their Catholic innards a tug when she hurled the last challenge at them. 'And where's our faith in ourselves? What's this about working side by side, guarding each man's dignity and saving each man's pride? Eh? Why are we singing that if we don't mean it?'

'But Sis, be reasonable. Doesn't it occur to you that we can be afraid?' Yean had voiced everybody's anxiety.

'Yes, we're afraid. Who isn't? We're human, but if we allow fear to rob us of the will to act, then dark forces will triumph. We're called to act and to choose. If we allow this web of fear to freeze us, then they succeed, without having to lift a finger.'

'Look, it's only human to be afraid but it's also human

to dare to dream and catch these dreams. Reason and logic are not the only paths to truth. Visions in the dreams that people dream may lead us to the truth too, so said Ibsen.'

It was a tussle between rice and poetry as she told Hans later, and in the Singaporean soul, rice would always win, she sighed. Peter and Ken had refused to join in the demonstration, calling it a hollow gesture. Mak had been glad for he long suspected them of being C I A or government agents. Mak then announced that there were other more committed student groups. emphasizing that these were committed even though they were not Christians, and challenging Hans to deny what he had said. Han wisely ignored him. Mak was a strange fellow, but they needed him. A good organiser who could speak fluent Mandarin, and various dialects to the workers. If only Peter and Ken had been as committed as Mak; it irked her that she had to be so dependent on Mak's fluency. Still if the convent participated she would have greater control; Mak was too emotional at times, so she had to ensure that things went smoothly. Their protest should be like a worm crawling up the streets seemingly harmless. And poems would be read and songs would be sung, the critique delivered peacefully. So people would realize that criticism and protest is not the same as Communism and violence. No, not at all. She had to save this spark of courage before it was extinguished by the good life and complacency.

'Marie, you're like a praying mantis trying to stop the carriage's wheels,' an old Chinese sister had told her. Well, still someone had to do it. She had to try even though her group had forsaken her. No, not all, there was still Yean, Kim and Aileen. The girls were more committed to poetry than the boys. They could see and accept more readily the symbolic significance of an act and not just weigh practical results. Still there was hope; and even if it were a mere flicker she would carry on for Man after all, she reminded herself, is lonely by birth. And tomorrow night with Mother Superior's support she would present her case to the community. And Lord, please, please, open their hearts and minds to accept what she had to say. Just a flicker of hope to go by, she sang as she waltzed down the corridor.

For Sister Marie-Therese this was enough.

★   ★   ★

The gong for prayer and assembly had sounded more than fifteen minutes ago. Sister Veronica, tall and square-shouldered with smiling Irish grey eyes, came out of her room and hurried down the arched corridor. She overtook the slight figure of Sister Mary who had recently taken over her post as principal of one of their secondary schools. Sister Mary, neat in appearance and precise in speech, was regarded as one of the modern principals par excellence who had a mind of her own and was not afraid to use it. No shilly-shallying with her. Her commitment to a given task was total. Sister Veronica smiled approvingly at this possible future Asian Reverend Mother of the convent.

'Hello, Mary, do you know what this assembly is about?

'Only vaguely. Reverend Mother did mention something about Sister Marie-Therese and some proposals she had.'

'Hmmm,' murmured Sister Veronica who had her own

reservations about young Marie-Therese.

'I wish Reverend Mother would tell her straight to concentrate on her studies and help with our catechism classes in the schools,' said Sister Mary, not without an undertone of disapproval at the softness of Reverend Mother toward her young charge.

They climbed the rickety wooden stairs and entered the dark gloom of the circular community room with its heavy, dignified chairs of the colonial period, just in time to catch Marie-Therese in fiery form.

'But this will be the first demonstration in Singapore in which we are not doing something for our own sakes!'

How times have changed. These young ones are so outspoken these days, Sister Veronica reflected a little sadly.

But Marie was at patience's end. She sank back into her seat, resting her arms on the huge cane chair, and crossing her legs to wait. She had nothing else to say. It was up to them now. She would take part in the demonstration come what may; and she looked round at the faces of the sisters. White figures huddled together, anxious to do the right thing, waiting as usual for outside sanction. The portrait of their archbishop stared down at them, waiting too. Couldn't they see this was the right thing to do? The community had to take a stand despite what the hierarchy had decreed about religion and politics! She was hot even though the windows all along the circular wall were open. Their community room looked dingy in the evening gloom. To her, the community's mind was as dingy as their furniture.

'We are a religious order, we can't take part in a demonstration like this. Besides, it's bound to be considered illegal and we can't get the school and community into trouble.' Sister Veronica was determined to curb the impulsiveness of the younger ones.

'But we have to commit ourselves one way or another,' Marie muttered almost under her breath.

'Yes, but not like this, we are committed to education. We have to keep our schools. You're being irresponsible to drag us into this.' Sister Mary had always disapproved of Marie-Therese spending so much time away from the community.

'Typical, this community only cares about its buildings and its security, hiding behind our habits,' Marie hit back.

'Now, that's not fair,' said Sister Aloysius, her thin voice quavering: she did not like arguments still less speaking up at meetings; she had devoted her time to cooking for the community. Marie listened to this Indian sister in surprise. She had never noticed her before. Sister Aloysius, her voice rising higher and higher, continued, 'His Grace is right, you know. We religious should leave politics to the layman. We should be humble. We know nothing about politics. We should not judge.'

Marie suppressed a groan.

'Yes, sister, you're right,' said Sister Anunciation briskly cutting her short. As a Mathematics teacher, she was used to seeing things in a clear-cut way. 'Our job,' she went on, 'is to take care of the spirit. We all know Man does not live by bread alone.'

Sister Anunciation's voice sounded so triumphant in its certainty that Marie could not resist retaliating.

'Man can't live by bread alone, fine! But man can't eat his bread without choking if he is stripped of his dignity.'

Her strident tone made the sisters shift uneasily in their chairs. Surely, this democratic sharing, this call to speak their minds and be as frank as possible, was getting a little out of hand. Sister Veronica longed for the old days when community meetings were simple acts of obedience with Mother Superior telling everyone what to do.

Marie looked round at the faces of the sisters and knew that she had hit home. She looked out of the window. Dark heavy clouds were gathering in the sky above, pressing down heavily upon the air: it would rain soon. She looked down into the garden and gazed at the granite grotto of Our Lady, praying that Mother Superior would come to her support. She was in the right; she would never give in.

'Look,' another sister was saying, anxious to bring a conciliatory tone into the tension. 'Is it worth jeopardising all that we've built up in order to let the world know where we stand?'

A logical question, but here was her logical answer. 'Yes, sister, especially in our context where everyone is afraid to take a stand in public. People say one thing and do something else in private.' Marie was beginning to feel tired of having to explain all over again why they must take a stand and why they must make it public. 'We must show that we care for the truth.'

'But what is your truth?' asked Sister Mary the school principal. 'It can be Communist propaganda. This is so anti-American. How do we know it is not Communism? How do we know? How true is your truth?' This futile meeting and the oppressive heat of an approaching storm was making Sister Mary burn with impatience as she thought of the pile of circulars waiting to be read from the Ministry of Education.

'Oh, must you go into abstract philosophy?' Marie groaned, ignoring their impatience which was swelling like a balloon, stretching the skin of their tolerance. Never fear confrontations, Hans had told her, they force the truth out of others; you Asians are too polite, he had once declared. Marie gathered herself again, 'In the Philippines, their priests and nuns – unlike us – flock into the streets. They form cordons round their demonstrating students to protect them from the riot police. If you really think about it, their presence in the forefront with their students speak louder than a thousand sermons on Sundays!' Her voice was tinged with contempt.

'Marie, aren't you being carried away by all these talks of revolution and activism?' Mother Superior asked quietly. She, too, was uneasy about such involvement in politics on the part of the religious.

'Marie, you're the one asking your students to demonstrate, not the other way round,' pointed out Sister Mary.

'They are brave in taking a stand which is more than I can say for this community of believers!' Marie flung out her words, careless now because she was angry. They were all against her, even Mother Superior, and she had expected her to be more positive after the hours spent in her office, explaining the Vietnam war and the workers' movement to her. She wished Hans were with her now.

'That was a most unfair statement, Marie,' Sister Veronica said. 'Demonstrating against an unjust war is important but it is not more important than some of the other sisters' work, caring for girls like your friend, Ser Mei. Your work is no more important than others.'

Murmurs of approval greeted Sister Veronica and soon other voices joined her: their order had never been afraid to take a stand when it was absolutely necessary. Hadn't we risked public disapproval when we started to educate the local girls in those early years? Hear, hear! Perhaps young Marie-Therese has lost her sense of perspective! Ours is a teaching order never a demonstrating one. What do we want to demonstrate for? Nothing will come of it! Perhaps Sister Marie-Therese does not know her community: she spends most of her time outside.

Why, another voice added, she often comes home late, parks her car here, and is gone again the next morning. Don't you think the community's car should be shared among more people? We have so many aged sisters.

Mother Superior got up. The meeting should end here; they would meet again when peace and generosity returned and their souls could reach out to touch each other gently once again. May the Prince of Peace hear our prayer, Amen.

Marie rushed into the darkness of the chapel and knelt down. Tumultuous feelings pouring out of her.

Malice!

Malice!

It was sheer malice that had made them say such things. The altar lights wavered, dimmed and swam in her tears. She put her head down on the pew and sobbed quietly. Why were they so petty?

Couldn't they see that she was not using the car for herself? Their order should not need a car. A car was simply too bourgeois! They had never approved of her work in Jurong. They did not want to become an industrial mission. It was not in their order's constitution. Now, Lord, isn't this too legalistic an interpretation? Marie asked, suddenly remembering that she was in the presence of the Trinity. Their rejection of her work was based more on fear than on mission. They were afraid of the government; afraid of being branded Marxist and Communist. But Lord, aren't we supposed to cast out fear? Aren't we supposed to teach others to take up their beds and walk? Wasn't this part of the Good News? Part of their mission? Her sense of mission was so different from the community's. How could she go on with them? This was a fundamental ideological split. She could never be part of a community too scared to act. Could she now, Lord, she asked.

The Lord hanging from His Cross did not answer. He only looked painfully heavenward.

'She's praying inside,' Sister Veronica said to Sister Mary as they walked. 'I do hope she will forgive us. We were rather harsh on her, poor pet. She's still very young.'

'But those things had to be said. She's been so insensitive of late. Poor Sister Beatrice had to take a taxi the other day because Marie had taken the car and you know, Beatrice's legs are weak,' said Sister Mary, who was younger and more impatient with human weaknesses. 'It's all this newfangled theology of revolution that's sweeping through the Philippines and Latin America. She's caught up in it.'

'I know, but surely she can see some value in working quietly with individuals and visiting the sick and the poor?'

'She calls it patchwork charity,' answered the other drily.

'Aaah, here is Sister Beatrice. Hello, sister, mana pergi?'

'Aye, aye, mana Marie-Therese? She not here, she not there. Hujan sa-kali! I look everywhere for her; dia belum makan,' the old sister complained as she hobbled into the chapel looking for her lost lamb.

'She's speaking more and more Malay as she grows older. She must have forgotten her Spanish by now.'

'She has decided not to return to Spain. She hates the Franco regime with Spanish passion. One of her brothers died in the civil war,' said Sister Veronica and after a pause, she asked, 'Now isn't Sister Beatrice as politicised as our Marie-Therese?''

The two sisters chuckled at the thought for they knew that in Marie's eyes, she and the aged Beatrice, devoted keeper of the gate, were poles apart.

A low rumble of thunder sounded. 'Let's get in; it's going to pour.'

★   ★   ★

The sky darkened ominously as the huge grey clouds, heavy with rain, rolled in from the sea. The spire of the Cathedral of the Good Shepherd stood high and solitary above the old pre-war shophouses of Victoria Street and Bras Basah Road, defying the onslaught of the flying clouds of a sumatran storm. Marie looked at it for a moment. If only the Church would be like its spire, but she quickly pushed the thought aside as wishful thinking. The Church would never be like that. It would stress the vow of obedience and carefully act within the limits of its grey walls and law-abidingly leave the teeming millions in the city's blocks and shop-houses to be organized and ordered by authorities other than herself. It was content simply to be a haven for the lonely individual squeezed dry by the city's machinery steam-rolling its way to progress.

Marie walked out of the convent quickly and turned up the road, a solitary figure on the ground, braving the gusts of sand grains which peppered her face. Lowering her head slightly she faced the oncoming cars and lorries in the full glare of their head-lights, metallic monsters rushing down the road ready to mow down the defenceless pedestrian. She was destined to move against such forces. Whirlpools of sand played about her ankles as she tramped on the squares of cement slabs with not a blade of grass between. Grey walls, grey road, grey sky! How she hated this grey neutrality! She moved along the kerb oblivious of the incessant roar which streamed past her, as she carefully avoided the trunks of those newly planted 'instant' angsana trees, their bare branches stretching out toward the sky like so many crippled arms appealing for pity, asking for leaves to hide their ugly naked trunks. But she had no pity tonight. None. None whatsoever, for all was malice against her. Her community had chosen grey neutrality but she was convinced that the struggle of faith and hope against the forces of fear and darkness was a struggle to the death! How could they expect her to remain silent when millions were dying in the north and thousands here were being subjected to a zombie life in the name of progress!

Contrary to what Paul Tan had said, she was no longer an armchair critic!

The thunder rumbled in the sky above, a dark solid mass, its edges softened by the glow of neon lights. Sharp cold drops stabbed her skin and splattered on to the road and pavements. The rain came down in glittering silver pounding the roof-tops of cars, stopped at traffic lights, fender to fender, windscreen wipers flashing in the orange tail-lights. Marie walked on in her wet clothes. Grit and determination. That was what she needed. A hardness of soul. No room for pity. Was this the price she had to pay? But someone must do it. Someone must break this web of fear and hopelessness; this hiding behind the vows of poverty and obedience. Poverty is not living behind grey walls. Poverty is to live life at the cutting edge, ready to be cast off by the rest. Her single act of fearlessness would push back the darkness and create another small corner of light. The rain pouring down in torrents, now rivulets ran at her feet. Soaked to the skin, she turned back, curbing the impulse to run for shelter, and walking steadily in the pouring rain, ignoring the honking of the cars, she passed under the arch into the convent – a Moses returned from the wilderness.

Jurong New Town caught in the ferocity of the same sumatran storm, was wet, naked and defenceless in spite of its towering structures of steel and concrete. Driving through it Mak saw how this planned and organized grid had become canals of bright orange mud swirling round the prisons of industry into which the workers filed each morning and out of which they rushed each evening. Jurong – this edifice of organized life – eight o'clock in, five o'clock out.
Cube, Block, Cube, Block,

Matsushita, Philips, T I, G E, Q R, C T,
Cube, Block, Cube, Block.

Mak drove on in the torrential rain, pressing ahead just
as these shapes pressed on him and he had to fend them
off; shout against, tear down and break free of all these
structures. He stopped the car, parked it under a tree and
got out. Holding his umbrella at an angle to ward off
the icy rain and battling the irrational wind in this rational land, he pushed against the gusting which threatened
to snatch his poor man's shield – his waxed-paper umbrella. But the steel frame of his determination would
not give in. No, he would never go with the wind. He,
too, believed he was destined to go against it. The dragon,
strong and wilful, would master the elements, would
even control them. And then, T H E Y, would have to
recognise him in his full majesty; T H E Y who had built
these towering structures! But now like the true impov-
erished cadre he would swim like a fish among the
people, incognito. Mak pushed on, soaked but proud.
And wasn't this a just and righteous feeling? While
Hans and Marie were cosy in their nests he had abandoned his car, this evening, to take the bus like the
rest of these workers battling for a toe-hold on the city-
bound bus. The rain, yes, the rain; he should remember
to tell his group this: the rain is the condition which
sharpens the contradictions between the haves and the
have-nots. The haves go home clean and dry and the
have-nots go home wet with the city's muck! They call
it Muck in the States; but we call it Dung here. This
grid is made to carry dung!

Unlike the workers, Mak had no immediate goal. He
was in no hurry to get home. He was here to observe.
He stood at the edge of the evening crowd that was

milling around the bus stop, necks craning, hair dripping wet, restless for any bus that would stop. The women were competing for the limited places on the buses and Mak was surprised that they were as hardy as the men.

'Femininity exists only in prosperity. Do you know this?' he asked the girl next to him.

She cast him a look, quite angry at this sudden intrusion by a complete stranger, and moved away.

'Seow-ay, don't know say what also,' she muttered to her friend.

Mak ignored the remark and smiled to himself – the smile of the unrecognised general. Wait, ah, wait. When he should give the signal for arms one day, she would remember that this was how she had encountered him, Mak Sean Loong, First Dragon. And was not one of the Chinese Dragon Emperors, Chien Lung, also one of those who moved incognito among his people like this? Satisfaction wreathed his face as he noted his own continuity with history, unaware of the contradiction in his comparison between a self-professed follower of Marxist–Leninist–Mao Tse-tung Thought and an emperor. He stood there in the rain, his glasses glistening in the evening light as he watched his people fight for a place in the buses. Ha! he would lead his people in the first ever attack on these prisons and let them see that they were not as invincible as they seemed. And Mak stood at the bus stop, in the midst of the restless crowd, feeling tall and strong despite the outward appearance of an aged gnome. Power to the People! he wanted to shout in exhilaration. He had confirmed his mission in life. He had found meaning! O U C H! Some idiot had stepped on his foot. He turned to see who the fellow was but too late. A bus had just stopped and the workers charged toward it and elbowed their way on.

In this onslaught of charging life, Mak Sean Loong, First Dragon, found himself pushed to the sidelines.

The storm which knew no social boundaries had also unleashed its anger in Kensington Park where Yean lived. The spacious gardens surrounding the mansions and bungalows were glistening wet in the lamp-light; their aged trees and shrubs gave the Park an air of organic grace and serenity for these had grown and aged through the years following the rhythm of nature, sheltered from the organized roar of the traffic outside the Park.

The storm lashing through the night was just stopping. Drops still fell from the trees, diamonds for a moment in the glow of her bedside lamp before they fell into endless night. Yean sat up in bed and listened. The house was quiet. Her mother's sobs had also stopped. She was relieved. She must have dozed off. When had her mother stopped crying? An icy drop of guilt fell upon her soul but its cold touched her for only a moment and then thawed, for all these troubles had nothing to do with her. She had always refused to be drawn into these family squabbles. Tai Yee, her elder aunt, had no right to lecture her like that! Why must she, the daughter, fight her mother's battles? Why should she confront her father for her mother who had chosen silence and respectability? She, the daughter, had rarely spoken to a father she had seldom seen. Gazing out of the window, she saw the solitary garden lamp throwing a ghostly yellow light on the driveway. Her father was still out.

'You have to watch his movements,' Tai Yee had advised her mother earlier tonight. 'Don't be so soft, fight.

He already has a number two. If you're not careful there'll be a number three. Our sister-in-law saw them both at the Tropicana, dancing so close together. She said that that female fox was about our Yean's age.' And at this her mother had cried bitterly. 'Ah, you must come with me to this medium the next time. His deity will help you to drive this fox out of your husband's life. His amulets are very powerful,' and she had stormed out of her mother's room protesting against such ignorant superstition. Why couldn't her mother confront father about his foolishness instead of resorting to this trickery? Why couldn't she deal with the truth head-on? Take a stand against his disgusting behaviour. Pure and simple. Such traditional submission and superstition was no way to fight a man like her father. She would never act like this!

Yean turned to look out of the window again. The gate had swung open with a soft metallic clang and she caught a glimpse of Hassan's silhouette against the glare of the Mercedes' head-lights. She glanced at the clock by her bedside. Nearly 2 a.m. Why couldn't he drive himself home? Now their chauffeur would have to sleep in the garage again; and all because he wanted to keep up this farce of being out on company business. Mak was right. 'Everything is personal from shitting to politicking,' he had said. Mak was mad but some of the things he said made sense. How could she remain uninvolved? Her father belonged to the exploiter class; just look at his morality! Another girl, her age. Ser Mei's name flitted through her mind and into the darkness outside as the garden lamp was switched off. The pain was too much for a daughter to think about. Going after another girl – Ser Mei's age – was that why she had left

Mei alone that Christmas Eve? Yean pushed aside the question. She was determined not to be drawn into her parent's sordid affairs with female foxes, mediums and deities! With great agility Yean's mind fled home and family into the university where rationality claimed existence.

Mak and Sis had met with her group. It was a disaster from Yean's point of view. Sis had always wanted the group to be the leaven in the loaf but it seemed as if nobody cared about this any more. Mak and Hans were too harsh perhaps.

'You think all this opposition against the war is none of your business?' Mak had asked, his eyes peering in vain through his thick glasses. 'Who is financing this war right here in this region where you and I live? Look beyond Singapore. Look beyond this little island. Who are the financiers of war? The multi-nationals! And their offices and factories are here! Just look at Honeycomb Corp.'

Kim and Aileen must have given him one of their apolitical stares for Mak was exasperated.

'Surely you remember what Dr Jones and Hans here have told you? Honeycomb Corp,' Mak had sounded like a tired teacher, 'which makes your beautiful cameras also makes your pineapple and spider bombs. And M D I which makes your textiles also makes parachutes and tents. And they're here. Their presence bloodies our hands. Aren't we helping to kill our own Asian brothers? Or are you so brainwashed that you see these white skins as our saviours?'

'Do you grasp Asian realities?' Hans had asked, supporting Mak's thrust. 'Do you feel that Asia is your homeland?'

Yean remembered how her group had bristled at Hans's question. After all, Hans was a westerner and an outsider.

'I will not be shamed or threatened into doing something I don't believe in,' Peter had declared, his face rigid with inarticulate anger. 'And I don't believe in demonstrations, it's unChinese.'

'Rubbish!' Sis had jumped in, eager to knock down Peter with this bit of inaccuracy. Then as if remembering her role, she had kept quiet and Mak had triumphantly continued on her behalf. And Yean knew that Mak was in love with Sis for his eager defence was his expression of love but Sis, of course, would not have known this. Poor Mak!

'All of you, hah, have forgotten the May 4th Movement in China. Didn't the Chinese demonstrate then? Who are you with names like Peter and Ken to determine what is Chinese or not? You can't even speak Chinese!'

'Please, please, don't get personal,' Sis had pleaded helplessly. And this was where Mak had declared, Yean remembered, his now famous statement: 'Everything is personal from shitting to politicking.'

Yean felt tired as she lay down on her bed again. Everything was indeed so personal and so confusing. But Sis had seemed so certain that what she was doing was right. Yean could not remember what else was said later for they had heeded Sis's plea. But Ken's fierce assertion to the rest of their group after Mak, Hans and Sis had left, stayed in her mind.

'He thinks he's local because he can speak Mandarin but I'm more local than he is, I speak Malay. And if we want to talk of a South-East Asia we're in a Malay-speaking world aren't we?'

And here was Hassan their Malay chauffeur sleeping in the garage because her father had had a late night out with his mistress, a girl her age, a girl Ser Mei's age! Sis was right. Money corrupts and corrupts absolutely! As much as she disliked it, she was on Sis's side. She hoped the rest would understand but already, she no longer cared for their understanding. Politics had a way of cutting across personal ties.

It was a bright blue and white Saturday morning, the kind of morning that came after the heavy rains. Yean drove down the tree-lined avenue leading to Dr Jones's house off the Bukit Temasek campus. She parked her car under a spreading Flame of the Forest, and smiling at its red blooms, locked her car door and went tripping into the garden which was ablaze with hibiscus reds and acacia yellows. The ground around the stone pillars of the kampong-style colonial bungalow was a hive of activity. The workers and students assembled by Mak had strung large strips of cloth between the pillars and were now busily painting red and black slogans on them. Others, working in groups scattered around the garden, were daubing waxed-paper umbrellas with huge blobs of red and black paint. The sight of everyone working together for a common purpose and their happy chatter and laughter assailing her ears warmed Yean's heart. She was glad that she could leave her family problems behind and join this band of committed people.

'This government, hah, makes everything good for the foreign companies,' Mak was telling the small group of men and women gathered around the steps leading up to the balcony of the bungalow. Yean sat down beside Pei Lan and Ah Huat, now recognised by Marie and Hans as the leaders of the workers and as fine examples of the success of the S W A project.

'They pay, hah, low wages and earn high profits, get

cheap housing and want everything hygienic.'

Everyone laughed but it was derisive laughter at an administration which was being short-changed by these grasping foreign companies.

'What, man, these ang mo sai come back from abroad think they are too clean for us. Roadside stalls, pasar malam all dirty they say. Beachee Load satay dirty now they say, must eat now in Ang Teng Tow; they forget that their ancestors for eighteen generations eat satay in Beachee Load and never die,' exclaimed one of the men in Hokkien whom Yean had never seen before. Everyone laughed again at this stupidity of the Western-trained administrators who had adopted the Westerners' concept of hygiene.

'Wah-lau, these people now hah, act tough only and got no heart,' another unkempt-looking young man chipped in. Yean guessed that he must be one of the construction workers brought in by Ah Huat. 'My old father lost one thousand dollars, hah, to those bastard inspectors. No license they say and broke all his cups and plates. All new. Three days in business. No license. One thousand dollars broken in front of his eyes. My old man cried like he lost his own father.'

The group which had grown larger now shook their heads sympathetically and the women murmured, 'Jing chau ah, jing suay ay,' while the men let off a volley of four-letter words in Hokkien and Teochew.

'Last time so good hah, you can make a living hawking the streets. No trouble. Now,' said the woman as she paused and looked at the crowd, 'you have to go here, go there, see this officer, that officer and sign-ah sign-ah this-ah that-ah form; pink, green, so many! Headache-ah!' and she beat her forehead.

'Ya, ay,' the crowd laughed. Yean smiled at this grass-root perception of bureaucratic red-tape and marvelled at the way Mak could get the people to speak out in this way. She glanced at Mak, seated at the top of the stairs and smiling his approval like a lord comfortable among his loyal subjects.

'Now ah money talk. You do this, it's money; you do that it's money. Throw rubbish even must pay money and we poor people suffer.'

'Oei, Oei, but you try to make more money, change job and they call you irresponsible lah and money-greedy lah say we go here go there not steady!' another young woman chipped in.

Yean had never met any of these workers before but she was pleased to hear so many of them speaking so eloquently about injustice in society. She had no idea that Mak and Ah Huat could gather such an articulate crowd. This success of the S W A had far exceeded her expectations.

'What man they want us to tighten our belts and eat less hah! The American companies want more profit!'

'Sure, that's their goal. They give us lousy third-rate machines and squeeze every drop of blood out of us Asians. That's why the Chinese fight them and the Vietnamese fight them. And we've got to fight them too!'

Mak pronounced his verdict, pleased that the crowd approved and seemed to accept his judgement.

At this point, Marie and Hans strolled in, hand in hand. Mak saw them coming toward him. A scowl flitted across his face. He turned to Ah Huat, whispered something in Mandarin which Yean could not catch, and the group got up and dispersed except for Pei Lan, Ah Huat, Mak himself, and Yean.

'Hi, morning,' Marie greeted them.

'How's everything?' Hans asked.

'All's well. Everything under control, boss,' answered Mak in mock submission. Pei Lan giggled and Ah Huat, the grimly silent man who spoke only when absolutely necessary, managed a smile.

'How's your end of things?' Mak asked Marie.

'I've already told them that my decision, though painful, is irrevocable. Our ideological split is too deep, I can never work with them. I know some of them are sympathetic but they're not willing to go all the way. As a community, they're more interested in social welfarism than in working for more fundamental changes in the social order.'

Yean listened, knowing that this was Sis at her eloquent best. Laughing, Marie recounted her confrontation with her community – a confrontation which she presented as her willingness to live at the radical edge of life as opposed to the sisters' clinging to the security of the set old ways.

'I said to them, look, you've locked yourselves in within the walls of the convent and the schools, pretending that what you do is important and relevant. Do you really think that you can make an impact on the education system? Do you think you matter at all now that a new pragmatic leadership has taken over?'

There was a short period of silence after Sis's speech. It was as if the group needed some time to digest her words.

'So when are you leaving the convent?' Yean asked finally.

'As soon as the council approves and accepts my decision. In the meantime I'm supposed to wait and pray. I wonder how long I'm supposed to wait.'

The undertone of irritation in her voice did not escape Yean. This delay in the execution of her will was quite unbearable. Sis looked up at Hans who smiled and squeezed her shoulders in possessive sympathy. Yean looked away, a little embarrassed at this open display of affection. Ah Huat and Pei Lan excused themselves and also moved away. Mak then handed a neatly typed sheet to Marie who read it in silence and handed it to Hans. That slight wrinkling of her nose betrayed her irritation again and Yean wondered whether Mak was aware of it. Yean knew that the contents of the sheet was what she and Sis had secretly laughed at as Mak's obsession, and to Yean it looked as if this morning Marie would no longer let it remain a secret joke between them.

'Look, Mak, you're getting paranoid. You really think you're that important in their eyes? So important that they'll spend all that money to employ someone to tail you? What have you done to endanger them? Nothing,' and Marie shrugged her shoulders. 'So why get all worked up?' She could no longer hide her impatience after all these months of Mak hinting at his own importance.

Mak sat slumped on the broad stone steps, hands in his pockets and legs stretched out. Yean could see his eyes which in contrast to his slack body burned with steely determination and anger.

Nothing? He, Mak Sean Loong, had done nothing important? Is that what she thinks? Mak suppressed his rage.

But Marie, aware only of the slack body stretched out on the steps and the beads of sweat on the oily forehead, seemed only to add oil to fire when she tried to push aside her own impatience to console him.

'Look, don't worry, give them some credit. They may be jealous but anyone with any sense can see the potential in this project. The students are encouraged to use their initiative to grapple with real problems, not just politicking among themselves in Union House. This is consciousness raising,' she ended with a term she had learnt from Hans.

'What about this guy, Santok hah?' muttered Mak into his handkerchief as he wiped the beads of sweat off his face. 'Santok is one of the scholarship students. He had been advised by the dean himself to beware of me – of Mr Mak's brand of politics – Santok himself told me. He had been advised not to do anything foolish to jeopardise his bright future.'

'So Santok has decided to drop out of the SWA – good for him. It just shows what a soft backbone he has – he's just more worried about his own future, that's all.'

Yean could see that at that very moment Sis had dismissed Santok from all her future plans.

'What about your jokers – Peter, Ken and the great inspector Paul Tan?' Mak retaliated.

'What about them? You're too suspicious, Mak. Ken and Pete had been my students and all my students support me. And Paul, well, Paul has always been like this – cynical – that's why we can never see eye to eye, but I don't think he will do anything against us,' concluded Marie as she turned to Hans.

Hans who had finished reading, looked down and winked at his fellow conspirator.

'Don't take this too seriously, Mak,' he smiled and turned to survey the activity in the garden. 'You've a piece of fantastic action here. They don't want to be locked out of the political process.' And, pointing to the groups painting slogans and umbrellas, 'Let's celebrate this instead of worrying about police spies and detectives. Don't worry about food or what you are to wear . . . ' he sang cheerfully the refrain from a Catholic hymn he must have learnt from Sis.

'Oho, I almost forgot. We can't stay, Mak, we've a wedding to attend this morning. It's a girl who had been a novice. She left some years ago and today she's getting married. We've been invited,' Marie said, pointing to Hans and herself.

'Ah hah,' Mak nodded with a smile which hid his rage at these two who had merely come to survey his work and to insult him. 'I've read somewhere that one of the Berrigan brothers is leaving the priesthood to get married too – some nun or other,' he said with a wave of his hand dismissing the frivolity of it all. 'I don't think your pope likes this at all,' he said grimly, examining his feet.

Marie and Hans exchanged a secret smile.

'I'll be back later in the afternoon,' Marie called out as she waved good-bye, dragging Yean along with her.

'You and I will have to see that Mak doesn't get out of hand,' Marie said as soon as they were out of earshot. 'I want to see that this demonstration is a peaceful and orderly one to show that we can discipline ourselves. Keep an eye on Mak and Ah Huat,' Marie whispered as she got into the car beside Hans.

Yean waved them off and stopped for a moment at the gate. That sense of camaraderie among committed people which she had felt when she first arrived this morning had disappeared. In its place was the sour taste of suspicion and distrust, but pushing this aside she walked back into Dr Jones's garden.

★   ★   ★

Inside his car, Mak pulled his sweater tighter round his chest. This pre-dawn cold was seeping through his T-shirt and icing his bones. He checked his watch for the umpteenth time. Still 4.31 a.m. Time crawled and stood still. Life had stopped. He was the only one breathing on that tree-lined road between the Cathedral and the SJI schoolfield – alone in a vast expanse of darkness. Even the Flame of the Forest on his left and the angsana on his right hardly dared breathe, waiting for Time to crawl by 4.33. To make it go a little faster he decided to pretend that he did not care for Time's speed. He would take no notice of its progress. He would instead watch the changing traffic lights ahead of him, up Stamford Road. He leaned out of the car window to see better. Good, the road was straight and clear of obstructions. There – right past M P H was his destination. That venerable bookshop and the darkened shophouses in the vicinity silently witnessed the drama of the changing lights:

Red – amber – green –

Red – amber – green.

One – two – three – four

he stuck to his counting, ignoring the impulse to steal a glance at his watch.

Twelve – thirteen – fourteen

deadweights dragging Time.

One change – two change – three

Red – amber – green

Red – amber – green.

Pushing away all thoughts and sensations of impatience

he counted religiously:

eighteen – nineteen – twenty.

He pulled up his sleeve and checked his watch again. 4.38. Shit! He jerked open the door and got out of the car. Under the ghostly glow of the street lamp, he looked warily up and down the road. Nothing moved in the gloom. He closed the car door with a soft click, and peered into the semi-darkness again, his thick glasses gleaming. Patches of dark shadows lay full of malevolent potential along the hedges and under the silent wheels of parked cars. Be careful now. Somebody was watching him. Staring at a particularly dark patch, silent and grim; did something move from behind the angsana? He would check. Nothing would be allowed to spoil the rising of tomorrow's sun. He strode across the road at an angle to Stamford Road, turned right abruptly, and ran behind the angsana tree. He found himself standing in the dark patch. Nothing was there. Relieved, he crossed the road again. Near his car he twisted his whole body round suddenly to look at the dark patch again. Ah, just a harmless shadow. He walked into the Cathedral grounds and strolled towards the gate opposite the convent.

The convent slept unawares behind brick walls spiked with broken bits of coloured glass; its ancient arched iron gate stood massive and grey. Shut! He was shut out! Shut out as he always had been. How often he had stood here watching the lighted upstairs windows of that curved building which was their recreation room, hoping she would at least look out. Various old sisters had peered out, distracted from religious pursuits behind those glass louvres, but never her. Never. He had always been disappointed. It had always been, 'Bye Mak, thanks, see you tomorrow!' And she had walked in without looking back. Not once had she done so while he waited in the car till he could no longer see her, before driving away, limp, impotent and angry. She had rejected him for H I M — that big white man — wishy-washy liberal posturing as the B I G   S A V I O U R — a mere Christian version of the B I G   S A H I B! These white bastards not content with taking his homeland, squeezing blood from his people, must also take his women. His Woman!

He unzipped his sweater, took out a handkerchief and mopped his brow. But come tomorrow they would know that he was not a man to wink about. Ha! They thought he didn't see them savouring that conspiratorial wink. Tomorrow she would know he was somebody — somebody with connections and influence to muster the crowd and move them into action. He would be the winner — the one in control! They had not suspected him. They had not realised that he was capable of more than what he had done. Ah, they dreamed and shared visions and talked and talked and talked, while he had worked like a mole. He had contacts and followers. He was recognised. All would support and follow him. He would be more powerful than H I M! Playing the benevolent white patron to people like himself — he had better look farther! His parents had not named him Sean Loong for nothing. He was a First Dragon.

'The Chinese Dragon will defeat the American eagle when the sun rises,' Mak muttered under his breath. 'Mark this Sister Marie-Therese Wang!' and he smiled for the first time the smile of anticipated triumph.

The dark night was turning grey, widening his horizon and sense of space, reflecting the sense of his expanding significance. Mak walked up Hill Street, ignoring the head-lights of the few cars speeding down the road. Time had hastened. 5.15 already. The green roof of the Chinese Chamber of Commerce building gleamed in the half-light. The solid building of grey granite guarded by two huge stone lions seemed immune to the force of Mak's anger.

Bastion of local capitalism! Those fat slugs in there – target number two – for sucking the blood of their kith and kin. Imperialist running dogs serving the American eagle clawing the flesh of his Vietnamese brothers! Vampires! Blood for blood! Bone for bone!
All will be avenged, my brothers!

The Flame of the Forest bloomed red and green as the light of the rising sun touched their tops. The American eagle in blue, red and gold shone from the glass doors of the embassy.

Perfect target for a flying kick! But he would wait. Wait till she saw him do it. See him reduce that American pastor into the puny guy he really was! He was strong and ready now. He would seize the time. In answer to the hundred deeds crying to be done he, Sean Loong First Dragon, would seize the day! He would A C T!

'And I would act now rather than wait till later,' declared Marie, sitting on the steps of the Cathedral of the Good Shepherd between Hans and Yean, waiting for Mak. She looked up at the statue of Michael the Archangel lancing a cringing Satan at his feet.

'There, look,' she pointed it to Yean, 'don't you think the Old and New Testament advocate that men act on their faith? I know some of the sisters think I enjoy power or what they call having influence over others. That's not true. I don't want power; I don't have the confidence which says that if God has given you this gift, use it.

I suffer from doubts.' And she looked up at Hans who smiled down indulgently at her. 'I don't know. I'm often not sure. Besides people who do God's will, who believe they're doing it; who are always sure they're doing it, always somehow suffer some defeat in the end. I often wish I were a Sunday Christian, then I wouldn't have to go through all this anguish of whether I'm doing God's will or not.'

Yean nodded; she, too, had often wished that for herself.

'I know I make mistakes,' Marie continued in a voice soft with this morning's humility. 'I often do all the wrong things but then if you look around and you're really the best available for the job, you just have to do it.'

And Sis looked down at Yean trying to instil a measure of her own confidence into her.

'I hope everything will be alright,' muttered Yean.

'Don't worry, I'll keep Mak under control,' Marie smiled.

'Hey, look, they are here,' Hans pointed to the four red buses rolling into the Cathedral grounds. Its sober, aloof air shattered by their roar.

Mak sprang up the steps of the Cathedral toward them, megaphone in hand. The workers from Jurong, the students from Yuan Tung, Nan Hai and Bukit Temasek spilled out, waving red and black umbrellas and unfurling white banners splashed with red and black paint and slogans.

Red on black
Violence from Evil hearts!
The banners proclaimed:
Death to all imperialists!
Death to all war-mongers!
Spillers of Asian blood!

From the steps of the Cathedral, Mak raised his fist in salute. A shout arose from the crowd.

'We shall overcome, we shall overcome!' sang the Bukit Temasek contingent.

'Line up, line up, please, everybody, don't sing yet. Listen to these instructions.' Marie shouted in vain, seizing the megaphone from Mak. She must give them last-minute instructions. There should be no chaos and no violence. Their protest should be as simple and clear as a classic statement in poetry – just the hard kernel of truth. She had not expected so many to turn up. Where had all these people come from? How did Mak get hold of them? She must trust him now. This was marvellous, simply marvellous! So many people! The sisters were wrong. She hoped they were looking out of their windows. So many people had actually dared to take a stand. Look at all these good people! She smiled and waved as people jostled to get into line behind the banners. She hoped this large crowd would obey her instructions and remain orderly. She handed the megaphone back to Mak. She could not speak Mandarin, but she told him what to say.

Mak gave a long rousing speech in Mandarin and then he barked into the megaphone.

'Alright, you people, link hands and don't give way. Just move on no matter what happens!'

'Nothing will happen. What will happen? Mak!'

'Don't worry. Good to prepare for the worst,' Mak answered cheerily as he hurried off with the crowd. It was good to see her dependent on him now. That American pastor was useless here. He was surrounded by his own people. The dragon was in his element now. He would rise before her and defeat the American eagle. That was his destiny.

Marie stood on the Cathedral steps, flanked by Hans and Yean, waving to the moving columns as they snaked their way up the road toward the M P H Bookstore. Umbrellas twirling in the morning light. Red and black spiralling grotesquely amidst shouts of YANKEE GO HOME! MURDERERS! The Bukit Temasek contingent sang to the tune of Yankee Doodle:

YANKEE MURDERER CAME TO ASIA
TO CHOP OFF HEAD AND SHOULDERS...

Marie winced at the words as she held Hans's hand. She would have to make sure that they would sing those hymns she had prepared; hymns that asked for golden peace. But where was Mak? At the top of the column the students of Nan Hai and Yuan Tung were singing Mandarin songs which she could not understand but their strident martial notes worried her. She half-walked and half-ran to catch up with Mak, leaving Hans and Yean to bring up the rear. At the head of the column she found their way blocked by a cordon of blue helmeted riot police wielding rattan shields and wooden truncheons. The crowd continued to sing and to press forward and Mak was arguing with an officer about unlawful assembly.

'WE WANT THE AMBASSADOR!
WE WANT THE AMBASSADOR!'

'You people go home! Huay Chia!' a Mandarin speaking voice boomed out of another megaphone.

'Go home! Move! Move! This is unlawful assembly!'

Mak seized the megaphone from Marie's hands and speaking both in English and Mandarin shouted: 'Don't move everybody! Stay where you are! We've the right to be here! This is our land. Sing! Sing!'

Marie was shoved back into the crowd as helmeted men tried to wrest the megaphone away from Mak. The crowd surging forward to help, pushed back the policemen who shoved them in turn with their shields and truncheons. Suddenly jets of water were fired into the crowd.

'Fire engines! The fire engines are here!'

Marie was knocked off her feet. A foot trampled on her hand. Struggling to get up, another powerful jet hit her. She was down again. Her jeans and blouse clinging to her. A strong arm pulled her up and pushed her to the side. It was Hans. He was wet too. Shouts of obscenity hit her ears as the men of Jurong battled with the police and the firemen. She saw a jet of water hit Mak.

'Fuck your mother's aged cunt!' he cursed. Marie winced.

Then she saw Mak take off his sodden sweater, hit a policeman across the face with it and run toward the embassy, breaking through the police cordon.

'Hao-ah, hao-ah!' cheered the crowd. Who were these supporters? Marie watched, horrified. Who were they?

Mak rushed to the front of the embassy, leapt onto the bonnet of a Land Rover, shouting: 'Fuck you! You bloody Americans! Cowards, come out and fight! Hiding behind those doors. These licking dogs,' pointing to the police running forward, 'these lackeys cannot protect you! C'mon workers of the people, break them! Break them!'

He waved to the crowd. The crowd surged forward. He leapt down from the jeep and ran toward the glass doors of the embassy. A police truncheon hit him on the back. He turned; took off his wet T-shirt, swung it round and hit the officer smack on the face. Some more men were running toward him. He looked around. No more weapons. No more T-shirts. Half-hopping, half-running, he unzipped his jeans, took them off, swung them around his head and hurled them at the officers. Zap! They fell back.

Ah ha! He had made his point.

The bastards had stopped.

He had mesmerised them.

They were all looking at him now.

He looked down.

Ahhh! His dangling manhood had kept
them at bay.

He never realized it could be so potent.

Hah! Who is the dragon now?

He would show them.

He turned toward the gold and blue eagle on the glass door and urinated. A jet of water, his own, made a beautiful arch and hit the eagle. Bulls-eye!

The Americans on the other side of the glass door looked in monstrous fascination at this Chinese man. Surely this couldn't be happening in staid Singapore!

Mak smiled in triumph as he let off a powerful flying kick. The American eagle broke into smithereens but Mak's smile froze on his face. Something had hit him. Then it was all dark. Silence.

Marie stifled a scream as Mak's nude body crumpled on the floor. Two policemen rushed forward and covered him with a red blanket. Marie turned and sobbed in Hans's arms. They had not listened to her instructions. They had not listened at all, she wept uncontrollably.

*   *   *

The two dirty yellow ceiling fans whirred incessantly. They were wet, embarrassed, silent and shivering, huddled in one corner of the police detention room whose bare grey walls were relieved only by the black and white portraits of the President and his wife, smiling blankly down at them. Yean looked at herself and the girls. With stringy wet hair clinging to their faces they looked like half-drowned chickens pale with fright, not looking at each other; each busy with her own private thoughts. That was how the powers-that-be robbed them of their dignity, dividing them with shame. She would demand that they be allowed to use the telephone as soon as the woman constable returned. Where was Sis? When the women had been separated from the men, Sis had been the first to be called in for questioning. The rest had been told to wait. Yes, wait here. Wait. Waiting in limbo. That was it. Just waiting powerless now like one caught in the grip of a nightmare, unable to stop the dream, unable to wake up. This must be a dream, this being rounded up by the police and herded together like common criminals. Lord, help us, give us strength, Yean prayed, wanting to believe this invocation would work and knowing that it would not. Man after all has to learn to bear the consequences of his acts. Why else was he given free will?

The door opened. Two women officers came in, carrying piles of olive-green towels and solemnly distributed these to the girls who tried to wipe themselves dry. Yean was the next to be called in for questioning.

She walked into the office and her heart skipped a beat. Paul Tan! She saw Paul dressed in the dark blue suit of a police inspector walk out with Marie. 'Thank you, Lord,' escaped from her lips involuntarily.

'Yes, what you say?' the woman constable walking beside her asked.

'Nothing, nothing,' Yean smiled for the first time. She had never expected such a speedy answer to her prayer.

Glittering blades pierced Marie's eyes as she emerged from the gloomy doorway into the noonday sun in the car park. Row upon row of neatly parked police cars with the light bouncing off their highly polished bodies. The potent power of steel held in a grid waiting to be released. Marie was surprised to see so many police cars assembled in the yard. Did they need so many machines against unarmed workers and students? Mak was right after all? Her little group must have been more influential than she thought.

'Use that side gate. The reporters won't see you from here. They're still waiting for you at the front office.'

Marie nodded.

'Bye, all the best,' and Senior Inspector Paul Tan held out his hand. Marie shook it stiffly.

'I hope you'll see the pointlessness of it all,' he said with a thin-lipped smile, pushing his glasses further up the bridge of his nose as if to see more clearly. A gesture all too familiar to Marie. Then he turned and went into the building.

He could not bear to see that half-defensive, vulnerable look, vacillating between stiff upper lip and appeal; that row of pearly teeth biting her lower lip fighting for control. He knew something like this would happen. He had done his best to warn her. But she would not listen. He could not help her now and he was as angry with himself as he was with her. He pulled open the door of his filing cabinet, drew out the file on Sister Marie-Therese Wang, threw it on his desk and strode out again. He needed a walk to regain his objectivity. The source of her missionary spirit, if one could call it that, was such a mixture of arrogance and ignorance. Her desire to do good to others was not the result of humility but the outcome of that strange perception which prided itself on being capable of leading others to a higher level of existence. So dangerous! But there you are! She was liable to go through life convinced that she had been chosen to save the rest of humanity. Always seeing herself and those with her either as the leaven in the bread or cadres to the cause of Liberty, Fraternity and Equality! As if they were the only ones worthy to be in the vanguard of society! Such pride! Such romance! As if Man's plastic nature could be so easily moulded. The great leaders had failed, yet she thought she could succeed with her own little coterie! Doesn't she realize by now that those born cows will be cows no matter what she might do? She had accused him of being cynical yet here she was, so impatient, so lacking in faith in her people, thinking she must save them from a loss of political will. What utter nonsense! Singaporeans are stronger than this. They will act when the time comes and only when necessary.

Marie too needed a walk. Out of the car park, through the side gate as directed, and down the quiet road with its two-storey pre-war shophouses. The muffled roar of traffic down Robinson Road reached her ears like distant sounds from behind a thick high wall. A quiet haven right in the heart of the city, strangely empty of traffic and people. The sun shining white and hot cast firm shadows on one side of the street, lined with lorries.

TAMIL TIMES PRESS
Black and white sheets of newsprint plastered its walls.
TET OFFENSIVE
BULLS IN GOLD MART
MILLION DOLLAR HEIST
Chinese characters in bright vermilion.

GUAN HENG EXPORT IMPORT CO. LTD.
CHOP BAN GUAN
KIM SENG ENGINEERING
KHOO KONGSI CLAN ASSOCIATION

The heat rising from the asphalt of the tarmac road choked her already dry throat – her only dry place she felt. The rest of her was wet with perspiration as the bourgeois termed it. Perspiration. Such a delicate term for a condition caused by insufferable heat and hard physical labour. She watched two red- and blue-clad samsui women clambering up the scaffolding on the opposite side of the road. Of course, those who worked in air-conditioned offices could afford such delicacy in language. Perspiration! What a refined word! Tiny drops of water glistening on foreheads or just a sheen on noses to be gently dabbed away with the help of Elizabeth Arden! This was Paul Tan's world not hers. And he had said, I hope you'll see the pointlessness of it all. She knew he would have added this other bit if his courage had not failed him at the last moment. You see where it all leads to? Betrayal! All commitment other than to the self is an illusion, as I've told you time and again. Yours is not the answer. All men work for their self-interest. Betrayal!

Self-interest!

All these he would have stressed.

Did he know St Peter's sin at all?

'Under the spreading chestnut tree
I sold you and you sold me
Under the spreading chestnut tree.'

Where had she heard that refrain? Such resigned acceptance of the inevitable. Had she sinned and not felt it? Had she done wrong and not known it? Had her conscience so hardened that she could not feel guilt any more? But here, Hans would say, was her Catholic guilt at work again – punishing her with remorse. Her grandma had often told her to examine a man's ten fingers whenever she felt she was being unduly harsh on others. Look, girl, she had said, not all the same length lah. Ada jari panjang, ada jari pendek. Some long some short. How true; she had to learn to accept others' shortcomings including her own. She had to admit her ignorance under questioning. What else could she do? They had seemed to know everything. And in Paul's presence – she just had to tell the truth. She did not know anything about Mak and his workers. She had no inkling that the illegal underground was involved. How was she expected to know? She didn't even know that Mak could be that crazy. It had never occurred to her. It was just too incredible. She had always looked upon him as intelligent. An incisive theoretician. A little eccentric, yes. Obsessed with police and spies, yes. Sinister? No! Loony? Definitely not!

Marie walked unseeing, intent only upon presenting her case to an imaginary panel of judges as she had done in debates long ago. And this was the most important debate in her life. She had to win. Mak had been a brilliant debater too whenever he wanted others to see things from his point of view.

'You think this war is none of your business? Did you know that G I s on R & R here had called up the girls' hostels in B T to book for dates?'

Marie could hear Mak's booming voice haranguing the girls as if his manhood was at stake. Could such a person be mad? Surely something must have snapped. Who was it who said that the irrationality of capitalism was reflected in the number of cuckoo cases referred to psychiatrists? Hans. Yes, Hans was right. In its very rationality lies its madness. Capitalism creates its own Shylocks and Edmunds. One had to be mad in order to be sane under such a system, Hans had said. Was she mad then? Should she have lied? Lied that she did know of Mak's connections? And jeopardised the S W A project?

Nothing cohered. Like grains of sand washed clean and clear, her mind was in fragments. The recent past was just bits of grit grinding into her. At this point it was difficult for her to even admit that she had simply lost control. She had paid too much attention to Hans and her own personal interests. In her mind she went back to the police station, being questioned like a common criminal. And he had come in, brisk and efficient, in his police blue and silver pips. He had sat, eyes down, shuffling his papers.

'You may go. We'll issue a summons when we require your presence again. Should it be sent to the convent or your parents' house?'

And she had winced. That was so unnecessary. Obviously, he had wanted to hurt her. She stood up and he had followed.

'I'll try to do all I can but I will have to follow the due process of law,' he had said in his familiar self-righteous tone.

'It's alright. I'm not begging,' she had replied.

A hit from the look on his face. Anyway, if looks could kill, he had already killed her. Her little hit was nothing compared to his brisk official tone in front of his superiors. He had to let her know that this was pure business. He would deal with her as with everyone else. She was no one special (as if she had not known it all along). He had to do his duty. His own position was at stake. He must show that he could put the public good before his personal interests. And yes, he was right. What is the point of it all? It was both a personal and official question but personal feelings and personal history no longer mattered. He had become a stranger. The O C – Officer-in-charge. Why? Why? Why must he strip off all her illusions? Sully all her experiences? Every encounter had brought pain. Nothing but pain. Couldn't he be satisifed that she had once loved him? Must they continue to fight even now? And she had wanted to remember him as someone she had once loved. Not this ugly career climber. This stooge, as Hans would say, exercising the power the real masters confer only on those of unquestioning loyalty. That would be Paul's definition of loyalty exactly – unquestioning obedience. She simply called it stupidity. No will of his own! Acting only according to orders. No, she would fight. She would resist. Workers and students must learn to exercise their collective will!

With that conviction, she hailed a taxi and headed for home.

*   *   *

Yean retreated into the seclusion of her bedroom, closed the door and windows, drew the curtains and switched on the air-conditioner. Its comforting hum flooded the room as she lay stretched on her bed with head resting on the back of her hands; one lone lanky body. And she clung all the more to this sense of an aloneness which for the time being would have to be her sole protection against the discordant voices of aunties, uncles, parents and anyone with any familial link to her pouring their unwanted filth into her ears. One word more now and she would leap up and tear the whole house down. There was this streak of madness in herself which she somehow couldn't quite explain. Perhaps she had something in common with Mak Sean Loong after all. Perhaps madness was infectious. She had caught it and her whole family had been infected by it. They were all mad. The whole lot of them. Mad. Mad. Mad.

'Yean,' her father had said, 'I've telephoned your uncle in California. You will join your cousins there next week or next month as soon as this business is over.'

Tyrant! Dictator! she had wanted to scream. Instead she had almost whined, 'But I want to stay with mother.' And then the bombshell. Her father had said, 'Your mother will go with you to keep an eye on things.'

What a scheming man he was! No wonder he was a manager! In a single sweep he had cleared away all obstacles. With Mother gone he would be free to carry on with his latest girl – her own age – young enough to be his daughter! And it was sheer stupidity on their part that made her mother and eldest aunt blind to her father's scheme.

'Ya, ya, very good idea,' her aunt had exclaimed. 'Sister-in-law here can go over and learn about the restaurant business from Tai Pak over there. His restaurant is doing very well.'

'Yes, very good idea, very good,' her second uncle had readily agreed. Agreed! Of course, he had to agree. He depended on her father for business. 'If my business improves, hah, I will send our Ah Pow over there too. Children nowadays very difficult to control. The gov'ment tell us to watch them. Ya, we're the parents we should watch them but so difficult now – not like last time.

What they do or think outside the house we don't know. How can we know what their hearts think! The gov'ment should not blame us for any wrong thing. I hope, Yean, you have not given your father any trouble.'

Toadying creature she had wanted to yell at him if only he weren't so elderly. And then her eldest aunt not to be outdone had to add, 'Aye, so troublesome when they grow up; they think they know everything.' They don't know and she had recited her favourite Cantonese proverb, 'When in trouble you find you call to heaven and heaven has no ears; call to earth and earth has no mouth. Then you know everyone is deaf and dumb in the face of trouble. Listen to us, Yean, we eat more salt than you eat rice. Now study when you can study. After your foundation is firm then do what you want when your pouch is full of money.'

Yes, that was their philosophy – to gird themselves with money, money and more money. Society was there as an opportunity for them to make money. People were there to be used for business or pleasure. Her family simply had never thought it necessary to make any returns for what they had taken or enjoyed. All they wanted was security through having more money.

The soft continuous hum of the air-conditioner soothed her jarred nerves and tired mind. She fell asleep thinking of Pei Lan and the others who had no money. Sis had not said anything about them at all except that they had been detained. Poor Pei Lan! If any of the workers should need help she would persuade her father to help out even if she had to agree to go to California.

A slanting ray of the five o'clock sun slipped between the partly drawn curtains and rested on Yean's face. Awakened by its gentle warmth, Yean opened her eyes and for a while enjoyed the dance of the dust particles. The sun was sinking and that patch of sunlight was moving though ever so slowly from her face to the edge of her bed. A joy must end eventually and with great reluctance she got up and changed. The morning's confrontation with her gang and family had robbed her of her energy. Poor Sis! She had been so confident. She was so adamant in maintaining that they had done nothing wrong. As far as she was concerned they were a group of people who had come together to protest against a universal injustice.

'What's wrong with that?' she had asked. 'We acted on our convictions. We dared to take the risk. If we didn't do this we would have allowed this worldwide phenomenon of the modern technocratic state to turn us into robots.' She had no answer to that charge but Sis, as usual, did not expect answers from her. Perhaps she saw her as her student who still needed teaching. Sis could be so blind, always focused on the cause, never the persons around. She couldn't help but be worried about what was going to happen now.

'Nothing to worry about,' Sis had blithely declared. 'They're trying to make mountains out of molehills. They have to justify their high pay, these officers. They are digging up everything from my past – from our first moratorium to I don't know what. Even my private relationship with Hans is suspect and blackened. They want to paint everything black and us as the agents of blackness.'

She had had to interject another question to stop another of Sis's blistering attacks on the modern police state. Sis would make a good lecturer. But what would happen to Hans, Dr Jones and Rev James whose houses had been used for so many of their meetings?

'Nothing much, I don't think they can pin anything on them. They were protesting against their own American government not ours. I don't think the police can make them out to be agents of subversion. But they can't leave the country yet, their passports have been impounded.' And what about Mak, she had asked.

'Oh, that is what I had come to tell you,' as if she had just remembered. 'I tell you they can't do anything, so they're releasing Mak on bail today. Hans and I are going to fetch him. I've called for a meeting at Jim's place tonight; please tell the rest. I'll see you there – about eightish.' And with that she had hurried away.

Yean closed her eyes for a moment, stretched her limbs and got up. She sat at the edge of her bed still feeling tired and heavy. She wished she had half of Sis's confidence and energy. None of her limbs wanted to move. She examined the big toe of her right foot and lifted it toward her closet. Ah, just long enough to open the door without having to move the rest of herself. She prised open the door and rested her leg. Now, what would she wear, and immediately chided her own frivolity. Typical spoilt bourgeois kid, that was what she was. No point denying it. She smiled to herself and lay down again on the bed as fragments of this morning's discussion with her gang drifted back into her mind. Gang! Why couldn't Sis see that there was no more gang. It was just an illusion that they could go on believing in the same things.

'To tell the truth, none of us are close to her these days. We don't know her work in Jurong.' Peter was being blunt as usual.

'Ya, don't you think she was rather mysterious in the past few months? Always so many meetings in Jurong with the Chinese students and workers and we don't even know their lingo.'

Aileen was right to some extent. They did not know Mandarin beyond the level of polite greetings but then neither did Sis.

'But she had Mak.' True, and she had to agree with Aileen.

'Mak is another suspicious character,' said Ken, but he had never been able to get along with Mak anyway. Then Kim had come straight to the point.

'I'm not going,' she had declared. 'I'm more concerned with people like Ser Mei than the war in Vietnam which I can't do anything about.'

She could see that Kim's social work experience was beginning to tell. Helping the individual was more important than changing the system. The system could not be changed; therefore help the individual to cope. Kim's response would have been spurned by Sis as easy compromise. There had never been any dialogue between Sis and the rest of the group. It was always a case of being for her or against her. She had always talked to them, never with them.

Yean got up from bed and stood in front of the closet, fingering the many blouses hanging inside. Finally she chose a red silk blouse and a pair of beige slacks.

Perhaps they were all dumping Sis now that trouble had come. But then these were basically decent guys. She had known them all her life. And anyway to be fair they had never agreed to the SWA wholeheartedly. Not everybody agreed with Mak. One of the workers had said, 'Mr Mak, scholar, big man, okay for him to talk like that about government. They from the big school always talk like that.'

'They don't agree with him but they support him, stupid idiots!'

But she did not agree with Peter's glib conclusion. Mak had his good points and the workers were grateful. He had helped them financially. He had gotten them legal aid, helped with the filling of forms, work permits and the writing of official letters; all of which were important and serious matters to illiterate men. Mak had guided them through this treacherous terrain so that they could eat their rice in peace and they were grateful. He was from the big school but he had treated them as friends and in the moral scheme of things as seen in the kungfu films, one would go to the gates of hell for such a man. Her Cantonese nanny used to say,

Owe another a gift of flower
Owe a debt of a thousand years' fragrance
Owe another a deed of gratitude
Then ten thousand years of remembrance is due.

Looking at Pei Lan's affection for Sis, she was sure that that was what made the workers support Mak and Sis. And yet somehow there was something wrong. But what?

Yean looked at herself in the mirror, peering closely with tweezer in hand, and pulled out a stray hair from her beautifully arched eyebrow. Her face looked rested now. The rings around her eyes, the result of many sleepless nights after the trouble, had grown faint. A dab of powder would hide them. There! Her face looked presentable now. Delicate and well-fed. Rest, good food and pleasant surroundings would always protect girls like her from the leathery skins and broad wrinkles of women slogging to make ends meet. One day Pei Lan, married with three or four kids, would become one of these hardened, loud-mouthed Ah Sohs with thick pink hands like her washerwoman. Angry with the unfairness of life, she proceeded to brush her hair. Always the poor and uneducated suffered the most. Her father was sending her to California! Nothing would happen to her! Nothing would happen to her gang! And they are refusing to turn up for tonight's meeting. But could she blame them? How she wished she could accuse them of being irresponsible. She was even more angry with Sis but she could not say which was the more annoying. She still agreed with many of the things Sis had said yet somehow, the way things were done . . . Ouch! she had brushed too hard. She stopped, replaced the brush on the dressing table and started to undress. Ever since the formation of the S W A Sis had become a different person. She always used to talk about being an individual but gradually politics had become an obsession with her. For the gang Sis was no longer the woman they had first known. Perhaps they were being stupid, her gang? Perhaps they had outgrown Sis and now they blamed her? They weren't giving Sis the freedom to grow and change. Why should everyone remain the same all the time? Yean felt a growing confusion. Whose side was she on?

Marie drove cautiously but impatiently through the snarling traffic, trapped in one of those after-office-hours jams; her Volkswagon nosing its way among the Datsuns, Mazdas, Hondas, Toyotas and Mercedes with tail-lights blinking red and orange. Signs of 'Men at Work' and 'Danger' and a long line of warning lamps hung at intervals had cordoned off a section of the road which had become a deep trench. In Singapore, one ignored such signs at one's peril. Those with the courage to take risks often discovered when it was too late that driving their cars out of line with the others or in a manner different from the majority of timid drivers could lead to tragic results in a trench. Life must always be lived according to rules and regulations.

Red – stop.

Amber – green – move.

That was how they were supposed to live here – just follow the signals given, and refrain from asking awkward questions if one had nothing constructive to say. Then you would prosper and be saved.

She stepped on the brake hard, jerking the car to a sudden stop, causing a blast of horns from the cars behind. She had almost hit the car in front. She had always been an impatient driver.

Leaning back into her seat she looked out of the window again.

The roads were always being dug up by various public departments. Why couldn't they coordinate and dig the road once and for all? Roads were always broken up and re-tarred, broken and re-tarred for the laying of sewerage pipes, water pipes, telephone cables, electric cables for this and that and this and that – an endless cycle of activity which they chose to call progress. Cars, gold and diamonds, looming blocks, stocks and shares, dirty factories, noise and dust, TV sets – buy, buy, buy. Must progress always be linked with the accumulation of things?

Marie released the handbrake, and the car rolled slowly forward for a few feet and stopped again. This orderly procession of cars, buses and lorries inching their way down the narrow road, glowed like a red luminous worm in the night. The dark grey clouds of an approaching storm had made the sky a low cover pressing upon the air and preventing the escape of heat from the thousands of engines and exhaust pipes down below. It was oppressive with the traffic snaking down the road.

Marie looked to her left and right, hot and impatient.

Cars in front, moved, stopped.

Cars at the back moved, stopped.

Cars to her right moved, stopped.

Cars to her left stopped and then moved.

Such was the varied life around her. Even then she could not move. She was trapped. She rolled down the window to let in some air but the heat and noise generated by the cars around her hit her like an invisible wave, flooding her in sweat so that she had to roll up her window again. If only she could fly she would soar above this mess and leave this over-crowded island for some far-off shore where for miles she would not have to meet with another human face or car; where she could

239

live with Hans luxuriating in the freedom of open space. Here she felt cramped and watched, compelled to follow the signs and rules of the game. Why couldn't people leave her alone? Always the questions in their eyes. And her taciturn father had not spoken a single word to her since her return. What you want to do, Marie, what you want to do in future? That was the only question her family asked; not how she felt or why she left. All they were interested in was what others would say, what others would think. And don't get into trouble with the government they told her. No one starving, people here got food to eat and clothes to wear, why you want to protest this and protest that and bring trouble on yourself. Not worth it. O God, why couldn't they understand that man can't live by bread alone; he must have freedom and dignity. But if wars were far away and their own sons were not being killed they couldn't be bothered.

Marie released the foot brake, touched the accelerator and let the car roll another few feet.

How was she going to get out of this jam? Her mother and grandma had begun to talk about engagements and marriages. These daily hints and questions which she could no longer ignore were getting to be tiresome. Why couldn't they let her be? She sighed for the anonymity of a big foreign city where people would not know that she had ever been a Sister Marie-Therese – pure, white and holy – as all nuns were expected to be; vestal virgins untouched and untainted by the filth of the earth! Why couldn't her father accept a daughter who was ordinary and human? Must she perform some extraordinarily heroic task before he would call her daughter.

A blast of horns awoke her from her angry reverie.

She drove the car for another few feet, stopped and glanced at her watch. 7.55.

She hoped Mak would be late too. What if he did not come? Why didn't he wait for her and Hans to fetch him? It was just like him to go off without a word. She hoped he had seen the message she left with his sister. Imagine, all this while she did not know that he had a sister or that his parents passed away when he was very young. Strange man; he never said anything to anyone. She hoped he would be alright now. She hoped everyone would forget about the embassy accident. They should have gotten over their shock by now. They hadn't stopped talking about it the whole week. She was glad no photo had appeared in the press and wondered whether Paul had anything to do with it.

Amber. Green. A deft turn to the left, she overtook the car in front, stepped on the accelerator and was through the bottleneck. Then zooming down the road, she rolled down the window pane for the rush of air to blow away the sweat, dust and heat. Now the car surged ahead on the near empty road, with Marie enjoying the speed and power of Hans's Volks, and finally turning into Princess Avenue, a quiet road lined with the dark irregular shapes of the Madras Thorn. Then slinging her black Indian satchel across her shoulders, she walked quickly into the church compound toward the manse.

Yean looked up as Marie came in. The whole group seated on the green carpeted floor turned toward her, full of expectation.

'Hi,' she called cheerily to everybody.

'Hi, hi,' everybody called back.

Like one of their usual party-cum-discussion sessions

and potato chips would be passed around soon.

'Sorry I'm late. Caught in a traffic jam as usual.'

'It's alright, we know your habit,' laughed Dr Jones as he made space for her on the floor beside him.

'You're born under a lucky star and the rest of us are doomed to wait for you,' moaned Rev James in mock despair as Marie gave him an affectionate punch on the arm.

Yean looked at the faces of the others. Peter, Ken, Aileen and Kim who had turned up despite what they had said earlier, seemed to be enjoying this banter between Marie and the two Westerners. Her group was decent after all. She examined the impassive faces of the five Chinese guys from Yuan Tung and Nan Hai. They didn't seem to find this light-hearted banter funny. Perhaps they couldn't follow what was being said. Perhaps they were anxious about Mak who had not turned up yet. Anyway she had always found these Chinese-educated guys more serious than those from Bukit Temasek who were only good at recounting soccer games.

'Where's Hans?' Sis asked, a trifle anxious since she did not know when he would be called up again for further questioning.

'He'll be here in a jiff, meeting some youths next door.'

'Getting them to join Christian Aid for Bangladesh.'

'Anyone seen Mak yet?' Marie asked looking round the group.

'Nope,' answered Peter, and Yean marvelled at his cheek for he had only come out of curiosity to see what this first meeting with Mak would be like. Nevertheless she was glad of his presence though she did not approve of his motives. The four of them made her feel less isolated. Strange that she should feel like this now. Hadn't she been the one to work alongside these people for the past year? Weren't she and Sis regarded as comrades in the S W A? Was she, too, moving away from Sis?

'Must we always dig for causes and reasons every time someone rebels? Am I a radical simply because my father is strict and unreasonable? I mean, look at the society as well.' Sis was arguing with Ken who was, as usual, trying to find a logical explanation for Mak's bizarre behaviour.

'Ya, ya, ya, Sis, how do we act when he turns up?'

'Act normal lah.'

'But isn't it difficult to act normal now? Won't they be watching us?' asked Aileen a little anxiously.

'Why should that bother us? We aren't doing anything wrong. Why should we let that intimidate us? Meet as usual and next time just get a permit lah and they can't accuse us of breaking the law.'

'Yes, you'll be a lawful assembly then,' laughed Dr Jones. 'I told Mike he should come down and write about us for his *Tribune*.'

It was as if everything had been a joke and it had been fun being arrested and questioned by the police. Yean looked at the three of them. Rev James was grinning like a schoolboy. Everything had been such a lark as the English would say in Enid Blyton's books. Yean turned to the Chinese students. They were not laughing. They must be thinking these Ang Mo were crazy and their perspectives inverted. Yean wished she knew enough Mandarin to be at ease with them.

'And are these all our future leaders?'

Mak's voice rang out, harsh as the clash of cymbals. The whole group spun round. Mak stared at them through his thick ringed glasses, his high forehead gleaming in the light of the overhead lamp. He seemed to loom large and wild with his hair in a mess and his body seeming to fill the doorway like an angry giant. Yean involuntarily shrank nearer to the wall, hugging a cushion closer to her breast.

'You call them leaders?' Mak shouted as if he were at the political rallies of the opposition parties. 'Those buggers pee all over the place like dogs. And the girls, hah! No bloody clean. Their bloody stuff all over the bowl! Sluts! All cocks and balls I tell you! The cats do it better!'

Mak glared at the whole group. For a while no one spoke. They held their breath waiting for the next explosion. Mak who had planted himself under the electric lamp looked like an avenger from the grave.

'Mak,' Rev James called gently, 'come, it's alright.'

'Ni de mah de! Zho kai!' Mak flung out an arm pushing an imaginary person away followed by a volley of Mandarin terms. The faces of the Chinese students told Yean that those were four-letter words.

'Ang Mo, you smell – go drop your shit somewhere else!' he shouted again.

Aileen let out a gasp and Mak turned on her.

'Why you worship their asses? They have shit on us, bloody spies and turncoats. Hah!'

Mak veered round and grabbed Hans by the shoulders just as Hans came in, not knowing what was happening.

'Here is the chief jackass of them all. You lied!'

'Hey, what's going on?' Hans tried to pry loose Mak's iron claws from his shoulders.

'Mah de! Ta gan wen wo ah! You Fascist pig! CIA agents! Running dogs of capitalism!' and Mak punched Hans in the stomach.

Hans caught hold of his arms and in the ensuing scuffle, Mak tripped and fell against the chair nearest to Marie. She tried to hold him down with the help of Dr Jones but Mak who was too strong for them, sprang up and grabbed hold of her satchel.

'You whore you! You think you're a Mata Hari? His balls are bigger? Didn't you see mine? You slut! Why? Why you work for them? They pay you better? I'm your leader! A Chiang Ching you don't want to be you want to be a pros! He fuck better?'

'Mak!' Sis's cry of pain rang out. The rest were silent and too stunned to move.

'Don't Mak me. Too late, too late to repent. I'm going to expose you lot. Ni men kan kan,' he said turning to the pale faced Chinese students as he ripped open Marie's satchel and flung out mirrors, books, combs, coins, notes – and then he held up a gleaming gold pack, lips curled in ugly triumph like a wolf going for his first bite. Sis's face went deadly pale and her mouth opened to cry but no words came. In the split second Hans and Dr Jones sprang forward and grabbed Mak from behind, locking his arms in a vice-like grip. He struggled with the strength of ten men, broke loose and fought with all the men, for by this time Peter, Ken and the Chinese students had recovered the use of their limbs. The gold pack fell from Mak's hands. Scuffling feet trampled on it and Yean watched as pale yellow pills spilled out of the pack and rolled in all directions across the room.

'Aiya, aiya! Lai, lai! He here, he here,' a woman came in shouting hoarsely to some people outside in Hokkien.

Four burly Indian men dressed in white pushed their way into the room with a green canvas sheet and belts.

Very quickly they wrapped the sheet around Mak and tied him up with the belts as he cursed the whole world in a torrid stream of Hokkien and Teochew, half of which Yean could not comprehend.

After the ambulance from Woodbridge had left, no one felt like saying anything yet no one moved until Kim, the efficient social worker, came to the rescue.

'Okay you guys better clear up the place, I'm going to make some coffee,' she said, bringing back a tone of normality into the room.

'I'll help,' Aileen responded with alacrity and went into the kitchen with Kim.

What should she do now, Yean thought, looking at the overturned chairs. Sis was sitting on the legs of one of them with Hans stooping over her, rubbing one of her hands. Sis seemed to be crying but she was not certain. Her view was blocked by Hans and Kim who were now busily picking up various objects from the floor and sweeping up the tiny pills into the dustpan.

'Move over, idiot,' Kim ordered, 'go re-arrange those chairs.'

Yean glanced at the contents in the dustpan. The pale gold packet had some tiny pills still in its plastic pockets marked by the days of the week – Mon, Tue, Wed.

'Move!' shouted Kim as she looked into Yean's eyes, silently ordering her not to say a word.

The five Chinese boys came forward, muttered a hurried good-bye and left. Mere spectators they seemed, not people who had worked with Mak and Sis throughout this year. Was this simply Chinese-educated reserve? Or a backing away from trouble? Yean was perplexed.

'A lift anyone?' Dr Jones asked. 'I'm driving down Bukit Temasek way.'

'Wait for me please, Dr Jones,' Kim said, raising her hand like a student answering a teacher's question.

Abruptly, everyone seemed to be going home, coffee was forgotten. Yean walked toward Marie but before she could reach her, Hans called out to the whole group. 'Night, Yean. Bye, everybody, I'll send Marie home.'

She was cut off, irrelevant. Sis didn't want her so she followed the others out of the room, leaving Sis hunched on the upturned chair with Hans standing protectively beside her: the final tableau in an Ibsen play. So Yean walked to her car, unlocked the door and slipped into the driver's seat. Her whole body was numb. Her mind too. The violence unleashed tonight had torn something apart; its fabric, rent. She sat there, motionless. Something had been smashed: a blue Ming vase dashed against the wall, its pieces never to be put together again.

* * *

NEWS BRIEFS

Anti-war Demonstration Aftermath
Told to leave

Church worker, Hans Kuhn of the American Christian Churches Mission to South-East Asia, has been told to leave by the end of this month, an Immigration Department spokesman confirmed.

Leaving with him is Miss Marie Wang, the former Sister Marie-Therese of the Convent of the Blessed Virgin Mary.

A university spokesman confirmed that Dr Tamney Jones's teaching contract which expires in May this year will not be renewed.

Suspended

5 students have been suspended for 6 months to a year following the advice of a commission of inquiry. Their names have been withheld.

Deported

3 men and 1 woman have been deported and barred from further visits to Singapore. They are Tan Chye Huat @ Ah Huat @ Bah Bah; Tong Tze Hai @ Tong Tze Chai; Khoo Teck Kim and Toh Pei Lan.

Marie got down from the city bus near the Capitol. St Andrews Cathedral looked white and serene in the middle of its shady field fringed by angsana trees, sentinels of the Church's serenity planted long ago by those nostalgic for the oak trees of the English countryside. Set in the heart of this busy shopping area considered as prime land by the developers of this country and protected by its fence of strong iron railings, the spire of the Cathedral rose high above the trees reaching out to things beyond this earth, above the petty concerns of man below. She turned away and crossed the road to the Capitol cinema which proclaimed the arrival of 'The Man From U. N. C. L. E.' in loud garish colours. Round the corner was the row of Indian-owned shops with their hotch-potch spread of cheongsams made of cheap-looking red brocade, black embroidered kaftans, trinkets, teak elephants, cameras and bras, all lumped into one huge incongruous display for the bargain-hunting tourist.

Marie wanted to avoid this part of the road so she crossed to the opposite side where she could stroll along the path running along the Stamford canal. This would be a most pleasant part of the city if only the Public Works Department would not widen the road again and chop down this row of Flame of the Forest whose blooms were like a streak of wild fire along the canal at sunset. Why, if one could just ignore the noise of the traffic one could even enjoy the illusion of walking down a country road with broad leafy runner grass at one's feet and an umbrella of jade green leaves above. But she knew these would not be allowed to remain for long so she bade them good-bye too. She remembered how she and Paul used to walk here in the evening to catch the last golden glow of brief twilight with a light breeze playing among the yellow-green leaves of her twinkling tree. A sigh escaped her. It seemed so very long ago when she had come here with Paul one evening to claim this tree as their own because its leaves seemed to glow with the fire of sunset and they were in their first flight of love like the young swallows that used to frequent the Padang. She pushed the memory aside; such a long time since she had last watched the sun set and the swallows gather. When had she stopped noticing such things? She had no time to walk leisurely through the city with Hans: they were always on their way to a meeting. If there were more time she would have liked to show this side of the city to him but there was no time now. She must make her farewells alone. She turned the corner to that side of the grey hallowed walls of the convent which permitted entry from the outside through its tri-ple-arched iron gateway. The row of 'instant' angsana was still there, amputated branches stretching hideously in the white heat of the morning. She ignored them and concentrated on the dust patterns at her feet. Grey serried lines of sand grains and the absence of waste paper; the road sweeper had done his job early and well. The highly acclaimed image of a clean green city was being effectively sustained by the diligence of workers who day after day push the grains of white rice into their mouths busily manipulating chopsticks or fingers with no other thought in their heads except that the rice bowls be full and the rice grains fluffy. And so they remain all the time on the level of the mundane and the pragmatic becoming the humble small men eating their lives away like so many beetles crawling in the rice bin. Where was their sense of the heroic? That awareness of their significance as the children of God, Creator of this island?

Marie passed through the gates and the roar of the traffic faded into the distance like a muted echo as if the secular world respected this pool of peace in its midst. There was no one around. The convent and its adjacent schools were deserted. Ah, this was still vacation and she was thankful that on this last morning she would have the whole place to herself. Even Sister Beatrice and Sister Gabriel were absent from their posts at the gate. She could not bear the thought of having to meet their enquiring looks. At the grotto of Our Lady of Perpetual Succour, laced with the bright pink lobes of Honolulu was a single lighted candle. Someone had come early to seek help and blessing. Dear mother, please, answer her prayer speedily; her empathy going out to that unknown soul who, like her, needed the help of Our Lady, mother to all in distress. She strolled toward the chapel and looked up. High up on this side of its grey walls a large patch of cement had fallen away revealing the orange bricks beneath, and wedging its way through this hardness was a green plant, a seed dropped by a bird perhaps, and now its bevy of leaves in the orange bricks was the focus of colour in that canvas of grey. Marie smiled palely at this plant growing precariously up there. It spoke of courage and endurance. She looked at it for a long time.

The sun was shining on one side of the driveway and Marie crossed over to the shady gallery with its ancient iron spiral stairway, its intricate pattern of flowers and leaves curling like creepers arrested in a climbing motion. She would not go into the chapel just yet; she would leave that to the last, walking past the low-roofed garage, now used as a storehouse. Ah, this open space separating the English primary school from its big sister, the secondary school. This was where she used to play tic-tac-toe and big balloon with all the other blue-clad girls as they waited for the bell of the afternoon session to ring.

'Hey, hey, jaga baik-baik, car coming. Don't run so fast, why you run so fast?' Sister Gabriel would scold from her post at the marble-top table below the statue of St Francis of Assissi: her shrill Tamil voice nagging the shouting, carefree girls was part of the normal order of things around her then.

'Sista, sista, see see my marmy give me this for my birthday.' She smiled at this recollection of childish voices. Dear Sister Gabriel. Once when they were late her gang had tried to bribe their way into the school hoping to escape Sister's long lecture on punctuality. She had offered Sister a stick of chewing gum which she promptly popped into her mouth like a Hacks. Then they had watched her suck, pulling in her cheeks and puckering her aged lips in a great expense of effort and energy because the gum had stuck to her dentures. And they had watched, not daring to laugh and not daring enough to move away. When at last she had extracted the troublesome gum from her mouth she had let forth such a torrent of Tamil-English that the whole gang beat a hasty retreat and for weeks afterwards they avoided her and went home by the side gate on Stamford Road.

At the school gallery Marie rang the bell, its single chime echoing round the empty gallery used for assembly and morning prayers. Sister D – when Irish eyes are smiling – they used to sing to her, presided every morning with Sister E standing solemnly at the side.

'Your breeding and sense of decorum show, girls, they show in your manners,' she used to tell them during morning assembly, standing straight in her modern white knee-length habit, shoulders back and breasts out while the Pre-U girls in the front row held their breath waiting for one of her buttons to burst again. It had been fun then. They were all so young and carefree and she had been so certain of what Life would hold for her. Like that black figure on the wall at the far end of the gallery she had been so certain of walking toward the light.

Into the secondary school now the same sounds of tick-tick-tack tick-tick-tack from Devi's typewriter greeting her as she went up the stairs as she had done years ago both as student and as teacher. These sounds and these grey walls had encompassed all her world then.

'Miss Lee, new cheongsam,' and she saw once again Miss Lee's demure smile as she answered with,

'Give me the properties of an equilateral triangle.'

'Aw, Miss Lee, it's just after Chinese New Year,' she had groaned. 'Well, you want Chinese dinner after the O levels or not?' Miss Lee's famous bribe rang in her ears once more. Marie had reached the cavernous school hall with its black curtained stage at one end.

'Presenting the Ugly Duckling in Swan Lake' she heard her own girlish voice of long ago announcing like the girl ghost she had always believed haunted the gallery upstairs among the stage props. She had been afraid of going into the Art Room too haunted by the ghost of a sister who had died during the Japanese Occupation. Her friends had seen her in the gloom of a morning at 6 a.m. sitting on the bare wooden floor upstairs combing her ghostly hair amidst the pots of paint and brushes belonging to Sister Valentine. The ghosts of dead years hung heavily in the stale air of the empty school.

Leaving the hall she went up to the school library on the fourth floor. Every morning as Head Prefect she had greeted the librarian, Sister Jude, smelling of Vitamin A and cod liver oil, her quivering voice matching her nervous movements among her beloved books. She had helped Sister Jude run this library once. And now standing alone among the chairs and tables midst the musty smell of books in ornately carved cupboards, the hopes and fears of those ancient days rushed back to greet her. With an impatient gesture she brushed away the tears that threatened; she was getting mushy. She turned and fled down the stairs running, running, and did not stop till she reached the ground floor out of breath. All those moments she had wasted! All those hopes futile. All her reading, her praying and her hoping turned to nothing! And these books. The lives of the saints! She had read them all, ardent in the first flush of faith and conviction that she was being called to the Saviour's side. St Joan of Arc. St Bernadette, meek and humble. St Theresa, pure as a lily. She had always wanted her as her model during those novitiate days. But she had failed Him even as she sat now too heavy to move. How could she have failed so miserably and fallen so low? She buried the question as she buried her head in her folded arms resting on her curled-up knees like one too ashamed to see the face of her Creator and yet inside her, she was crying like one afraid in the dark: Lord, Lord, where are you? Do not abandon me.

'The path of the spirit is stony and full of briars;

the way of the flesh is broad and smooth and lined with primroses,' Father Ariola had said in catechism classes. 'The sacrament of marriage, girls, is sacred and holy. God's blessing was bestowed upon this permanent union of man and woman. Nothing should take place until God has blessed them,' staring awe into their eyes. Yes, she had sinned and sinned grievously. She had sinned in the ripples of those exciting vibrations stirred by his gently exploring hands; and the restless ocean that had been caged in her for so long swelled, rose and surged through her, drowning the both of them in a passion which she had since discovered, was not always as gentle as she had dreamed. The imperative of demand from those we love and who claim to love us in return had shocked and dismayed her although she still held on to the belief that love-in-service-to-others contained that kernel of freedom she had always sought. It was, however, pointless quarrelling now and wasting time in regrets. Time, the nursemaid and gravedigger of all thought and action, God's expression of futility. But her sacrament of marriage would be for real and always. This she vowed to make sure.

With this new determination she rose from the step upon which she had been sitting, walked briskly down the school corridor, passed the school office, crossed the deserted gallery once again and retraced her steps till she reached the chapel. Entering, she genuflected and slipped into a pew at the back. Then kneeling, she let the tears flow freely down her face in the privacy of the chapel's holy gloom. Here was where she had been born into faith, into the loving arms of her long suffering Saviour. He alone understood her loneliness now. He alone saw what was aching in her heart. And like a ravished pilgrim, beaten and robbed along the way, she abandoned herself to the silent comfort of a loving Saviour whose presence in the tabernacle was signified by the flickering light of the red altar lamp. In that silence she rested her head on the wooden pew and sobbed her heart out.

After that night's debacle, she was still feeling raw and naked as if Mak had raped her in front of them all in the full harsh light of that electric lamp above his head. Its mere recollection burned into her brain and she had to hold on to the pew to steady herself. A nut, dehusked and shelled, she was empty and hollow inside. Lord, is this my punishment? Is this a sign of your displeasure? Her silent question went unanswered as she looked at the figure hanging on the cross bathed in the blue light from the stained glass windows. No, it couldn't be, she reassured herself, for my God is the God of love not vengeance. That was the work of man – deranged and demented man. He was destroyed, Hans had said, by circumstances beyond his control and she had nearly drowned in his whirlpool of filth. She could not bear to see him again even when Hans visited him, not when she still felt his dirt clinging to her. It would be years and years before she could wash it all away. But before I go I will walk these streets and these roads, stamping my good-byes on them, burying my past with every drop of filth that oozes out of my pores. O Lord give me strength, just give me strength. She wished she could vent her anger on him but she couldn't. He was mad! Stark staring mad! Why, Lord, why? Why did they have to push him over the brink? To show their power? O these vindictive men! These small-minded beetles scuttling in self-importance, destroying the fabric of her life. How she hated them! Yes, Lord, she hated them even if it meant being condemned to hell for it. She hated this society they had built. Built on fear; claustrophobic as a garrison with walls going up higher and higher. They were misers grasping, accumulating, perpetually fearing the loss of their hard-won treasures. Their fears condemning the rest to live in prison. So, perhaps then this was indeed God's way to get her out of a society she had grown to resent? Perhaps it was His Will that she should serve the cause of freedom and justice in another land? At least America would be a freer society. There she could follow her conscience and her will.

In this way, she reasoned herself out of sadness and nostalgia and into a willingness to face the new and the unknown so suddenly forced upon her. She got up and left.

'Hey, you're here already? Did you wait long?' she asked Yean outside the chapel.

'No, not long,' Yean replied, trying to read Sis's face. But she had failed again. If she had expected sadness she did not see it for Sis looked cheerful enough that very moment.

'Have you said your good-byes?'

'Only to that part,' Sis pointed to the secondary school. 'I haven't been to the other side yet; I used to walk around that field at night.'

'Shall I wait here while you say good-bye to the convent?'

'No, no, I'll do that tonight. Hans and I are having dinner with them. But we can walk round the field together if you like.' So Yean got up and walked beside her with mixed feelings, resenting this obvious privilege even though no one else had been invited. After all these years, she was still clay in Sis's presence. She had never had the strength to confront her with anything, and felt disgusted by her own ineffectiveness. Now after all that had happened she was still silent. If she had had the strength she would have asked: all these people have paid a price for you. Are you aware of it? Do you appreciate it? Are you going to waste their love, affection and loyalty? Are you still angry with Mak? He loved you too, only you were not aware of it. He did not act out of sheer madness. Jealousy was in it too. Did it ever occur to you you could have been part of his breakdown? You only heard his big dreams and ideas, his thesis and antithesis, but did you see the man? The person? I'm disappointed. You, who have spoken to us so touchingly about the importance of the soul and the individual; you were not aware of him at all.

Yean walked beside Marie, silent, listening to her plans for the wedding next week. This would be their last meeting together without the presence of the others.

If this was to be their last meeting what was the use of saying anything: there would be no chance of another meeting to clarify any angry feelings. What was the point then of stripping another person of her illusions if she were not going to be there to take care of the consequences? Sis would have to deal with her own illusions as best as she could. Anyway she had Hans which was more than most have. Besides, it was arrogance to think you're the only one capable of helping someone see clearly. When you are ready to learn your guru would come, the yogi always say.

'See, this is where we used to sit at night,' Marie was saying, pointing to some stone seats in the tennis court, intent upon sharing with Yean this aspect of her life in the convent. Yean nodded dumbly, thoughts drifting on.

Was this her own rationalization? Perhaps she had grown indifferent? Perhaps she had already distanced herself from Sis like the others? Perhaps she was just not prepared to walk with her through the difficult journey of self-discovery and therefore had chosen the easier path of charity – leave her her illusions; she may need them to make a new life abroad.

They strolled across the field in the glare of the noonday sun. With Yean, Marie felt some of her cheerful optimism returning. No, Mak had not destroyed her. She still liked what she saw of herself. If trouble and crisis were the true sons of Shiva, then all the mirrors we held up to ourselves would have been smashed as so many illusions. Marie was clinging all the more to favourite images of herself. She looked at Yean, inarticulate, awkward though fiercely loyal. Why should Yean be any different now? All the same, on this their last morning together, she wished Yean would make an effort to say something; to say what was in her mind so that they could be more honest and less awkward with each other. If only Yean had been able to pour out her thoughts and feelings then, Marie too, would have been able to confess: I, too, have learnt something. I dream a dream but my dream is many-faceted. Different parts of my dream attract different people. I know I attract them but I do not make them like me. How can you, Yean, in your silence blame me? Can you blame the Flame of the Forest if passers-by admire its blooms and stop in its shade? Why blame me for Paul, for Ser Mei, for Siew, Mak, Pei Lan or yourself? Must I carry the burden of others' loves and hates? Don't I have enough guilt of my own to carry already? You would say I encouraged them. I encouraged them to grow. Is that a crime? Should I have left Pei Lan alone, stagnant in the help-lessness and obsequiousness of her slave mentality? Now at least she is sharper in her perceptions, more critical and more aware of herself and her society. Isn't this a good thing?

Yean was pursuing her own thoughts as they walked silently around the school field. Pei Lan and Ah Huat had been deported to Malaysia, marked forever by their government as dissidents and trouble-makers. They would have difficulty getting jobs. Have they benefited from your dreams? Haven't they been harmed in some ways – their rice bowls cracked? Are they happier for having been made more aware? More critical of things around them?

Yes, Marie was thinking, yes, they would have been happy left alone; happy as only the ignorant are happy; ignorant that they are the faggots of war and the digits of labour to be moved like chess pieces by those who have mastered the economics of survival. Is this freedom and dignity? Is this what man is all about?

But since no one spoke their thoughts, their arguments remained unsaid, unchallenged.

★ ★ ★

That had been their farewell. Yean felt a vague sense of disappointment. No, not vague. If she were true to her feelings she must admit that she was hovering on the brink of bitterness. What had she just experienced? Was that a good-bye between old friends who were sup-posed to have shared commitments, dreams and visions? Why hadn't Sis said a single word even remotely connected with themselves and their relationship? Their meeting was simply the bright bubbling of a shallow stream of words about her coming wedding and her continued involvement abroad with the SWA. 'Having a grasp of Asian realities I would be in a better position to establish contact with concerned Americans there and in this way contribute to developments here,' and Yean had found herself nodding out of long habit. But nodding to what? To what was she agreeing? A war in Vietnam. Refugees in Hongkong. Communism in China. Hunger in Bangladesh. Dictatorship in one place. Corruption in another. Harsh Asian realities. And Yean remembered Paul's words at the police station.

'You people, you think you can change things in one grand gesture of defiance. It's an illusion. Marie celebrates the greatness of the great individual – herself. But here in Singapore it is only in the day-to-day behind-the-scenes workings of many men, each one doing a small part of the job that real change comes.' Harsh words then, but how true!

Yean had been so enmeshed by Sis's dreams and vision of an ideal society that she had been blind to what was going on in the SWA. Where was Mak now? Why was it no one wanted to discuss Mak? Where were his Chinese students? His loyal supporters had vanished into thin air. She had never bothered to keep track of those who came and went in the SWA (because we should trust everyone, Sis had insisted) so now she did not know who they were. How was it that none of them foresaw his madness? Surely there must have been signs? No one, as far as she knew, no one simply became mad overnight. And his sudden attack on Hans and Marie as if he had never trusted them, as if he had hated them

261

all this while. And now Sis's obvious indifference to his fate – all these she found difficult to accept.

Mak's attack had split the SWA. Now she saw there had always been two camps. She had always known this; it was only that her brain had refused to register the fact because it would complicate things for her. It would have meant facing up to her uneasiness about Mak and his Yuan Tung and Nan Hai supporters, opening herself to being criticised for English-educated arrogance. It would have meant admitting that in the SWA there was contention for power and influence as in any other political group. They were not there simply because of a desire to save the suffering masses. She realized now it was not Marie nor Hans nor Mak even – their group of four – who had held the SWA together. They were the visible articulate ones but the invisible members from Yuan Tung and Nan Hai were the backbone with Mak as their spokesman communicating only as much as he thought useful for his own purposes. Now with their disappearance the SWA had also died out. Even if Sis had stayed she would not be the rallying point she still thought she was. No, she and Sis had been the waterlilies floating atop a deep lake teeming with voracious terrapins capable of devouring all attracted to the waterlilies. Yean felt used. Was Mak really mad? And why had Sis seemed so unconcerned just now? Didn't she care any more? She hadn't even asked about Pei Lan and Ah Huat.

'She doesn't really care. All she wants are stooges for her grand ideas!' Ken had been harsh but still she had to admit that Sis had changed. Look at Ser Mei and Yin Peng; she had forgotten them. She didn't make an appearance for Yin Peng's birthday and Yin Peng had wanted to show her that she needed only one crutch to walk now instead of two. Nor had she come for Ser Mei's anniversary mass and they had waited for her. And now Mak. Why this silence? It looked as if Peter and Ken had been right to move away from Sis. She had just said good-bye to Sis through a brick wall. Their group spirit was broken. They were going their separate ways. Was this part of growing up? Inevitable? She felt old as if witnessing the passing of an era. What was the cause of this sense of loss? What had she lost? And all she could remember and cling to was that night when she had looked up into the eyes of Miss Marie-Therese Wang and thought her the most beautiful person in her universe. She was waking up into an imperfect world of fleeting relationships where even the best of good-byes contain the seed of bitterness. In the end only images of key moments would remain, illuminating the greyness of the past.

Yean was bound for California with her mother. She, too, would fly.

Taking off his glasses, Paul Tan proceeded to wipe them. He was sweating despite the air-conditioning in his office. A glance at the wall clock told him that he had just two hours to finish his report. Wearily he took up his pen again holding it poised, ready to write, but he continued to stare at the half-written sheet in front of him. Nothing would come into his head. He glanced at his notes but it was useless. His usually quick mind seemed inert this morning. He read what he had written. Always highly praised by his superiors for his cogent situation reports, his words now seemed superfluous simply filling the pages. He was hot and tired, enmeshed in the sticky lethargy of the mid-morning heat caused by the recent dry spell whose crushing pressure had squeezed the few remaining drops of moisture in his already arid soul. The struggle to remain cool and alert this morning was proving to be too much of a strain. With a sense of defeat he put down his pen and swivelled his chair to look out of the window. No tree cheered his spirit. There were the usual scaffolding and machinery at work banging out a dull thud, thud matching the throbbing of the vein in his left temple. He watched the slow circular motion of the yellow crane's gigantic arm swinging a huge cement block into place in the midst of piling machines hammering steel rods into the foundation of yet another multi-storey office block. Such activity had always bolstered his confidence in an affluent Singapore. But today these signs were dreary reminders of Marie, vehemently critical of this frantic tearing down of the old to build the new. This thoughtless erasing of the past, she had scolded, would only leave us with economic gods to revere. They had always fought. Constantly wearing each other down, unable or unwilling to concede even an inch of ground. He hoped she would be happy now.

A wry smile creased his face as he turned back to his desk. He must get back to his writing and not allow thoughts of Marie to distract him. Reading the page again he stared at it for a long time till the pale blue vein in his left temple stood out and began to throb again. He could feel its dull hammering on his nerves. He glanced at the clock again as if for release but the minute hand was moving as slowly as his mind. He still had plenty of time to finish his work. He had no excuse for leaving his office yet. He was not suffering from lack of time but from too much of it. He would be released once the wedding was over.

He flung away his pen. It was useless. He could do no writing today. He re-arranged the sheath of papers and put it back into the file, closed it and returned it to his drawer. He cleared the scraps of paper from his desk and returned the pen to its proper box. He had always liked the order of a neatly arranged desk. He abhorred anything which suggested mental or physical disorder. Discipline should control the chaos inherent in life, he thought, as he kept himself busy re-arranging all his official papers in an attempt to keep all other thoughts at bay. No, it was useless. Who was he trying to kid? Pushing back his chair, he got up, opened the door of his office, nodded to his astonished clerks and strode out to see to it that Marie leave Singapore with Hans Kuhn in accordance with his department's deportation orders.

*   *   *

In the church he allowed himself to be conducted to his seat in the third pew. He caught himself stretching his lips slightly and briefly, mere reflex action, an imitation of a smile. They had invited him and he had come. He would be civil. He saw Marie's father turn round and nod. He returned the nod but made no effort to speak. There was no point now although in the past he would have done so to gratify the old man's vanity knowing that Mr Wang, the senior government clerk, liked to keep in touch with rising young professionals. Sitting in his allotted place with arms folded and his back rigidly straight, his face was an impassive mask.

Conscious of being invited as an observer not as a participant in the proceedings, he watched the crowd fill the church to capacity with many latecomers standing along the aisles.

The entire congregation of a Sunday mass had been invited to witness the event. The crowd and the heat in the church oppressed him further, exacerbating his throbbing temples. The ceiling fans fitfully stirred the warm turbid air thick with the odours of a sweating crowd. Nevertheless, Paul, sweating profusely himself, did not fidget like the others.

The central aisle of the church was decorated with sprigs of white daisies and golden showers. A brand new red carpet stretched from the entrance of the church to the altar rails. The altar, draped in red and gold cloths embroidered with the golden chalice and white host – the symbol of love and sacrifice – had all the trimmings of a grand wedding, the solemnity of a traditional high mass.

But Paul saw none of these things. Staring ahead, stoically waiting for the inevitable to close a chapter of his life. At precisely eleven o'clock he heard the bells, not ringing but tolling. The organist, however, struck up a gay march. Members of the choir, dressed in yellow and white muslin, tripped in, laughing and waving to their friends in the congregation. Every head turned in anticipation. They all expected the usual solemn white parade into the church with the bride shyly leaning on her father's arm. In this case there was little or no solemnity. All was laughter and gaiety. The choir burst into song as the bride and groom entered, dancing into the church. Dressed in beige *kurta* and *dhoti*, elaborately embroidered with gold threads, the bride and groom held hands and danced merrily down the aisle, waving to their friends and relatives. In their trail came ten little bridesmaids and pageboys, dressed in red and white, scattering flowers into the crowd. Surprised and then pleased by this unusual spectacle the crowd clapped. Thunderous applause followed as the bride and groom turned to face their audience and took their bows.

Showy! Beige and gold! How ridiculous Hans looked in his *dhoti!* An American in Indian garb! Nothing will change the paleness of his skin though, Paul thought, as he straightened his back and folded his arms a little more tightly across his chest.

The music and clapping stopped. The Reverend James entered resplendent in white and gold cassock and surplice. For the next half hour, Paul watched as the congregation stood, bowed and knelt following the order of the marriage service. He followed all their motions, mouthed the words of the service as they appeared to him and followed the letters which had no meaning for him, imitating the mouths and lips moving around him. He stood rigidly at attention as in a police parade watching the bride and groom walk up to the altar still holding hands. Holding on to each other so tightly as if afraid the other would fly away. So, it's because of this American that she had left the convent! He watched them sit down on the two chairs reserved for them. Through a haze he saw various people going up to the microphone placed at one side of the altar to speak as at any secular gathering. Words, words, torrents of words tumbling out of their mouths setting the crowd laughing and clapping. Hah! They had even engineered a praise-name calling session. Typical American you-stroke-my-back-and-I'll-stroke-yours. Definitely not Chinese! The choir sang as he strained to listen, observing the people singing. But when he opened his own mouth no sound came from his parched throat. Again he struggled to listen, to pay attention, but he heard nothing distinctly, only muffled noises. He was trapped in an air-tight bell jar, observing all that was happening through the glass but cut off from the pain and sounds of life around him. Nothing could touch him. Good. He would have no part of this revolting carnival. He did not belong here. He raised his eyes from the hymn book on his lap and gazed out of the window at the cheerless branches of the few dying trees in the church compound; their ugliness reflected in the metallic brilliance of the row upon row of cars parked in the hot sun. The light hurt his eyes. He turned away and glanced at the woman sitting beside him. Like the others she was engrossed in the spectacle around the altar. He looked at the congregation. Typical Singaporeans! They would be impressed by the show and ritual! He was disgusted to see the sacred moment of a whole life's commitment reduced to a performance of the hour to please the vulgar crowd. To propagandize their politics. The inane speeches, the shameless dancing and the theatrical bowing and applause smacked of the vulgarity of the mass weddings organised by the local Chinese press and tourist agencies. Why couldn't she realize, he raged inwardly, that in turning a quiet moment of commitment into a gala event, that American, Hans, had degraded her. And she in turn had degraded him! To think that not so long ago he had shared with her all that he had held dear and private! He, too, felt cheapened.

His head still throbbed with a dull ache as the whirring of the ceiling fans continued to plague him. He swallowed hard to rid his throat of its parched feeling.

'Friends! Everybody!' Rev James's voice boomed over the public address system.

'Hans and Marie invite you, all of you, who are their close friends and comrades, to join them in this celebration of life and love. You are invited to break bread with them.'

No one moved. The organ played softly. Its music filling up the vacuum of silence which followed the announcement. The crowd fidgeted in the heat. They were hungry now. It was nearly lunchtime. The service had taken much longer than expected. Paul sat still; his back stiff and straight, his arms still folded, listening to the hungry rumbles in his own stomach. The organ continued playing. Nobody had moved. Nobody had gone forward. The priest, the bride and her groom stood at the altar, waiting.

'Come,' invited Rev James, 'don't be shy.'

Parts of the crowd giggled like awkward schoolgirls hiding their embarrassment. But still, no one moved. Hans whispered something to the Reverend who smiled and nodded.

'I'm sorry,' the Reverend James confessed. 'I've forgotten to explain. This is an ecumenical celebration. All Catholics and Christians of all denominations and all non-Christians are invited. All those devoted and dear to Marie and Hans come,' the Rev James hailed through the microphone, spreading out his arms in an expansive gesture to embrace the whole congregation.

Paul winced. The tone of that hail-fellow-well-met voice jarred his sensibility. This was all wrong. Why do they so desperately need this public affirmation of their popularity? Must they prove that they are well-liked here before leaving? Was this his doing? Or hers? Paul looked up at Marie. Their eyes met. He turned away and proceeded to examine the contents of the hymn book on his lap. He could feel her eyes on him still. Unable to bear this tension any longer and angry more with himself than with her, he looked up and met her eyes again. Swallowing hard he tried to turn away again but he could not ignore those eyes. They were appealing to him as once before. Do something! Break this impasse, her eyes pleaded with him.

Small and soft she had been whenever she needed him. Once like a hurt sparrow she had come quivering into his arms and he had enclosed her protectively, shielding her from the clucking sympathy of all those busybodies after that failure to obtain her scholarship. And she had nestled in his arms sobbing quietly while he stroked her hair, wiped away her tears and still she had clung to him as he kissed her, drinking in the perfume at the nape of her neck whose tiny hairs felt like soft down. How he longed to hold her once again in his arms!

Before he realized it, he had stood up and was motioning the woman next to him to go forward.

The crowd burst into applause as if he had done something heroic! He felt like a fool and was glad when Ken and Peter joined him. Eventually the rest of them flocked forward. Paul looked up once more at Marie, saw her smiling, her eyes glittering with the triumph of this affirmation of her popularity. Their eyes did not meet this time. She was too busy smiling to the rest. Paul kept his eyes on the ground, not even looking up when he received his piece of unleavened bread. He held it in his hand, paused to murmur a prayer of thanks, put it in his mouth and swallowed hard. It grated against the walls of his dry throat. Swallowing again and again, he made his way out of the crowded church. The service could end without him.

*　　*　　*

From the safe distance of the airport's main stairway Paul watched the crowd milling once again around Hans and Marie like groupies following their favourite idols. Fools. They were all fools like him. He was still seething with anger over his own foolishness this morning. But now dressed casually in a batik shirt, he looked like any bored loafer haunting the Paya Lebar International Airport to enjoy its excellent air-conditioning and to observe the regular parade of friends and relatives come to bid the traveller Godspeed in a babel of languages and dialects. His body leaning against the banister was languid but the eyes which casually surveyed the crowd were alert, picking up the plainclothes men he had stationed at all the entrances and exits. Not that he expected any trouble but like any good police officer he was not taking any chances. After this morning, he was all the more determined to perform his duty and see to it that Hans and Marie boarded the plane without any incident.

A sudden commotion at one of the entrances made him turn round. Another large group of students had arrived to bid the couple farewell. Like all of Marie's departures this was going to be another of those dramatic occasions, Paul thought resignedly, for he had long ago stopped fighting her propensity to create drama out of every occasion. But this time he would have no part of it. Standing beneath the mosaic picture of Singapore's harbour at night, Paul watched as groups of giggling factory girls pushed each other forward to shake Hans's hand. Towering above them, he smiled down, accepting everything as his due. What he lacked in depth of character he made up for it in height. That was the only good thing Paul could think of him since to Paul, Hans was like any other American who had come out to Asia for a short stint and left, convinced that he now knows the continent and its people. Various groups of people had dragged Marie away for photographs. She and Hans flashed smiles and 'peace' signs liberally as though they were at a victory parade. Then she looked up and saw him. With a warm smile of welcome she waved and beckoned him to go down. This time, however, he resisted the impulse. He turned away and walked up the stairs. He had barely reached the landing when he heard.

'Everybody, thank you for coming. We are touched by the courage you have shown in coming to our wedding and now to see us off.'

Paul quickly went down the stairs again in time to see Marie standing on one of the airport benches, addressing the crowd. A glance told him that his men were poised to act as instructed should she touch on anything political in her speech.

'Your presence here speaks louder than words. Despite the presence of the authorities,' and she glanced up defiantly at him, 'you have the courage to demonstrate your friendship and solidarity with us, you have not cast us aside. Hans and I will never forget this moment.'

She paused to wipe away her tears. The crowd was moved. For a moment there was silence as the onlookers waited. Then with another defiant glance in his direction she continued: 'We pledge that in the States, we will continue to fight for the cause of freedom and justice. My wings have been clipped here but they will soon grow and I will fly again!'

The crowd clapped and burst into song:
'It's a long road to freedom
A winding steep and high
But when you walk in love
with the wind on your wings
And cover the earth with the
songs you sing
The miles fly by . . .'
Paul turned and walked up the stairs once more.
He would have nothing to do with her little triumph.

*　　*　　*

From the airport Paul drove straight to his club where he played a furious game of tennis before relaxing in the warm shower. Calm and refreshed then, he sat sipping coffee in the club's lounge, drinking in the dulcet tones of a piped organ solo, not unlike a husky-voiced mistress whispering words of endearment in his ears. Dim lights, air-conditioning, pots of green plants and ferns, white cane chairs and tables gave this room the atmosphere of a cool indoor garden. An oasis away from the heat outside; protected from the hustle and bustle of life along Orchard Road and served by discreet attendants, Paul sank deeper into his seat and, stretching his legs, enjoyed the gradual release of taut muscles. If he had to slog like a dog for five-and-a-half days per week in order to enjoy this, then enjoy it he would. Fortified by this sense of well-earned comfort, Paul's mind returned to the morning's wedding. From the safe distance of his club, he viewed Marie again and wondered why he had never noticed those determined lines around her mouth; pursed and unsmiling when she could not have her way. An attractive face with eyes which had once fascinated and mesmerised him. But that desire for attention, for approval, admiration and adoration was all revealed to him in that victorious gleam behind the smile with which she welcomed those who went up for communion this morning. That gracious smile had repelled him. It belonged to the world of Hollywood and cheap politics. It was the kind of gracious smile which First Ladies used to woo their public and within it he could no longer find the artlessly idealistic girl-woman he had once loved.

A brief laugh made him look up from his coffee and glance at the two women sitting at a table from across him. With a pang he remembered that it was the very table where he and Marie had sat during their last confrontation. The two women in question were Marie's age. But unlike her, they were fashionably dressed in contrasting tones of blues and reds and were heavily made-up. Paul studied them for a moment before dismissing them. He did not find them attractive at all. Such women and even some of his more tastefully attired colleagues had never managed to gain his attention much less his affection; he had never bothered to ask himself why.

'Aiya, I'm so mad with them!'

Paul looked up again. One of the women was apparently recalling the most distressing episode in her life as she wrung her hands flashing diamonds.

'How can? I asked the matron. I'm entitled to first class and they dare put me in second class with everybody else! I was so mad! I absolutely refused to budge from the labour ward until they found me a first-class room. So maddening it was!'

Her companion laughed in obvious enjoyment and approval of her friend's insistence on her rights and privileges.

Paul stared coldly at the two women as they continued to talk and laugh, oblivious of their observer. Their well-made-up faces repelled him. Their loud voices repulsed him. Why were they so vulgarly snobbish? He thought of what Marie had said of such women – they are the products of your economic system which inevitably creates such *nouveau riche* vulgarity. He looked round the lounge uncomfortably. He could no longer relax in it. It did have this air of consciously created class; of separating the few from the many. So, Marie was right. He got up and walked out of the club.

She might have been wrong about many other things but in this instance she was right. Vulgarity, nothing but vulgarity, he thought angrily as he viewed the fashionably but garishly dressed women crowding into C.K. Tang's Department Store, eager for its bargains.

Walking up Orchard Road, brisk and unseeing, he passed the Thai Embassy, the row of imitation French cafés and decrepit shophouses selling imitation antiques and porcelain wares. He turned into the suddenly tree-lined hush of Nassim Road. The winding of this shady lane soothed his irritation. Disregarding the tourist attraction of Jade House he strolled slowly up the road, every step bringing him nearer to a happiness irretrievably lost to him. Such a gulf had separated them. They had been irreconcilable right to the end. And now she had gone. Why hadn't he seen things from her point of view a little more before? Why had he withheld agreement so totally? They did not even say good-bye. He walked slowly under the silent trees and felt parts of his logic and good sense crumbling. It was on this road a long time ago that she had taught him to enjoy the company of these august trees, to walk in the rain and catch its drops on the tip of his tongue and to listen to the song of the birds. In her company then, he had never felt foolish doing such things. He paused, listening to the evening hum of the myriad invisible insects and gazing up the grey trunks of the angsana trees he tried to recapture those rare moments of harmony but in vain for, was there really harmony if it was built only on a rain-drop and a birdsong? They had not even touched each other's core and she had remained defiant to the end. But without searching his heart too deeply he knew why he was still clinging to her last look of defiance flung in his direction.

And standing still as at a war memorial, he bowed his head and waited for some minutes. He could hear nothing except the loud chirps of the crickets and the whining of a mosquito around his ears. Her birdsong was no longer there among the trees.

He was alone in Nassim Road.